ENTANG

OF

FATE

CHRIS BROOKES

Gretton Court
LIBRARY
Girton

A SCHNAUZER PUBLICATION

First published in 2013 for Schnauzer Publications
by FeedARead Publishing
An Arts Council funded initiative

Copyright © Chris Brookes 2013
Cover design © Chris Brookes 2013

Typeset in Minion Pro by Steven Levers, Sheffield
www.stevenlevers.com

The author asserts his moral right under the Copyright,
Designs and Patents Act, 1988, to be identified as
the author of this work.

All Rights reserved. No part of this publication may
be reproduced, copied, stored in a retrieval system, or
transmitted, in any form or by any means, without the prior
written consent of the copyright holder, nor be otherwise
circulated in any form of binding or cover other than that in
which it is published and without a similar condition being
imposed on the subsequent purchaser. All brand names and
product names used in this book are trademarks, registered
trademarks, or trade names of their respective holders.

A CIP catalogue record for this title is
available from the British Library.

All enquiries to:

enquiries@chrisbrookes.info

ABOUT THE AUTHOR

Chris Brookes was born in 1960 and lives in Sheffield with his wife and two children.

After spending time in the army, Chris embarked on a career in musical theatre production and began co-producing touring shows. However, after discussions with his bank manager and the revelation that a mortgage needed to be paid monthly, it was agreed he would also seek a 'proper job'. Soon he found himself working in service delivery management, but all the while continued to pursue an interest in the stage, writing scripts and organising shows. He also worked on his other passion of painting and has produced numerous limited edition prints of his work.

Chris is currently busy writing the sequel to 'Entanglement of Fate', as well as a three-part TV script based on the life of Luisa – Crown Princess of Tuscany.

Acknowledgements

When I look back, writing this novel has been about working with people, most of whom I have never actually met in person, but they have all made a massive contribution in their way.

Firstly, I have to say a big thank you to Kristina Train, singer/songwriter, who was always my vision of Mary. Her music, along with that of fellow Sheffielder, Richard Hawley and the late Harry Chapin, took me to great places in my mind and allowed my imagination to run riot.

I have to acknowledge two editors with whom I have worked throughout – Michelle Goode, who has such a talent for developing structure and offering guidance and Helen Hancock (her of the red pen!) who has patiently taken my writing and skilfully made changes.

My thanks to Jan Chatterton for her time, endless re-reads and corrections. To Bill, my father-in-law, for first introducing me to the story of Walter. Thanks also to the many friends and other people who have helped research and check facts and my gratitude goes to those who have read and reviewed my book, pre-publication.

Finally, thanks to whatever it is inside me that drives and inspires me to write.

Dedicated to Kate,
without whose love, support and encouragement,
the following pages would not exist.

CHAPTER 1

STREET ARAB

Past midnight was no time to be running over the wet, slippery tiles of the city's terraced rooftops, trying to apprehend a criminal; and particularly not one who moved over the ridges with the agility of a cat. But such was Constable Reynolds's challenge, as he struggled through the shroud of rain, soaked in a sulphurous stench.

The sound of muffled clicking on the roof tiles overlaid the never-ending thud of foundry hammers in the distance. They were strange, random clicks with no rhythm, the sort that would annoy anyone who liked order and pattern. The noise stopped for a moment, then began again, becoming more and more audible. Finally, it had a beat – click, click, clunk. Through the veil of lashing rain, Reynolds caught sight of a slim, bedraggled figure, running and balancing with ease, his heavy hobnailed boots clicking against the slates.

The figure stopped to catch his breath and looked back

at Reynolds struggling behind him, the flickering light from the constable's torch bouncing erratically round. In the back alleys beneath, dogs began to bark in disharmony at the sound of indistinct police whistles, whilst on the street, a dozen policemen grouped together, all fighting to keep their faces out of the biting cold wind, half-heartedly moving their torches back and forth to throw a dim light up to the rooftops. Three nights this week they had been called out to catch the man they now dubbed the Street Arab. Each time, they had failed. One minute he'd be up on the roof, the next at the bottom of a drainpipe two hundred yards further on than you'd believe he could be.

As the rain eased and bright moonlight broke through the clouds, the Street Arab drew back to hide in the shadows until, once more, darkness could give him cover. He pushed his drenched black hair away from his youthful, swarthy face with its dirty half-grown beard. His dark sunken eyes glared out in anguish as he wedged himself flat in the gully, well hidden between dormer and roof tiles.

Least impressed this night was Sergeant Drake, a portly man who constantly ran his fingers through his thick handle-bar moustache. For him, this nonsense had to stop once and for all. And stop it would, by fair means or foul. He was determined that this 'toe rag', as he called him, would see the inside of a cell. He looked upwards and bellowed out to the rooftop, 'Reynolds!' There was no response. 'I can't see a thing. Where the bloody hell is that lamp?' he demanded. Finally, a constable handed him a heavy-duty torch, which he fiddled with until at last it came on, flooding the rooftop with light.

'Reynolds! Can you hear me? Where are you?' bawled Drake, becoming more and more agitated.

A sorry-looking character finally appeared above; trying to balance over the roof ridge, one hand waving about, the other desperately trying to focus his torch.

'I'm here,' responded the thoroughly dejected Reynolds, as Drake's torchlight finally picked him out.

'Well! Where is he?'

'Er…he's gone, Sarge.'

'Gone! What do you mean he's gone? Where the bloody hell to?'

'I don't know, he's just…well, disappeared as usual.'

'Disappeared as usual. Lord, give me strength,' the Sergeant spluttered, ready to burst at any minute. He looked towards his group of men, all now utterly miserable, and singled out Jenkins. Pointing towards the house door, he said, 'Go in there and ask them, nay, tell them, you need access to the roof from their dormer.' Jenkins obliged, thankful for any opportunity to get out of the wind even for a couple of minutes.

The Street Arab, meantime, dared not move, knowing that any minute the light of the Sergeant's torch could pan across and pick him out. But, equally, he realised that only back on the ridges would he have any chance of escape. Suddenly, with a forceful push of his hands, he was back on his feet again and running. Immediately half-a-dozen torches moved in the direction of the noise. A voice shrieked, 'Look, there he is!' Drake's light easily exposed him, clambering to the ridge.

He reached the apex of the roof and started running along it, only to pull up abruptly. In front of him was the end of the terrace. Beyond, only the gable of the next line of houses, but not before a twenty-foot gap. He surveyed the drop. Dear God, at least forty feet, he reckoned. Looking up again, he saw the drainpipe and considered if he could make it, all the while conscious Reynolds was closing in on him from behind. He knew he could double back and easily bypass him on the ridge, but he couldn't be sure there weren't more policemen further down the roof.

His decision was suddenly made as the dormer window opened and Jenkins crawled awkwardly out onto the roof. It would now have to be the jump to the pipe, however daunting. His eyes opened wide with anxiety. Jesus Christ! he thought, taking another look at the drop. Blood pumped through every part of him. His body tingled. Gently he rocked back and forth, ready to propel himself across.

'It's now or never. I won't be caught,' he said to himself. That much he was determined about: he wouldn't go back to that hell!

'The toe rag's only going to jump,' Drake exclaimed, looking upwards. The next moment the Street Arab was in the air, arms outstretched. Faces below looked up agog at what he'd just done.

A grimace showed the pain as he thumped hard into the pipe. Pain was something he was all too familiar with; but this was in a league of its own. He pulled back to see the damage – a bracket crushed hard into his torso, the wind taken out of him so badly he couldn't even utter a moan. He tried to make sense of what he needed to do next, but all he understood was the need to cling onto the pipe.

Drake flew into a rage. 'No! No bloody way! He's not escaping this time.' Frantically he hollered out instructions, 'You, up that pipe! You lot, get in every house with a dormer and get on their roof! Come on, run!'

His directions, however, weren't needed. The Street Arab was going nowhere. His only possibility was to hold onto the pipe. The pain in his chest was now so severe, he was on the verge of passing out. Finally, he had to concede and slowly slipped down the pipe towards his waiting captors. Only harsh treatment awaited him on the ground. He was frog-marched in front of Drake, who circled around him, like a hyena waiting to attack its prey. Without warning, he unleashed a punch to the man's stomach. The captive's head slumped; his body flopped like a puppet suddenly without strings. Drake pulled up the bowed head by the hair. 'Right lad, your game's done,' he said, and pushed the head back down forcefully, as if it were on a rag doll. 'Get this scum to the station!' He spat out the instruction to his men.

For the Street Arab all pain was gone – the darkness of unconsciousness fell over him.

CHAPTER 2

The Enigma

The police station cells held no comfort for detainees. They were dark, cramped and, above all, freezing cold. The walls were so riddled with damp that any paint had disappeared long ago. In the still of night, only an intermittent flicker of light from a duty constable's lantern offered any small hope of discovering where the sound of scurrying came from, although the occasional scream from a prisoner signalled a rodent's presence was closer than was desired. Certainly not the place for one fearful of rats.

Robert Elliott, accompanied by a young nurse, waited patiently to be led down to the cells. Elliott was undeterred by such conditions. During his seventeen years as a police court missionary, he had become accustomed to even the most atrocious of prison cells. As he saw it, the inmates' futures were his primary concern. Reform of prison hygiene was for the politicians and statutes.

The young nurse, Mary, on the other hand, was horrified. It was all she could do to prevent herself from retching at the vile smell of urine and faeces that suddenly hit her as Drake opened the corridor door.

'Are you all right, Mary?' Elliott enquired.

Clutching a handkerchief to her face, she nodded, although the draining of colour from her cheeks suggested otherwise.

It struck Elliott as slightly strange that Mary should react in such a way. After all, as a nurse, surely she was used to these things. But perhaps it was understandable in one so young and not conversant with the harsh reality of detainment. Maybe it would have been prudent to offer her some insight into the reality of police cells before asking her to assist him.

His job consisted of a weekly visit to the men and women awaiting prosecution in the courts. After an appearance before the bench, if the charges were trivial enough, the magistrates would release defendants into Elliott's supervision. Then, with church mission support, he would offer them help towards a new beginning.

However, this night was somewhat different. The request was, simply, to offer his account of a detained man who was reportedly deaf and mute. The case seemed intriguing, but with no real experience of the deaf, he had invited Mary to sign for him.

Mary O'Driscoll was indeed well suited to the task, having given much of her spare time to helping in the mission's school for the deaf. Over the last year, she had become very proficient in signing, to the point where she now taught the techniques to parents and schoolmistresses.

Mary forced herself to regain her composure and followed Drake and Elliott along the corridor, her nostrils, at long last, becoming accustomed to the awful stench. Elliott stopped at intervals to look through the cell door hatches.

'With the men, it's generally idleness, drink or gambling that causes their detainment, Mary,' he explained.

'Really, Mr Elliott.' Her tone sounded more apathetic than sympathetic.

He opened a hatch to reveal a young lad eagerly scratching his name on the wall with a rusty nail.

'And with the lads, it's evil home influence, lack of discipline, and above all, lack of worthy companions and friends that lie at the root of their misdoings.'

'I see,' replied Mary, a little more enthusiastically.

Elliott pulled up by a cell from which a woman prisoner shouted abuse and obscenities. He spoke with despair. 'As for the women, it's most often prostitution or theft following abandonment that brings about their undoing.' He gestured to Mary to look through the hatch. She reluctantly accepted and braced herself for what depravity she might see. Her instinct proved right.

A ragged old woman was sitting on a pile of filthy sacks, and smiled to expose her blackened, decayed teeth. Mary offered a delicate smile in return, half through pity, half through revulsion.

'Want to see, do you, luv?' said the woman.

'See what?' Mary enquired innocently.

Without hesitation, the old woman whipped up her threadbare skirt and started to urinate. Mary, aghast, slammed the hatch shut. The old woman laughed hysterically and shouted, 'What's a matter, luv? Never seen an old gal pissing?'

Mary leant her head back against the wall for support, the horrified look on her face giving evidence of her sheltered upbringing. As a nurse at the city's hospital, she had witnessed some crude scenes, but nothing quite as vulgar as this. She turned to look at Elliott for reassurance, but saw he was now some way down the corridor. She quickened her pace to catch up with him.

Elliott saw she was flustered. 'Are you sure you're all right, my dear?'

With her soft Irish lilt, she told him, 'Yes, I'm fine.' Then she thought for a moment before finally taking a stand. 'Well no, actually I'm not fine. You see…quite frankly, Mr Elliott, I find them disgusting.'

'Sometimes the path we're on is not the path we took by choice. Remember, Mary, let one not judge another without first knowing their plight.' Elliott's words were spoken effortlessly for her consideration.

'But can't anything be done for her?'

'Sadly, some people are beyond any help I can give them, my dear.'

Drake stopped by a cell. 'This is him, sir, our mute. The Street Arab as the men here call him.'

Elliott gave a slight frown of confusion.

'Because he's dark. Has Arab looks, you see,' Drake explained, and drew the hatch up. 'Hardly moved he hasn't for two days. Just crouches there.'

Elliott couldn't altogether see the Arab link as he looked through the hatch. For him the thin shaft of street light from a tiny barred window only showed a prisoner with a dirty, unshaven and anguished face, crouched in a corner, holding his stomach. Drake pulled out his large set of keys to unlock the door and swung it open to reveal the box of a cell. It was nine foot by six at best, Mary guessed, as she surveyed the contents – or more to the point, the lack of them. Her heart felt for the poor wretch inside.

'The slop, Sergeant,' Elliott shouted, meaning for Drake to remove the bucket. Even without Mary, Elliott wouldn't have been prepared to conduct an interview with that present. As Drake took out the bucket, Mary wondered how many hours a day a prisoner had to suffer such indignity.

'And perhaps a chair for Miss O'Driscoll?'

'Of course, Mr Elliott,' Drake replied, being forced to acknowledge that a visitor should at least be afforded a chair.

Elliott walked slowly into the cell, taking careful note of the man still crouched in the corner. He took his cane and gently moved the man's head to one side. A graze was instantly obvious, high on his cheekbone. He allowed the man's hair to fall and cover it.

Drake returned with two chairs.

'Has this man been beaten?' Elliott offered the question without looking at him.

'Injuries sustained whilst resisting arrest, nothing more,' an indignant Drake answered.

'So, the man is violent?'

'No, I didn't say that. Just plays up a bit, that's all. Probably on account of him being hungry.'

'And why would he be hungry?' said Elliott, keen to understand. He turned to look at Drake and continued with authority, 'You know, Sergeant, it's against the rules to deny a prisoner food. So again, why would he be hungry?'

Mary flinched at the sudden and unexpected change of tone in his voice.

Drake pulled up his large frame, wanting to show

disobedience. 'Look, Mr Elliott, I need to know who this man is. I thought a day without food might bring him to his senses, help him find his tongue and all.'

'And has it?' The sarcasm in Elliott's voice cut Drake straight back to size.

'Well, no, but…,' Drake protested.

Elliott didn't allow him to carry on. 'No, exactly!' He ended the conversation abruptly. Drake swept out of the cell, the door shutting firmly behind him.

Mary gingerly took a seat, trying to avoid the prisoner's gaze. And why wouldn't he want to fix his eyes on her? A young woman in her early twenties, about five foot six, and beautiful, some would say stunningly so; but by any judgment she was very pretty. Mary had features you couldn't help but look at with interest. Her dark hair was swept up at the back and tucked under a nurse's cap, but enough was left exposed to show that when let down, it would be long, silky and wavy. Even in the dim light, her olive complexion was flawless. And finally: her eyes! She had eyes that few women could fail to envy – large, deep brown, dreamy eyes with never-ending depth, set under perfectly formed eyebrows.

Even with all the hopelessness of his situation, the Street Arab still found enough vanity to gently stroke down his tousled hair. Finally, he released Mary from his stare and let his head fall forwards.

'Are you ready to start then, Mary?' Elliott broke the silence, whilst taking off his cloak and gloves.

'Yes, I'm ready, Mr Elliott.'

Elliott raised the man's chin with his cane, making him look again at Mary. She began to sign in earnest as Elliott spoke. 'Good evening, young man! My name is Robert Elliott and I am a police court missionary from the Court of Assize. This lady here is Nurse O'Driscoll. She helps at the deaf school and will be able to sign for us. Do you understand?'

There was no response from the man, who just gawped at Mary. She signed once more as Elliott repeated, 'Do you understand?' The man averted his gaze, until the cane made him look at her again. 'Mary, please ask him his name.' Still there was no response. 'Perhaps then, he could state his age.' Mary signed the question at a slower speed but to no avail.

'I'll try a different sort of signing, Mr Elliott,' she offered.

But she wasn't given time. The man was up on his feet in seconds. Mary gasped, clearly shocked at the swift transformation in him. She pushed back in her chair, frightened, as he approached Elliott. Suddenly, he opened his mouth wide and began frantically to push his fingers in and out. Elliott remained totally undeterred – no flinching, barely a blink. He just watched the being before him continue to gesture with ever-growing animation. The whites of the man's eyes were yellow and terribly bloodshot.

Elliott was no stranger to witnessing odd behaviour. His years of observing the criminal classes had exposed him to many an uncomfortable situation. He'd been threatened with all manner of things, anything from knives to jagged tin cans, once even by a wooden leg! But, strangely, he had never been physically attacked by anyone. Not that you'd want to try, weapon or not, for Elliott was an imposing man, well over six foot, with broad shoulders. Even in his forty-eighth year, his torso was still relatively v-shaped. His pleasant, dignified face remained authoritative as the prisoner carried on his vigorous miming. Time and time again he pushed his fingers in and out of his mouth.

'Ah! I see. Yes, I understand. You're thirsty.' Elliott acknowledged the game. He walked to the door and banged it with his cane. 'Constable, some fresh water if you will.'

The cell door eventually opened and a young constable dutifully stood there with a jug of water. Mary, now calm, looked at Elliott with interest as he took the water and offered it to the man. 'Here. Water, just as you asked… Well, why hesitate? Take your fill.'

Suddenly, the mute man swiped the jug to the floor and made a dash towards the door, only to be thwarted as Elliott swung out his cane to trip him. Next minute, Elliott was towering over the sprawled body, his cane posed aloft ready to beat him.

'No! Please, Mr Elliott, no,' Mary screamed.

'My patience has been tried. Sign me your desire,' demanded Elliott of the mute. The man, accepting defeat, retreated to a corner of the cell and sat hunched up, visibly protecting his stomach, docile once more.

'Perhaps he just wants some food,' Mary suggested.

'I dare say he does. But I want him to sign and tell me so,' came Elliott's swift reply.

Gently, she lowered herself in front of the man and began to sign her words at quarter speed. 'Are you hungry? Do you want food?'

Elliott rolled his eyes upwards in frustration. To his mind, what was needed was a quick cuff across the ears and some tough talking. However, patience came over him.

Mary dropped her hands with marked disappointment as the mute yawned.

'I'm sorry, Mr Elliott, but he doesn't seem to understand anything I sign. I've tried all the different ways I know.'

'Yes, quite the mystery isn't he?' Elliott replied, now convinced it was all an act. He knew just how tough life was on the city streets. To survive was a constant battle for many an able person, let alone the disabled or afflicted. For a deaf and mute person to have any chance, he would need to understand at least some sign language.

Elliott picked up his cane, 'Come, Mary, it seems I have wasted your time.'

'Oh,' Mary replied, rather surprised at the abrupt end

to things. 'I feel I've let you down,' she said, waiting for Elliott to attach his cloak.

'Nonsense, not at all, my dear.'

There was sympathy in her voice as she asked, 'What will become of him now?'

'Oh, he'll be remanded here while I make fuller enquiries. That will take a few weeks. Then, of course, he'll go before the Bench...' He drew his prognosis out, like a Shakespearean actor, '...who will, no doubt, adjourn for an expert view. I'm afraid he may be here some time, Mary. But don't you go fretting now. These situations always work themselves out in the end. Right, let's see if this constable can find us a nice cup of tea,' he finished.

The constable snapped to attention, having been totally engrossed in the mute's whole charade – without doubt, the best bit of entertainment he'd seen in this station for a while.

'Wait!' A voice suddenly shouted out from behind them after the cell door slammed shut. They turned to see the man's face at the hatch peering out. 'All right! You win,' he said.

The constable was beckoned to reopen the door and Elliott strolled back into the cell. Mary, totally perplexed, followed. 'Well, well, a mute suddenly to speak. Isn't that a miracle, Mary?' Elliott sarcastically remarked, circling around the man.

'My name is Walter…Walter Stanford. I'm twenty six years. There, happy now?' concluded the man, speaking in a condescending manner.

Elliott huffed his disapproval. 'Such remorse from one who chooses to waste my time.' Then he continued with authority, 'You would do well to remember who is in a predicament, my lad!'

Walter considered the comment before he again went and crouched in a corner of the cell. Mary, now thoroughly intrigued, again took a seat on the chair, as Elliott moved steadily round the cell.

'Well, Walter Stanford, you'd better explain yourself,' Elliott announced.

'I just thought it a prank, that's all. A chance to have the authorities baffled. Give them something to fill their wooden heads with,' replied Walter.

'You obviously have a low regard for authority.'

Walter didn't answer, realising now that Elliott had the measure of him. He suddenly grimaced with pain and held his stomach.

Mary decided she would join in the inquiry. 'You hold your stomach all the while. Are you…?'

She didn't get time to finish her words before Elliott interjected, '…from around these parts?' He had no intention of suffering any more play-acting.

'Nearby – Ecclesfield,' Walter replied, as his pain subsided.

'Yes, I know it…and whom do you want me to notify 🖉 you've been detained?'

'Nobody!' Walter shook his head. 'Please, no…I don't want my folks to know I'm here.'

'And why is that?'

'Let's just say I've brought enough worry to people. Whatever trouble I'm in, I'll deal with it alone. I always do.'

'You're no stranger to trouble then?'

'No.' Walter deliberated for a moment before continuing, 'I suppose I ought to tell you, it will come to light anyway…' But he couldn't finish. Another stabbing pain appeared to strike his stomach, this time totally winding him.

'Please, Mr Elliott. Allow me to take a look at him,' Mary pleaded, convinced there was something wrong.

Elliott sighed but conceded, 'Very well.'

She knelt by Walter, desperately hoping it wasn't a trick. Placing her hands on his soiled shirt, she slowly pulled it up to expose a massive bruise covering the width of his chest and tracking down to his navel. She drew back to allow Elliott to see. 'This man is injured, Mr Elliott.' Gently, she put down his shirt.

Walter looked into the deep pools of her eyes. 'It's not good, is it?' he said, pulling his hand back over his stomach. She offered him a half-smile in acknowledgement. Again, he winced and then began to cough. Suddenly he was barking uncontrollably. Blood splattered from his mouth.

'He needs to be seen by a doctor!' Mary shouted. Walter slumped into unconsciousness. 'Without delay!' she insisted.

Then the drama was all over. Just as quickly as it had started, it ended. Elliott watched as Walter was dispatched to hospital, Mary at his side.

The quietness allowed Elliott to ponder on what to make of the lad, and how he would offer any meaningful opinion to the courts. As he paced the cell in deliberation, his eye was suddenly drawn to an object on the floor. In the dim light, it gave off just enough of a twinkle for him to investigate further. Bending down, he now made it out. It was a chain and locket, or rather half a locket, slightly dented in one corner but otherwise well cared for. On the inner side was a red velvet lining. Fumbling around the floor, he searched for the other half; but there was nothing to be found.

He studied the locket and thought it looked familiar, but couldn't really think why. Eventually, he concluded that most likely, it was somebody's little trinket which Walter had stolen and since damaged. He wondered whether, when he came to interview Walter again, he would be able to find out the rightful owner and return it.

The locket's plain and simple design was in complete contrast to the complexity of its secrets.

CHAPTER 3

STRANGE SENSATIONS

A clock on the wall of the hospital receiving room showed 11 o'clock. Everything was ready for the following morning, when members of the public would surge through the doors, seeking any available medical help. Matron Hanson flicked over the pages of the large register on the lectern-type bureau, her bony finger moving down over the columns, checking for the slightest mistake.

'Ah, Matron, Matron! Just the person.' A refined voice broke her concentration. 'Sorry! Did I make you jump?' he carried on, devilishly, knowing the answer.

'Oh, Mr Sharpe,' said the shocked matron, her hand fixed firmly over her heart.

He proceeded to look around the desk, turning up papers, then discarding them, much to Matron's annoyance. 'Is it something in particular you're looking for, Mr Sharpe?' she asked, putting the papers back in order.

'My notes for tomorrow's lecture,' he continued, whilst rifling through more papers on the desk. 'They're somewhere round here, I'm sure.' Tom Sharpe was a brilliant general surgeon, arguably one of the best outside London, but alas, he was also perhaps the least organised where paperwork was concerned.

Matron couldn't take any more, her orderly world suddenly violated. 'Mr Sharpe! Please!' she exclaimed, then added calmly, 'If I may be allowed to assist you.'

Then, once again, her calm was shattered as, without warning, the double doors to the room burst open with a bang. Through them rushed a policeman pushing a trolley. On it lay Walter, still unconscious. Behind followed Mary, looking somewhat dishevelled after the night's ordeal. Matron, her eyes wide open, breathed deeply, before looking down at Walter, then at Mary, who had blood spatters on her uniform.

'Nurse O'Driscoll, what on earth…?'

'I'm sorry, ma'am, I can explain,' Mary answered, knowing full well she was going to be in serious trouble. Being in uniform outside work hours was bad enough and very much against regulations; but to bring a patient in off the streets, no matter how ill or injured, was always taboo and considered a severe breach of protocol.

'I'm sure you can, Nurse…in my office tomorrow morning, at precisely 8 o'clock!', Matron curtly concluded.

Tom, however, saw things differently; he only saw a patient in need of help. He felt Walter's neck for his pulse and checked the beat with his watch until, finally, he frowned and began to circle the man, surveying every inch of him. Taking his pen, he slowly parted a soiled, blood-stained shirt and quite casually remarked, 'Acute haemothorax.' Then turning Walter's head to one side, he touched a trickle of blood in the side of his mouth and rubbed it between forefinger and thumb, testing its consistency. 'Erm...possibly with some damage to the gastrointestinal tract or spleen. Very well, to the theatre with him then, please, Nurse.'

'But Nurse O'Driscoll is not on duty, Mr Sharpe,' Matron tried to explain.

Tom looked over to Mary, 'No, neither am I, dear...shall we?' He gestured the way forward. 'Oh, Matron, would you be so kind as to call Doctor Belling and tell him he's required in theatre.' Matron Hanson gave him the sort of glare only she could.

It wasn't unusual for a nurse, even a probationer, to find herself assisting a theatre surgeon in an emergency. Often, junior nurses found themselves witnessing the most gruesome of surgical procedures, with no real experience. Mary, however, did possess enough medical knowledge to know what was to come. It was the level of her own involvement that she was quite unprepared for.

'Come on, Mr Belling,' Tom muttered, scrubbing his hands harshly with carbolic soap and glancing at Walter, who now gave the occasional moan. Drying his hands, he announced his intention, 'Right! We can't wait any longer. You'll have to administer the anaesthetic, Nurse.'

'Me!' Mary responded, quite shocked.

'Unless you can see anybody else,' Tom declared.

'But Mr Sharpe...I...well...I haven't any skills in such matters,' she answered with trepidation.

'It's quite simple,' he said, handing her the leather bag and face mask. 'Don't worry; I'll talk you through it step by step.' He then proceeded to cut away at Walter's shirt and inspected the bruise, 'Erm, quite a trauma...all right, mask on...and a gentle squeeze.' He carried on, 'What did you say happened to the poor chap?'

Mary, desperately trying to make sure she followed his instructions precisely, blurted out, 'Did I...I mean, I didn't...oh, I'm sorry. Mr Sharpe, would you mind awfully if I were to just concentrate!'

He smiled generously and began to hum out a melody as he unravelled a tube. 'Another gentle squeeze now... feel his pulse...right, now hum with me.'

Mary looked at him perplexed but nervously began to join in as instructed. 'That's it...can you feel it beating in time?' he asked. She nodded in agreement. 'Good, then just let me know if it begins to race or fade.'

With that, he picked up his scalpel and started to talk to himself. 'About here will do.' He made a small incision into the side of Walter's chest. Blood immediately began to spurt out. He plunged the tube quickly into the hole, allowing the bright red liquid to feed through and drain into a bowl on the floor. 'Everything all right at your end, Nurse O'Driscoll?' His comforting tone made her visibly relax.

The sudden sound of hurried footsteps coming towards the theatre caused Tom to joke, 'Ah, it sounds as if we have the charge of the light brigade, Nurse. And just as we were doing so well together!'

'I'm terribly sorry, Mr Sharpe...,' Doctor Belling said, as he entered the theatre and rolled up his sleeves in readiness for action, 'Seizure on Vickers Ward, I'm afraid.' He took over from Mary, administering the anaesthetic without any acknowledgement of her efforts. Tom carried on calmly with the operation, not once looking up at Belling.

'Perhaps, well done Nurse O'Driscoll might be appropriate in the circumstances, Dr Belling!' he sarcastically remarked, not being one to suffer bad manners and lack of recognition.

'Yes, of course, absolutely...well done, Nurse!' Belling humbly replied and nodded to Mary, although inwardly he seethed that he should be openly embarrassed in front of a mere nurse!

It took another fifteen minutes of all his surgical skill before Tom was finally able to suppress the additional bleeding in Walter's stomach. Relieved, he began to stitch him up. 'Swab please,' he said, holding out his hand. But nothing was forthcoming. He looked up at Mary, 'Nurse, a swab please!' Mary stood next to him in a trance-like state, her eyes wide open and her gaze straight ahead.

Belling called out sternly, 'Nurse O'Driscoll, will you…,' but Tom interjected, raising a palm to silence him.

'Miss O'Driscoll, is everything all right?' he asked, thoroughly intrigued. Getting no response, he waved his hand in front of her face. 'Where are you, Nurse?'

Finally, Mary replied, 'I'm here,' her eyes still firmly fixed forward.

'And where is here, exactly?' Tom enquired.

'In the theatre of course.'

'What, in between me and Doctor Belling?'

'No, by the sterilising equipment.'

Tom looked at Belling, offering a raised brow. Belling in return gave only a shrug of confusion, for the equipment was at the other end of the theatre.

'He's going into arrest,' Mary said coolly.

Tom again looked over to Belling, who felt Walter's healthy pulse, 'His heart rate is absolutely fine,' he concluded. Tom glanced over to the clock. It read 11.50.

'What time is it on the clock, Miss O'Driscoll?'

'11.55.'

'Not 11.50? Look again,' he instructed her.

'No, definitely 11.55,' she added.

Tom was now utterly beside himself with excitement. For all his skill as a surgeon, his passion was for neurosciences and the unexplained workings of the mind. Mary's trance-like behaviour was research material of the highest order.

She moved away and sat in a chair.

'What is going on, Mr Sharpe?' Belling begged.

'She's having some sort of out-of-body experience,' Tom explained.

'A dream?'

'Yes, effectively.'

Suddenly Belling cried out, 'I'm losing his pulse!' Frantically he moved his fingers over Walter's neck and tried to locate the pulse point. 'No, it's gone.'

'Amazing...absolutely damned amazing!' Tom muttered and promptly thumped down hard on Walter's chest before bracing his hands together and starting to push up and down in an effort to resuscitate him. He looked over to Belling. 'Anything?' Belling just shook his head.

'He doesn't die.' Mary spoke out and walked over to Tom.

Tom carried on pumping, until Belling confirmed there was still no pulse.

'No, Mr Sharpe, don't give up! He does make it,' said Mary.

Tom looked into her eyes, which stared intensely at him.

'Please believe me,' she requested calmly and with conviction.

If nothing else, Tom realised he was witnessing something unique; and he did believe her. Again, he clasped his hands together and began to pump away at the limp body of his patient, to the utter frustration of Belling, who rolled his eyes in disbelief.

'This is utterly ridiculous,' Belling said, taking no trouble to hide his contempt for his superior – who carried on regardless. 'There's nothing, Mr Sharpe, absolutely nothing,' he added, feeling for Walter's pulse one more time.

Tom glared at Mary. With all his bravado, he couldn't now help but begin to feel that Belling would be proved right. 'When, Nurse? When?' he called to her anxiously.

Mary walked away and slumped deep into a chair. 'Do trust in me, Mr Sharpe,' she answered and gently closed her eyes.

'Come on! Come on, damn you!' Tom shouted at Walter, still pumping furiously.

'Am I honestly expected to witness anymore of this nonsense?' huffed Belling.

CHAPTER 4

FRUITFUL INVESTIGATIONS

Elliott started making further enquiries about Walter, realising he would ultimately be sent before a judge. His initial assessment was that the man was no more than an intriguing criminal. However, he would need to provide more than an absorbing tale when summoned to the Magistrates' Court.

He had little to go on, other than a name, an age and possibly a location, any one of which could be false; although he did remember Walter saying he was from Ecclesfield, and he himself knew of the village. It was thirteen miles or so away, and his old friend Canon Charles Brockwell lived there. It seemed a logical place to start.

Walking down the leafy lane to the vicarage, he wondered why he had never come across Walter before. Ecclesfield fell within the area served by his court, and he could recall all the cases that had gone before the bench for many a year. Unless, of course, this was the lad's first encounter with the law; but somehow he doubted that. Turning the corner, he reached the pretty ivy-clad house, with its velvet lawn gardens, beyond which the tower of the ancient village church was casting its shadow.

Canon Brockwell was delighted to see Elliott as he opened the door to him. 'Well, well, I'll be… It's been some time, but it's altogether good to see you,' he said, offering a firm handshake. 'Do come on in. How are you, Robert?' They went into his study, a large impressive room with a floor-to-ceiling library of books across one wall and a lovely old ornate fireplace on the other.

'Can I offer you a drink?' Brockwell asked, pouring them each one, regardless. Elliott accepted, his expression that of one not wishing to disappoint.

'Not a word to Mrs Brockwell, Robert,' added the Canon, furtively looking through the French windows. 'What is good for my soul is best the dear wife doesn't see!'

As they caught up on all manner of things, an hour soon passed, although Elliott, more often than not, was forced to be the listener rather than the talker.

'How's the research going?' Brockwell enquired, remembering his friend's passion for delving into the background of his house.

'Oh good, I'm back to 1854 so far.'

Brockwell gave an impressed smile, and Elliott took advantage of the pause in conversation to broach the purpose of his visit. 'I was rather hoping you could shed some light on a lad that I've chanced upon in custody. Apparently from these parts. He'd rather me not involve any of his people, so I haven't a deal of information to take to the courts.'

'Intriguing. What's his name?' Brockwell enquired.

'Stanford...,' Elliott began, but he wasn't allowed to finish as Brockwell interrupted him.

'What! Walter Stanford?'

'Yes, you know of him?

'I certainly do!' Brockwell's look turned quite sour.

A brief description of Walter quickly confirmed to Elliott that they were referring to the same young man.

'I dare say if he's crossed your path, Robert, the lad's met with trouble again?'

'Trouble that's landed him in hospital, I'm afraid.'

Brockwell offered what he knew of the man, and soon made it clear that Walter had taken to a life of crime out of deliberate choice; there being no reason other than mischief and his pure love of it. Walter had received an excellent education and begun a career with a successful commercial house, rising quickly in the organisation. By the age of twenty-two he had a considerable repertoire of foreign languages, and it was said he spoke and wrote German like a native.

'His mischievous nature was his undoing on most occasions, though,' remarked Brockwell.

Most occasions actually meant nine times: this being the number of convictions apparently recorded against Walter. Elliott learned the man was a total abstainer and non-smoker, had no interest in gambling; his only vice – burglary! Such was his climbing ability that he would enter premises through an attic window and then flee via the rooftops. Elliott wondered how he was always caught, until the Canon explained.

'There would be no catching him if he weren't such a fool as to come back peeping round a corner where the police were, just for the fun of seeing them baffled.'

'Well, the lad appears nothing if not intriguing, Charles,' Elliott commented. 'Thank you for the information; it will prove most useful.'

'You're welcome, Robert,' replied Charles, pleased he was able to help.

Canon Brockwell, however, knew much more of Walter's past than he was prepared to divulge to his friend, and there was good reason for his silence.

~~~

Another visit the following day to the commercial house filled in more gaps for Elliott and offered further insights into Walter's character. He waited patiently to see George Mills, the owner's son and an old school friend of Walter's at Trent, and later Rugby. Before long the pair were deep in conversation, Mills affectionately recounting bygone days and fond memories of weekends spent with Walter.

'I could tell you a hundred stories or more about his pranks, sir,' Mills concluded.

'So what happened to make him go so disastrously astray?'

Mills got up and walked to the window. Staring out, he continued, 'If only I knew! You see one weekend he went on a sailing trip to Devon and simply never came back!'

'Resigned?' Elliott asked.

'No. Well, by definition, yes, I suppose he did,' said Mills, remembering the confusion at the time. 'Nobody could believe it: Walter held awaiting trial on a charge of entering premises with intent to steal.' He returned to his leather chair, sighing, and threw his hands firmly down on the arms. 'Mr Elliott, Walter had a peculiarly constructed mind. For all his intelligence, he could also be such a fool.'

Elliott listened with interest as Mills explained further. Walter had been seen to climb to an open skylight on the roof of a house. Police officers were called and, going in the door, met him on the stairs, coming down from the attic he had entered through the skylight. Asked what business he had there, he replied that he was searching for friends he'd met on the pier, and with whom he proposed taking supper – he thought they lived at the house. Quizzed as to who the friends were, and being unable to name them, he was marched off to the police station. Further reflection couldn't help him remember his friends' names, yet he stupidly stuck to his tale in court.

'The truth was, Mr Elliott, Walter just couldn't resist an open attic window. Unlike you and me, who look at the pavement when we're walking, wherever Walter goes his eyes naturally turn upwards. He just feels bound to show people they're mistaken in their view that nobody can get in there. It's a case of being ruined by a gift for climbing and the challenge of getting into a place.'

Elliott gave him a look of confusion.

'I know it sounds ridiculous, sir, but that's how Walter is. It would never occur to him he was doing wrong – that ordinary mortals do not act as he acts,' Mills explained.

'Is he a thief?' Elliott asked, pointedly.

'No, I don't believe so…well, certainly not to start with, at any rate. I dare say more recently he has had a need to steal to survive.'

Elliott pulled out the chain and locket from his pocket, explaining, 'It's just I found this in his cell. Perhaps you would take a look, and tell me if you can remember him ever wearing such a thing.'

Mills took the locket and studied it for a moment, then smiled.

'Aye, this is Walter's all right. It was given him by his mother.'

'Really?' responded Elliott, realising he had made a wrongful assumption when he found it on the cell floor.

'Yes. If you only knew how many arguments this caused with the masters on the rugby fields,' Mills remembered, with an even bigger smile. 'He'd never take it off, you see.'

'It's rather unusual, just half of the locket.'

'The other half belonged to his sister, he reckoned.'

'He has a sister?'

'Did. Yes, Victoria. She died a few years ago. He worshipped and protected that sister of his, Mr Elliott, she being frail with consumption and all. I never saw anyone so devoted… I believe it was Victoria's death that changed him. After that his whole outlook on life became…well, dark, for want of a better word. He certainly grew ever more eccentric and distant, that's for sure…Took himself off yachting or climbing at any opportunity. I guess that's when we started to drift apart as friends.'

Mills then described how Walter's mother had been crushed by the news of his first arrest, taking to her bed and unable to attend the court hearing. His father, although devastated, bore up well to all outward appearances and duly attended the proceedings. Ultimately, though, he was as bemused as everyone else by his son's behaviour and could only agree that Walter's excuse must be a lie.

Knowing the court system, Elliott could appreciate how Walter's lying excuses would irritate the bench. They would think the story nothing but impudent invention. However, he was surprised to hear Mills recount that a sentence of three months' imprisonment with hard labour had been given, and he could only assume the magistrates had been somewhat overzealous. The sentence was harsh, and had shocked Walter, but he heard it like a man and left the dock with a contemptuous look on his face. All his previous good character counted for nothing with the man who presided over the bench.

'You think I'm a criminal? Then watch, and I'll act the part,' were his final words before being led away.

'I did write to him in prison, Mr Elliott, as did his father. We begged him to go straight when he came out of prison, and return to work, where all was understood.'

However, what Walter's father and Mills hadn't realised was that prison officials religiously observed regulations preventing the delivery of letters to short-term offenders until the morning of their release. Walter spent those three months of his detainment brooding, having only his father's reproachful incredulity at the trial to contemplate.

When, finally, Walter was handed his letters, he stood expressionless, reading his father's message, which was plain enough; but what Walter failed to realise was how ill his mother remained, and he could not understand why he was asked not to go home. He was not to know that the doctor had said his mother was too weak to bear the excitement of seeing him.

So, on being discharged, Walter vowed to put as many miles as possible between him and any place where he was known before his imprisonment. By now, he felt the injustice of his imprisonment keenly, and his mind turned to rebellion. He kept his word to act the criminal and, within weeks of his release, he was again in front of magistrates on the south coast.

Elliott duly thanked young Mills for his invaluable insight into Walter and the start of his troubles.

'I sail to the Transvaal tomorrow for six months, on business, but I would very much like to see Walter again on my return,' said Mills, as he opened the door for Elliott.

'I'm sure he would appreciate that, Mr Mills,' Elliott replied, realising theirs had been a true friendship and that Mills undoubtedly felt for Walter's current plight.

The two visits had changed Elliott's mind about Walter: there was something to make of the lad after all. At the small desk in his study, he contemplated the case. He had often been angered by magistrates. To his mind, their decisions, on occasion, represented a backward-looking attitude to resolving problems, particularly through the dispropor-tionate use of prison. With just a little consideration of root causes, he felt, many a young delinquent could be moulded to a better future. This certainly appeared to be the case with Walter. Elliott concluded that he must have elected to be dealt with summarily by a magistrates' court, most probably on the offer of the charge being reduced to one of being on enclosed premises for an unlawful purpose. This was a mistake, but understandable for one with no experience of court procedure. He would have stood a better chance at a higher court, with a jury. Elliott was convinced that, had he had able counsel, this travesty of justice would scarcely have been possible. That said, Elliott now knew Walter was his own worst enemy.

~~~

Elliott believed a visit to Walter's old school, Rugby, would provide some evidence of the lad's past high achievements. Enough, at any rate, to allow him to include a balanced character view in his report to the courts.

Dr Seymour walked with Elliott through the halls of the resplendent building with its views of the hallowed rugby fields spectacularly framed by large windows. The tall, thin teacher stopped by a row of plaques and slid his glasses over a furrowed forehead and onto his wispy, greasy hair.

'Stanford bordered on genius, Mr Eniott,' he pronounced.

'Elliott,' came the correction assertively, this being the third time the teacher had made the error.

Seymour took no notice and instead commented, 'Languages in particular: no tongue the boy couldn't master. One seldom witnesses talent of such a high order.'

They looked up at the empty space where a plaque was obviously missing. 'His honours award?' Elliott enquired.

Seymour acknowledged, 'For rock climbing, as I recall.'

Elliott wanted to know why the plaque had been removed.

'News travels fast, Mr Eniott,' Seymour babbled.

Elliott, now weary of the mispronunciation of his name, wondered if there was an honour for school idiot.

'The school has the highest reputation to uphold. We couldn't be seen to be honouring a criminal!' Seymour said, in a callous tone. 'A brilliant education, wasted! Social grounding obviously missing,' he hissed.

Elliott was unimpressed by Seymour's attitude and his obvious failure to look into the circumstances of Walter's downfall. He looked over to the man constantly on the lookout to chastise the next boy he caught running, and held out his hand to him.

'Well, I do thank you for giving me your time, Mr Sagemore. Goodbye!'

Dr Seymour looked offended at hearing his title disregarded and his name mispronounced. Elliott turned away and smiled.

~~~

When something troubled him, Elliott would pace up and down continuously, turning at each end of the room with the precision of a soldier. His wife had learnt long ago that, when he was in this mood, it was best to leave him to it. She would, however, always have the maid turn the carpet rug around 90° degrees the following morning to ensure even wear of its pile.

One thing that had nagged at him for the ten days he had been investigating Walter was the lad's chain and locket. He was convinced he'd seen it before somewhere, but he just couldn't remember where. There again Elliott had a long-term memory like a sieve. He picked up the locket and studied it hard, squinting one eye and rolling his tongue against his upper teeth in deep deliberation; but no memories were forthcoming.

Finally came his most peculiar habit, and the one most annoying to many who witnessed it: he pushed his hand deep into his pocket and brought out his loose change, carefully laying out the coins in order of size, then threw them all back into his pocket, only to repeat the whole exercise, again and again. In exasperation, he sat down, his hands in front of him, and began tapping his fingers together.

Elliott was no different to most men, and before long he had reached his boredom threshold. He opened his hands wider and wider until he was eventually conducting an orchestra. Then, quite softly, he brought them back together and started to make shadow shapes on the wall. Suddenly, like a man possessed, he cried out, 'Of course! Lucinda!'

Elliott had remembered the girl who had taught him to make the shape of a running horse with his hands. It was Lucinda Trevill. She was the owner of a chain and locket exactly like this one, a gift he'd given her many years previously.

'How strangely the mind works!' he laughed. For a while, he allowed his thoughts to drift back to his youth and his first meeting with Lucinda, at the local toll bridge, as he made his weekly visit to his uncle's farm. At one end of the bridge, in a field, was a tinker's horse-drawn caravan. It was home to the girl and her father and, in this tranquil idyll, the man would ply his trade of sharpening knives and odd bits of tool-making, whilst Lucinda would intercept travellers and attempt to sell them anything from shoelaces to lace handkerchiefs. She was a spirited girl, with a beauty that suggested Romany origins. Each week, as he approached the caravan, he melted under the effects of a growing infatuation; and eventually he had the finest collection of shoelaces!

Throughout those spring months, Lucinda would greet him with a drink of water on his arrival at the toll, and they would stay chatting for a while. One weekend, he plucked up the courage to ask her to stroll with him by the river. The die was cast for an innocent summer relationship. She was the butterfly, dancing and flirting; he the smitten eight-een-year-old eternally chasing God's beautiful creature. By the end of summer, he would have to return to college in

Ripon and their brief friendship would end; but not before they had exchanged gifts, pledged their devotion and promised to write letters to each other. Alas though, the butterfly, now adorned with his present of a chain and locket, would soon find her wings again and dance elsewhere.

Whilst Lucinda might have been his first love, Elliott had long since found his true love. She was Ann, the woman he adored, and they had been married for eighteen years. He looked out of the window at her on the lawn, playing catch with their two young sons, and knew he was a lucky man. She chased their youngest, Cecil, up and down, until finally she caught hold of him and spun him around in her arms. Several tickles later, they were both laughing outrageously and cuddling cheek to cheek. The elder son, Henry, couldn't quite see what was so funny and slouched off to read his fishing book.

Seeing them together at that moment made Elliott realise just how much Cecil looked like his mother. It was then that a possibility suddenly entered his thoughts, and he recalled Mills' words about Walter getting the locket from his mother. 'No, surely not!' he said out loud. But the more he thought about it, the more he was convinced he was right. He visualised Lucinda again, then Walter, trying to see a resemblance. Even though he had seen him only briefly in the cell, and despite his face being covered by dirt and blood, it didn't take much imagination to see the similarity. He was absolutely convinced that Walter was Lucinda's son. And from what he'd learnt of Walter so far, it seemed the lad had inherited the same desire for life and adventure as his mother.

Elliott went to sit in his chair and took a few minutes more to consider the likeness between the two. He took hold of the locket again and smiled. Finally, he resolved he would try to help Walter as much as he was able. If it were within his power to get him back on a straight course, then he would do so. In the meantime, however, there were plenty of other court cases requiring his attention as a missionary and, as always, he needed to write reports to present to the magistrates.

One report he wasn't looking forward to writing was on a once-sweet mother, Alice Harper, employed as a housemaid by Canon Brockwell. It had been quite a shock for him to meet her in the cells that week, now a destitute woman and held on a charge of petty theft.

'How on earth did this happen?' he enquired. 'You were a respectable woman in the employ of the church. Does Canon Brockwell know of your situation?'

The woman explained that she was no longer in service at the vicarage and began to pour out her absolute loathing for the Canon. Her comments shocked Elliott and, had he not known Brockwell, he would have thought she was describing a monster.

'There are things I could tell you about the man, Mr Elliott, things I wasn't meant to see or hear,' the woman said, with bitterness. She wanted to say more, but held back, suddenly realising that, if she went on and Brockwell were to find out, he would carry out the threats he had made to her. Elliott had tried to probe, unwilling to accept such a statement without foundation. But the woman refused to give further details, and thereafter only gave disparaging general comments. In the end, Elliott could only presume that a once perfectly good master-servant relationship had somehow become strained to such an extent that things became untenable. Dismissal from service was, therefore, inevitable and ultimately brought her into hardship. Given this, he wasn't surprised she sought redress through unkind words. However, this was only a superficial explanation. Had the woman not feared for her life, she would have told Elliott much more, and taken his investigation of Walter down a different path altogether.

As he left the cell, Alice uttered parting words that would stick in his memory, and that one day he would appreciate in relation not just to Alice, but also to Walter.

'In the future, Mr Elliott, perhaps not in my lifetime, maybe not even in my child's, but one day, women will have a better deal of things.'

CHAPTER 5

A CHARMING PATIENT

Had Tom Sharpe been organised and on time, he would have been at a dinner party the night Walter lay all but dead on his operating table, and the lad's fate might have been altogether different. As it was, fortune had blessed Walter with a skilled surgeon and, like Mary O'Driscoll had predicted, Walter's heart had eventually begun to beat again, just at the point when Tom was ready to admit defeat. Now, two weeks later, he was making steady progress towards recovery.

Sitting up in his bed, he looked a great deal different to his former self. Gone were the ashen look and yellow tinged, blood-shot eyes. In their place was a healthy, handsome face, clean-shaven and well nourished, his chiselled features framed by clean and somewhat shorter hair, although not cut as short as Matron Hanson had prescribed. The Matron had yet to witness his roguish streak and was unaware that, days earlier, Walter had convinced a young nurse that, because he was required in a police line up, a truly short haircut would infinitely change his appearance, therefore, would not be permissible. Such was the charming patient in their midst!

That morning he was in especially good spirits and ready for any fun that could be had. Deep down he knew all too well that his time in the hospital was nearing its end and that several months, perhaps more, in prison lay ahead. 'No jollity in that hotel,' he would say to four or five fellow patients crowded around his bed listening to his yarns.

However, all of them would quickly depart on hearing the clatter of footsteps. An army of footsteps meant it was time for the senior surgeon's rounds, and therefore, they had to prepare themselves to appear sufficiently unwell not to be discharged. For many a patient, another day in hospital would mean three meals and a last opportunity to feel the comfort of a bed with clean sheets. Discharge for many meant a return to the streets or back to the workhouse. Either way, their future would be as desperate as could be imagined.

Tom, with an entourage of students and junior doctors, breezed into the ward, where the Sister was preparing to accompany them on their round. They were met with patients suddenly coughing and whining, as if auditioning for a play. The surgeon, however, was having none of it. Despite being only 29 years old, he was far too experienced to be taken in. He picked up the clipboard from the end of a bed, the occupant wheezing relentlessly.

'What you must always remember, Doctor Grayson, is that not all the best actors are on the stage!' Tom declared to the young man, before handing the clipboard to the Sister. 'Another dose of castor oil and fennel, and then he can be released,' he concluded without emotion.

'Ah, Mr Stanford! And how are we today?' Tom asked Walter, approaching his bed.

'Well…,' said Walter, '…the food is good, the bedrooms are of the finest order but, as you can see, the entertainment needs improvement.' He finished with a sweep of his hand through the air.

'Indeed, I agree. Right, Miss Kramer! This patient had an acute haemothorax…' He lifted up the sheet covering Walter and continued, '…with complications of bleeding in the upper gastrointestinal tract. In your opinion, this is caused by…?'

The young German student began to attempt an answer but became flustered and blushed. 'Look at the location of the scar for a clue,' Tom suggested. All eyes fell on Miss Kramer. She hesitated before stuttering a very unclear response in broken English.

In perfect German, Walter joined in. 'Don't allow him to intimidate you, my dear. Tell him, he is but an ass for embarrassing you so.' Miss Kramer gave him a slight giggle, as she stood amazed at the fluency of his sentence – every word of her mother tongue perfectly pronounced.

'Very impressive, Mr Stanford. And may we enquire what you said?' Tom asked.

'I simply told her the answer.'

'Did you now! Then perhaps you could share your medical knowledge with us,' Tom suggested.

Walter needed no further encouragement and promptly told the assembled trainees, 'A ruptured spleen.' He would have been quite ignorant of the answer, of course, had he not previously heard the surgeon discussing his case when he was presumed to be asleep.

'Exemplary! I can see we will need to be more careful what we say within earshot of you, Mr Stanford,' Tom sarcastically replied, before moving on to the next bed. Suddenly, he caught sight of Mary in the corridor. 'If you'll excuse me. Carry on Doctor Grayson…Examine the chest and lungs and give me your prognosis,' he instructed.

'Nurse O'Driscoll,' he called out, before finally catching up with Mary.

'Yes, Mr Sharpe,' she replied.

'I was hoping to have a word…about the other week,' Tom began. He had not seen Mary since the night of Walter's operation. She had hoped that the matter had been forgotten and looked at him sheepishly.

'I do apologise, Mr Sharpe. It won't happen again!'

'What won't?' Tom replied, rather bemused.

'You have to understand it was a very long day and I…', Mary tried to explain, but Tom interrupted.

'My dear nurse, whatever are you talking about?'

'My falling asleep on duty.'

'As I recall, you weren't on duty.'

'Then you won't report what happened to Matron?'

'No, why on earth should I?' he asked, taking from her hands a pile of towels that was creating a barrier between them.

'Thank you,' she said softly.

'Tell me, do you dream, Miss O'Driscoll?' he asked. Mary's puzzled look made him realise his question sounded rather intrusive and needed further explanation. 'Of course you do. Sorry, what I meant was – that night in theatre, can you remember dreaming?'

'Well…yes, a little,' she said, but she was being less than honest. She remembered everything, and vividly. In fact, so real was her recollection that it had frightened her for several days afterwards. 'Why do you ask?' she enquired, innocently.

Tom could see she was uneasy. 'Have you heard of a phenomenon described as an out-of-body experience?'

'Vaguely.'

'Because that's what I think happened to you.' Tom explained further, 'You see, dreams – of all kinds – are

49

something that really fascinates me. Perhaps I could help you understand the things you dream.'

'Please, I really ought to be going,' Mary implored, taking back the towels.

'If it happens again, would you allow me to do some research?' Tom eagerly asked.

'I'm sure, Mr Sharpe, it was just fatigue, that's all…I don't anticipate I could assist you in the future,' she said, abruptly ending the conversation.

Mary had no wish to be analysed in such a way. She could be an intensely private person, neither courting comment about herself nor worrying too much about what others said. However, she was not to be able to blame fatigue for her next strange experience.

Mary's shifts over the following days saw her working more on Walter's ward, where she observed him with interest. He was not at all what she had first assumed – a mere criminal; quite the contrary. Sometimes she would find herself help-lessly staring at him, as though quite smitten. Then, when he noticed, she would blush like a schoolgirl. She became more and more fascinated by him, trying to fight her infatuation one moment, whilst the next she would do anything possible to be in his company. She would listen to him intently when he spoke, captivated by his voice, allowing his words to be absorbed into her thoughts.

One evening, as she watched him, standing unseen

beyond the entrance to the ward, she fell into another out-of-body experience, seemingly drawn, in her trance, to an intense light which appeared around him. She walked forward through the entrance to the ward, and the next moment she was standing in a large, splendid ballroom, dressed in a lovely chiffon gown, and looking onto a scene of waltzing couples. Walter, in evening dress, suddenly appeared, smiling, in front of her and he held out his hand. She placed her own hand in his, and allowed him to lead her onto the dance floor. Their eyes locked as they danced together, and to Mary, everything around them was a blur, except for a young woman, who stood watching them, smiling. Yet during the whole fantasy experience, Mary was, in reality, simply standing on the ward with an expressionless face.

'Hello Nurse Mary,' said Walter's voice, softly. She didn't respond, her eyes fixed forward.

'Mary!' he repeated, waving a hand in front of her face.

Only then did she regain consciousness. She looked at him in disbelief and gasped, 'Oh dear Lord!'

'Well, not quite,' laughed Walter, but Mary was too stunned to react to his teasing.

'But I'm on the ward!'.

'I'm afraid so. Are you all right, Mary? he asked with some concern. 'You look as if you've seen a ghost!'

Mary shook her head and put a hand to her mouth

'What is this all about?' she asked, glaring at Walter.

'I'm so sorry if I startled you,' he said.

Mary slowly began to take control of herself again 'What are you doing out of bed, Walter?'

'Oh, I couldn't sleep, my mind being preoccupied with thoughts of…well, you know, back into custody and so on.'

Her composure regained, Mary searched for something apt to say. 'Yes, I'm sorry you have to leave us in such circumstances.'

Like a remorseful puppy, he looked downwards. 'I'm not a wrong 'un, Mary. A rogue and a prankster, perhaps. Even a misguided fool. But please don't think me a true wrong 'un.'

'No, Walter, I don't believe you are,' she murmured. As he looked up again, she began to melt, wanting only to hug him, to share his tragedy and relieve his pain. But, of course, she dared not move towards him.

Loud shouts from the adjoining ward broke their tender moment. Mary stood up straight as Nurse Abrahams came running over. 'Can you help please, Mary?' she panted.

'What is it?' Mary asked.

'It's the foreign patient. He's ranting.'

Mary set off with her fellow nurse and Walter, intrigued, felt impelled to follow.

The foreign patient was an old Polish man in the last, agonising days of cancer, his pain-riddled body now begging to be released to its maker.

'Mr Pedawicz, please calm down!' Nurse Abrahams cried, trying to restrain the man's thrashing arms. Totally blind and in delirium, he continued to call out. Before long, three nurses were restraining him. He shouted out ever louder, in his mother tongue. Sister Lester finally took control.

'Get the straps, Nurse Abrahams,' she instructed.

Walter watched the pitiful scene as attempts were made to strap the patient down. Eventually he had to speak out. 'He just wants his son.'

Sister Lester spun around in surprise. 'Mr Stanford, what are you doing here? Please go back to bed.'

'All he's asking for is his son,' Walter reiterated. 'Please let me talk with him…in Polish. It will calm him.'

Sister looked at the junior doctor who was now on the scene. He shrugged his shoulders and conceded, 'Why not?'

Taking hold of Mr Pedawicz's frail hand, Walter spoke softly to him. 'You must stop shouting.' Instantly the ranting stopped as the old man recognised his native language.

'Ivan! Ivan! My boy, is that you?' came the man's emotional reply. His hand clasped hard onto Walter's. Walter took a deep breath and paused for a moment. He didn't want to deceive, but he knew that, for the sake of the man, he had to.

'Yes, Papa, it's me, Ivan.'

Mr Pedawicz let out all his agony, wailing repeatedly, 'Take me home.'

'Let's walk, Papa,' Walter suggested, trying to choke back his tears. 'Imagine we're walking home together. Can you hear the birds singing, Papa?'

'Yes, I hear them,' the old man replied, the whites of his blind eyes positioned upwards. Then his lip began to wobble and he started to sob.

'What is it, Papa?'

'The house, our little house…Over there! Look!'

Walter realised Mr Pedawicz was reliving happier days. 'That's right. We're home again and Mama will be waiting for us,' he said.

'Ivan, wait!' He pulled on Walter's arm, then suddenly blurted out, 'Bread…We haven't got Mama the bread.'

'Don't worry! I'll get the bread, Papa. You go in and take a rest now…Close your eyes.' Walter held him and softly started to hum. Then, with a final squeeze of hands and a slight grimace, it was all over. The old man had found peace.

Walter looked over to the small gathering of staff. They hadn't understood a word of what had been said, but all were nonetheless touched by the tenderness of it all.

'Thank you, Mr Stanford,' Sister Lester finally acknowledged.

~~~

Two days later, Mary would meet another charming young lad. It was a meeting that seemed nothing out of the ordinary, but was actually far from it.

As she walked to work each morning, Mary would purchase a daily newspaper from one of the young street sellers and take it onto the ward for Walter to read. It was just a little gesture of kindness that was much appreciated by him. He loved to study the foreign correspondence columns.

The boy, probably no more than nine or ten years old, shouted out, 'Telegraph! Get yer Telegraph here!' and thrust out a folded paper towards passers-by. As Mary approached, he pulled off his cap and let his tousled hair fall down around his cheeky face. 'Always something interesting to read for such a beautiful lady as you, miss,' he said.

'Then I must take one. Thank you,' smiled Mary, and she looked at the boy with some interest, not being able to recollect if she'd seen him on the streets before. He looked far more scruffy than most of the other boys, and with clothes that, even as hand-me-downs, appeared strangely dated. Still, she gave him little more thought and took the newspaper, dropping her money into a little ink-stained hand, that, even allowing for the black newsprint, did not appear to have been washed properly for weeks.

'Thank you, miss,' the boy said with enthusiasm, seeing that she had given him two pennies more than was necessary. As she walked across the street, she heard him shout out after her, 'You will show it Walter, won't you, Mary?' But when she turned back, a trolley bus obscured her view.

Only when it had passed could she see that the boy had gone, vanished as if into thin air. She was rather unnerved and wondered if it had all been yet another vision, but if that were the case, why was she still holding a newspaper?

When Mary entered the ward she placed the paper on the desk, ready to take to Walter after the doctor's rounds. She hadn't even glanced at it, and so did not notice that it did not have the usual layout and type. Had she looked more closely, it would have been immediately evident that the paper was some twenty-odd years old!

A busy and eventful shift that day meant she completely forgot to hand over the newspaper, and wasn't even aware it had gone from the desk. It was only when she was called into the Matron's office that she was prompted to remember it.

'Yes,' answered Matron Hanson to Mary's knock on the door. 'Ah, Nurse, come in,' she continued as she saw who it was.

Mary began cautiously to enter the room, but stopped abruptly as the man sitting opposite the Matron's desk turned to look at her. It was Canon Brockwell.

'Well, do enter girl,' hissed Matron with impatience, as Mary just stood there, half in, half out of the doorway. Eventually, she moved forward and closed the door behind her.

'This is Canon Brockwell,' Matron said.

Mary looked at the Canon uneasily and her stomach began to churn. She had no reason to feel this way; it was simply her reaction to his presence.

'How do you do, Canon,' Mary eventually said, her eyes fixed on his.

Moving his head slightly from side to side, the Canon began to stare at Mary in an intense way, making her feel even more uneasy. As he continued to stare, it seemed to him that he had met her before, so familiar did her face look. Finally, he took control of himself and said, 'I'm so sorry, my dear, but as I look at you, I have to ask, have we met before?'

Mary tried to remember a past encounter, but eventually, she had to admit, 'I don't believe so, Canon, but do please forgive me if we have.'

'No matter. At my age I'm always mixing things up,' he replied, not convinced.

'Well...,' interrupted Matron, keen to get to the reason why the Canon was here and why Mary had been called, 'I need to establish something, Nurse.'

'I see. Then how can I help?' asked Mary.

Matron began in a sarcastic tone, 'It's the ever charming Mr Stanford. The Canon believes he may have some jewellery that doesn't belong to him.'

'Indeed,' babbled Brockwell.

'Oh!' Mary said in surprise.

'You seem shocked, Nurse,' said Brockwell.

'Well, yes, I suppose I am.'

'Mr Stanford is a criminal. You are aware of that?'

'So I understand,' Mary had to concede.

Matron once more brought the conversation to its point. 'You saw Mr Stanford when he was in the police cells and again when he was admitted and operated on. Did he have any jewellery on him or in his belongings?'

Mary thought for a second before answering, 'No, I can assure you he wasn't wearing any jewellery and, as for belongings, well he hasn't any, other than the clothes he wore when brought in. May I ask exactly what jewellery is he supposed to have?'

'It really isn't relevant. If you say he wasn't wearing any, then I must have been misinformed,' Brockwell replied.

'Well, I'm sorry we couldn't help you on the matter, Canon,' concluded Matron, sitting back in her chair.

'That's quite all right, Matron. I hope you understand that I had to make sure.'

The whole visit had now gone wrong for the Canon. What better way, he'd thought, to get hold of Walter's locket than under the pretence of Walter having stolen it from someone he knew. The flaw, however, was that he had never imagined Walter wouldn't be wearing it: the thing he now so desperately sought.

Walter had visited Brockwell some months earlier.

He had always been intrigued by his locket's past and, in particular, by the writing on a small note hidden behind the velvet lining. Believing the words might have some religious connection, he had hoped the Canon would be able to help. But the situation had come as a shock to Brockwell. As he was handed the half locket to study, his eyes opened wide with astonishment. He was holding jewellery he knew very well, and which had been worn by someone who had witnessed his wicked past. Whilst the words on the piece of paper would make no obvious sense to other people, they did to him, and he was worried that Walter would somehow unearth their meaning. He had held his secret for many a year, and he wasn't prepared to let anyone discover anything that would expose him now. Consequently, he had told Walter one lie after another. The lad seemed satisfied; but Brockwell knew he would feel much better if he could destroy that little note.

'Well, that will be all, thank you, Nurse,' said Matron; but suddenly she remembered there was something else. 'Oh yes! Nurse, is this newspaper yours?' she enquired and pointed to her desk. Mary looked over and saw the newspaper, as did Canon Brockwell; but his reaction was one of blind panic. On the front page was the headline "THE TRAGIC TRUTH OF 24 NEWSOME STREET."

'Dirty old newspapers on the ward just won't do, Nurse,' Matron reprimanded. 'Whatever possessed you to leave such a thing lying around?'

Brockwell braced himself, as they all looked again at the paper.

'Walter…,' Mary started to say, then stopped on seeing Matron raise her eyebrows. 'Sorry, Mr Stanford, likes me to bring one in for him to read.'

'The thing is filthy,' said Matron, picking it up, to Brockwell's horror. His leg was now trembling with anxiety. She read the date and pronounced, 'It's over twenty years old!'

'But I don't understand,' said Mary in confusion. 'I only bought it this morning, ma'am, from the street sellers.'

Brockwell offered a simple explanation: 'I think you've been duped by those urchins, my dear.'

Mary couldn't really think of any other reason, unless the boy was yet another strange vision. After all, he had looked as if he were from the past. 'Oh I don't know,' she said to herself, 'Perhaps the Canon is right and I have simply been duped.'

'I'll take it to Mr Stanford right away,' Mary suggested.

'You'll do no such thing, my girl. That newspaper will go nowhere other than in a rubbish bin. Do I make myself clear?' insisted Matron. Mary gave her only a look of disappointment.

'This Mr Stanford seems to have all my nursing staff quite smitten, Canon Brockwell,' Matron huffed.

'Indeed,' said Brockwell, but he was barely paying attention to the Matron. His mind was preoccupied with Mary. Was it just coincidence she should appear out of the blue with an old newspaper mentioning Newsome Street? How well did she know Walter and what had she learned about him? Had Walter solved the puzzle of his locket and asked her to find a newspaper highlighting the events at that place? The possibilities were agonizing. In the meantime, he had to make sure Walter did not read the paper.

'I really should be getting along Matron. I do thank you for your time and attention. Please, allow me to dispose of this for you on my way out,' he said and firmly clutched the newspaper as he stood up to make an exit.

'That's kind, thank you, Canon. I'm sorry we weren't able to help with your jewellery matter,' replied Matron, holding open the door.

'Not at all,' he replied and then turned to address Mary. 'Perhaps you would be good enough to show me to the hospital entrance, Nurse. I really have no sense of direction in these places.'

Mary had no option but to agree, though she felt most anxious at having to accompany the man by herself. There was something about him that made her skin creep. As they walked down the corridor, Brockwell skilfully quizzed Mary. To his relief, it appeared she knew nothing.

All the same, he thought it would be wise to discourage any future association with Walter. 'If I were you, Nurse, I would keep my distance from Walter Stanford.'

Mary looked at him with dismay as he continued. 'You see, I happen to know Walter very well and…how shall I put this? Let's just say he has a rather blemished past, one that I am sure, a well brought up and wise young woman such as you would not wish to be tarnished by.'

'I'm sorry, Canon, but am I to believe you think that Walter and I are somehow…?'

'No, my dear, not at all. What I am trying to say is merely that many women fall for Walter's charm and, ultimately, come to regret it, if you understand my meaning?'

Mary pulled up sharply. Firmly she replied, 'Yes I do understand your meaning, Canon, and might I say that I am not like many women, sir.' She pointed forward and down the corridor, 'The exit is just down there and to the right. Good day, Canon Brockwell.'

He gave her an insincere smile and made his farewell. Of course, he had lied about Walter. Although the lad was, without question, a blatant charmer, he was not the sort of man who would take advantage of a woman. In fact, at twenty six, his experience of women was very limited. However, the Canon's defamation of Walter's character had been enough to at least sow a seed of doubt in Mary's mind.

CHAPTER 6

FURTHER DREAMS

Mary's home was just two small rented rooms in a less than desirable part of the city but they were cheap and near the hospital. She had been happier in the Nurses' Home on the hospital grounds. However, after finishing their training, nurses were expected to make way for the next intake of students. Her rooms were high in the attic of the house, accessed by a twisting staircase. In winter, they were freezing cold, in summer stifling hot. With only a small dormer window and a skylight in the main room, she often felt uncomfortably hemmed in, and she looked forward to the day her trust fund could be accessed and she would be able to afford something better, something more like what she had been accustomed to back in Ireland. Sadly, legal wrangles meant it would be a while before this was likely to happen.

Nevertheless, she made the best of what she had, creating pretty furnishings in her free time to brighten things up. Towards the back of the room was a large screen, which she hated, but it did divide off the kitchen area and was to some extent disguised with an emerald green drape with motifs sewn on it – a small reminder of home. Above the fireplace a small single shelf held various precious knick-knacks. Mary did so love to see the glow of a fire, but seldom had much time to prepare one, except on her day off, when she would curl up in front of the comforting flames and read a book. The rest of the room was functional, having a table, a couple of chairs and a sofa. Perhaps most important to Mary, though, was the bookcase, full of her neatly stacked books.

Mary's bedroom was a more cheerful affair, and quite spacious. Unusually for a rented property, it had an impressive Georgian wardrobe, which she adored. She often wondered how Mrs Walsh, the landlady, had managed to get it brought up the stairs and into the room. Perhaps the difficulty of moving it was why it was still there, she thought. The double bed was covered in a beautiful patchwork quilt, a gift to her from the deaf school. Alongside was a freestanding full-length mirror and a tallboy, the top of which displayed not the usual array of small items you would expect of a young woman, but a casket containing numerous letters, carefully placed on a piece of embroidered linen.

The envelopes, bound in bright green ribbon and tied

with a bow, were her treasured possession and the link with her past. Inside were letters from her devoted parents, both of whom, to her great anguish, had been killed in a freak landslip accident whilst out walking on a coastal path. At one time, she had read and reread the letters endlessly, but now, three years on, the memory was not quite as painful and she only opened them occasionally, mostly when she needed her spirits raising. From her father's letters she drew support for her vocation as a nurse, whilst from her mother's she found the strength to discover new experiences.

Returning from the hospital on the day of her encounter with Canon Brockwell, Mary sank onto the sofa, took out the pins from her nurse's cap, and allowed her silky dark hair to fall. She shook her head and leant back, her arms lying limp beside her. Thank the Lord, she thought, grateful to be out of the bitter cold. However, no sooner had she closed her eyes than it started – the most annoying thing about her rooms: the hot water pipes! A series of clunks and clatters finally gave way to a continuous vibrating sound that couldn't be ignored. She went over to the pipe by the sink, took off her shoe and began to bang sharply. This caused the usual shouts of disapproval from Mrs Walsh down below, and the usual angry retort from Mary that it was high time the pipes were mended.

After an evening spent reading, Mary climbed into her bed and drifted into a deep sleep. Then her dream was instant. She stood watching him, a young Walter, at Rugby School, climbing up the facade of the masters' building. On the ground were three of his school friends, including George Mills. She wasn't one of the group; but with just a slight twist of her body, she was able to soar into the sky and observe the scene from any angle. Once again, Mary was having an out-of-body experience. But this time her dream related not to the present but to the past.

'What's the wager I make it then, George? How about I walk out with that lovely sister of yours?' Walter shouted down.

'I think you're deluding yourself there, dear chap,' was George's lofty response.

'Be careful, Walter,' Mary heard herself saying. Yet the words didn't come from her mouth. Instead, they were spoken by George Mills. It was if she were pre-empting the dialogue.

'Oh, stop fretting. Don't forget, I'll be climbing the Matterhorn one day,' Walter joked.

'Matterhorn! Listen to him! Thinks he's Edward Whymper, no less,' his other friend, Jim, joked, as Walter scaled the balustrade and finally reached the roof.

With another twist, Mary was able to bring herself up alongside him, watching him pull at the half-open skylight. The next moment he was inside Dr Seymour's room, looking around. He spied a pair of long johns and then the master's cane. 'Ha!' he said to himself, glancing back at the skylight. 'I wonder?' In a flash he had tied the under garment to the cane and was wedging the cane into the window casing. It took only seconds for Walter to be out of the window and scrambling back over the guttering, leaving the long johns to blow merrily in the wind.

Back on the ground, Walter re-joined his friends as they moved away from the masters' building towards the courtyard. Mary was now beside him, not exactly walking but more floating. It was a bizarre experience, yet one that felt quite normal, quite real.

Dr Seymour looked up as a boy drew attention to his long johns billowing out in full view. He went a deep crimson colour at the roar of laughter from the boys all around, and then, enraged, he stormed off.

'You are a rogue, Walter Stanford,' Mary said.

'I know, but surely a loveable one?' he replied and smiled. 'Hello, Mary.'

Mary was shocked. Her dream now suddenly allowed her to talk to him!

Then, just as in a cinema show, the scene changed. Her dream was back in the present, and she felt the warmth of Walter's naked body next to hers, his legs drawing her closer to him. She murmured softly as his lips gently brushed her neck, and his warm breath caressed her shoulders. She felt the pleasant sensation of a finger running down her spine, as his other hand slowly outlined her breast. Tenderly, his lips nibbled down her rib cage. She gave a sigh of delight as he rolled her over and ran his tongue over her now erect nipples.

Then, just as Walter was working his way down her body, Mary opened her eyes and was wide-awake. Utterly confused, she pulled herself upright and could feel her heart beating fast. Her nightgown clung to her sweat-covered body. Still panting, she mopped her brow. What on earth has just happened? she thought in bewilderment. Eventually she realised it must have been a dream. Half of her was disgusted at the mere idea of being in bed with Walter; the other half desperately wished the dream hadn't ended and she were free to continue the passion of those few minutes. She began to sob, her emotions confused and overwrought.

Finally, Mary began to try and put her experience into perspective – for such was her nature. She knew there must be a good reason for what had happened; she just needed to find it. She made herself a cup of tea, and flicked through her medical books, remembering what Mr Sharpe had said about the phenomenon of out-of-body experiences. To her surprise, there was little documented beyond a general definition of: 'The feeling of leaving the confines of one's body.' To her frustration, her books could offer her no real insight. She dropped the last book in disappointment and sipped on her tea, realising she would need to visit the library to read further on the subject. Perhaps a visit to Mr Sharpe would offer the most information, she considered.

The thought of such a visit did not appeal much. Mary knew she would be terribly embarrassed discussing any details of a sexual nature, even with a woman, let alone with a man! Unlike many Irish people, Mary was not a Catholic; but she had had a strict moral upbringing. As such, any exposure to relationships of a sensual nature had been through romantic fiction. However, no novel she had read could be compared with the dream experience that she now recollected so vividly. It was only as she calmed down did she realise that, if she did speak with Tom Sharpe, there was no need to go into graphic details.

Knowing she would see Walter again the next day did, however, make her anxious. It also filled her with a warm expectancy that she couldn't quite comprehend. What was it about this man that had suddenly turned her world upside down and thrown her otherwise well-organised life into turmoil? She sat for a while pondering the enigma of him, before finally falling asleep. This time she slept without event, or at least none she could remember the following morning when she awoke.

Mary steeled herself as she walked into the ward. 'It was just a dream, that's all, nothing more,' she kept saying to herself.

'Morning Nurse Mary.' Walter was the first to speak, watching her sort the daily pile of clean bed linen.

'Yes, morning to you, Walter,' she courteously replied.

'I shan't be troubling you all much longer…so I'm told,' he mentioned, casually. His words cut through her like a knife, making her realise that what she felt for him was more than just imagination.

'I see.' She wanted to say more but resisted.

'Yes, apparently Mr Elliott will be here at three o'clock on Tuesday to prepare me for trial.'

'You talk as if you'll be on trial for murder.'

'It may not be murder, but the outlook's still grim - prison!'

Pulling a curtain part of the way round his bed, Mary asked, 'Walter, may I ask you something?'

The swift change of subject took him by surprise. 'Of course. What is it?' he said, seeing that something was obviously troubling her.

'When you were at school, did you get up to any pranks?' Mary enquired.

Walter laughed, 'My dear Mary, where do you want me to start?'

'Anything that included climbing? Perhaps a teacher was involved?' she asked.

Walter thought her question over for a second, then recalled, 'Well yes, there was the time when I climbed up to old Seymour's room. Thinking back, it was a bit childish.' He started to laugh as he remembered the situation, 'I actually tied his long johns on his cane and...'

Mary joined him in finishing his sentence, softly muttering, '...hung them from a roof window.' She took a deep sigh, remembering her dream, and worried that, if the prank actually happened in reality, then surely so did their passion in bed. She put a hand to her mouth and quickly hurried away.

A bemused Walter could only call after her in concern, 'Mary, where are you going? Is everything all right?'

Alone in the corridor, she leant her head back against the wall and closed her eyes for a moment. 'What was the significance of it all? What is happening to me?' she asked herself in desperation.

CHAPTER 7

EXPLANATIONS

'Come in,' Tom shouted, in response to the delicate knock on his door. Slowly, it opened, until, finally, Mary peered in.

'I'm sorry to bother you, Mr Sharpe, but I…,' she started to say politely, hoping that Tom would give a welcome and ease her nervousness.

She needn't have worried. Tom immediately held out his hand and cheerfully replied, 'Nurse O'Driscoll, what a surprise! Do please come in.' It was a genuine surprise for him to see her out of uniform. He couldn't help but admire Mary, who looked more mature dressed in a nipped-in, hip-length, plaid jacket and a matching circular skirt that showed off her tiny waist.

'I do hope I'm not putting you to any inconvenience; I know it's against the rules,' she said, entering the small room and looking around at the mass of papers, books and journals strewn everywhere.

'Oh bother the rule book! Here, let me find you a seat,' he offered, moving a pile of papers off a chair, and not feeling a bit embarrassed about the state of his office.

'Quite a collection of…well…things, Mr Sharpe!' Mary observed jovially before sitting down.

'Perhaps I could offer you some tea?'

'You have a kettle?' she remarked, coyly, looking about for where it might be hidden.

Tom had to admit he wasn't the tidiest of people. 'It is around somewhere.' He sat down, pushed back his blond hair and joked, 'Well, Nurse, to what do I owe the pleasure? Should I assume you're here to whisk me away to some distant paradise?'

Mary gave only a hesitant little smile in response, not yet being attuned to his sense of humour.

'I have been thinking about what you said,' she explained.

'About the kettle?' he asked.

Mary looked at him bemused.

'I'm teasing, Miss O'Driscoll.' Realising he should stop his playfulness, he leant forward and clasped his hands together. 'Your dreams, you've had one again, haven't you?'

'Well…yes,' Mary said softly, casting her eyes down, 'That's why I'm here. I was hoping you might be able to help me make sense of it all.'

'I certainly would like to try,' he responded.

'You see, I've looked through some books on the

phenomenon you mentioned, but they haven't really told me much, well, at least, not much I can easily grasp,' explained Mary.

Sitting back in his chair, he thought for a moment, then started to pour out his knowledge on the subject. 'There is still a lot of research to be done on out-of-body experiences.'

Mary was relieved that the conversation had got around to why she was there. 'I thought they were supposed to be associated with the moment just before death,' she suggested.

Tom smiled at the simplicity of Mary's assumption. Where most psychologists would readily have diagnosed Mary as suffering from a form of psychosis, he was more inclined to pursue the relevance of dreams or visions as an influence on her life. It was an alternative theory, and considering alternative explanations fascinated him.

'Let me try to explain. What you experienced feels very real, but it's still, effectively, a dream.'

Mary was immediately drawn in, eager to learn anything she could.

'You see dreams can be broken down into types,' Tom carried on, 'Once we know the type, then we can theorise on the dream's meaning. So, tell me what's happened since we last spoke?'

Mary wanted to tell him everything, but stopped herself.

Instead, she replayed Walter's school prank step by step. 'I mean, why should I dream something that happened to somebody some time ago? I've never met him before; I know nothing of his past.'

Tom wasn't ready to offer any answers yet. 'And that was it? Then you woke up?' he enquired.

She turned her face away, not wanting to answer.

'Then you woke up?' he asked again.

'Well, no, I mean…yes, obviously I woke up but it was after…oh, I can't remember exactly,' she stammered, her face now bright red with embarrassment.

'The dream went on?' he probed.

'Yes,' Mary finally answered.

'So, tell me. Explain what happened then.'

'Just things.'

'Things! That's not altogether helpful.'

Mary really didn't want to be drawn further, but Tom wasn't going to leave it; he simply waited for an answer.

The lengthening silence finally prompted her to say, 'Things like you read in a novel.'

He stood up, walked across the room, picked up a reference book and flicked through the pages, sarcastically repeating her words: 'Things like you read in a novel.' He shut the book and added, 'No, nothing in here about that.'

'I don't mind being teased, Mr Sharpe, but I haven't come here to be ridiculed,' she said sternly.

'Then enlighten me, please.'

'Things that happen to women in novels, was what I meant,' she eventually clarified.

'Forgive me, I'm not a reader of romantic fiction, but I can only assume that you mean your dream went on and things of a sensual nature happened with Walter,' Tom suggested in his usual forthright style.

She paused, sank back into her chair and let her head fall. 'Yes,' she said, uneasily.

He didn't pursue his questioning, at last realising that for her to expand further would be a bridge too far. Besides which, he very much wanted to maintain her confidence in him. 'Let me assure you, Miss O'Driscoll, I've read many case studies on these types of experience. What you've been dreaming is nothing to be afraid of and perfectly natural.'

Mary lifted her head and begged, 'I just want to make sense of it all.'

Tom explained further. 'You're combination dreaming: flitting between states or types of state. Mostly you're having an epic dream. These dreams possess much beauty and awakening from such a dream can give you a feeling that you've discovered something amazing about yourself, almost a life-changing experience.'

'But why with him?' she asked.

'Theorists would debate this all day, my dear. But I

follow the work of a young psychologist called Jung,' he replied. Mary looked at him, none the wiser.

'Jung believes that dreams, in whatever form, are a way of communicating and acquainting yourself with the unconscious. They guide the waking self to achieve wholeness and offer a solution to a problem you're facing in your waking life.'

'It all sounds very intriguing. But I didn't think I had a problem that needed a solution.'

'Oh, but perhaps you do!' he said calmly. 'It is called desire, love, even lust.'

'Mr Sharpe! I can assure you that I'm not that kind of woman,' was Mary's firm response.

Seeing Mary all but ready to leave, he knew his words would need further explanation. 'Please, allow me to make things clear.'

Tom offered various learned theories of Freud, Jung and Adler, some of which left Mary more confused than ever. His final sentence was one that certainly confirmed he needed to work on his presentation of facts. 'Dreams are a way of overcompensating for the shortcomings in your waking life. They offer a form of satisfaction that is more socially acceptable.'

Mary gave him another look of deep disapproval. The truth, though, was that Tom was right. Mary did have shortcomings where men were concerned and had never had any real romance in her life thus far. Even in her mid twenties, her desire for a fulfilling relationship seemed the last of her priorities. Her apparent lack of interest in men made her oblivious to any innocent wooing and, for this reason, she was often considered too aloof for any honourable advance from a possible suitor. This did not discourage Tom, however, who was becoming very much taken with Mary. His eyes studied every inch of her as she thanked him for his time and bid him goodbye.

'I'll pull out some papers, Miss O'Driscoll, so you can read up on these matters, if you'd like,' he said, looking for a reason to keep her talking.

'Well, if you're sure. Thank you, Mr Sharpe.'

'Please call me Tom, when we are not on duty, and perhaps I should call you Mary?' he attempted.

Mary simply replied, 'Oh, I don't know if that would be appropriate, Mr Sharpe.'

~~~

In the mission hall where she taught her sign language classes, a performance by Mrs Dorothy Winters, a celebrated spiritual medium touring the county, was eagerly anticipated. Word of Mrs Winters's alleged psychic powers had captured the imagination of the whole area, and the two hundred available tickets had quickly sold out.

On the night of the performance, all available volunteers were mustered for duties, including the ever-sceptical Mr Elliott, who was assigned back stage duties, with strict instructions to keep his 'poppycock' opinion of spiritualism to himself. Mary offered her help and was busy arranging the rows of chairs when Mrs Harris, the event organiser, escorted a rather plain-looking Mrs Winters into the hall. The medium liked to see how things were laid out, and to ensure she had easy access to her audience. Her performance was a theatrical endeavour, with much laying-on of hands, whilst she imparted messages from the other side.

After pacing back and forth around the hall, Mrs Winters began to observe Mary from a distance until, eventually, she went over to her.

'My dear girl,' said the medium, taking Mary by surprise.

'Oh! I'm sorry, I didn't realise you were talking to me,' replied Mary, standing up to face the woman. 'I was miles away.'

Mrs Winters took hold of Mary's hand gently and pressed it between hers. 'Let me help you.'

Mary assumed she was offering help to lay out the chairs, but was confused as to why the offer should be made with such emotion. 'I'm sure I can manage but thank you all the same,' she said and tried to pull away her hand, only for Mrs Winters to hold on more tightly.

'I can see so much anguish in your life. A great many things are troubling you, Mary. It is Mary, isn't it?'

Mary was quite speechless and rather uncomfortable as the woman's eyes studied her.

'Well, yes, my name is Mary,' she muttered nervously and began to realise to whom she was talking.

'Please don't be afraid, my dear. It's simply that my spirit guides wish me to talk to you.'

Mary looked at her with trepidation until she found her rational voice. 'Do please forgive me, but I don't believe in the occult.'

A lovely sense of reassurance radiated from Mrs Winters, as she gave Mary a warm smile. 'Oh, occult is such a horrible word. I'm merely a medium, able to feel and hear thoughts from the spirit world, that's all. I use them to help people overcome difficulties in their lives.'

Mary looked unconvinced.

'Difficulties like understanding your dreams!' said Mrs Winters, waiting for Mary's curiosity to get the better of her, as it did.

'But how do you know about my…?' Mary started to say until interrupted.

'Let me hold your hands again, please.'

A little unsure, Mary finally relented and held out her hands to allow Mrs Winters to hold them, tenderly, her thumbs pressed onto the palms. Mrs Winters slowly closed her eyes. There was a long silence, although it wasn't uncomfortable or frightening to Mary; in fact, just the opposite: she felt a calm serenity embrace her.

Mrs Winters finally opened her eyes and stated, 'I know your dreams are confusing to you, Mary, but there is good reason. You see, Walter isn't receptive to the spirit world, therefore, everything has to be channelled through you.'

Mary took a slight step backwards in surprise, releasing her hands from Mrs Winters's seemingly psychic touch. 'How do you know his name?'

'Am I wrong?'

'Well, erm, no,' Mary was forced to acknowledge.

'Then why doubt me?'

'It's just…well, you've taken me by surprise,' replied Mary. And why shouldn't she be shocked? One minute she was quietly arranging chairs and the next, she was in a conversation with a clairvoyant about her dreams, the spirit world and Walter. It was all a bit sudden and she stood there bewildered. Yet, it was all so intriguing, something she couldn't help but want to learn more about.

'I tell you simply because the spirit needs closure.'

'Closure! Of what exactly?' Mary enquired and then felt another soft squeeze of her hands.

'My guide connects me to a troubled young spirit, someone we class as being trapped in sadness, unable to move through to their final spiritual resting place. She lets me know that Walter and you have to come together to seek justice.'

'I'm sorry, but I really don't understand. Justice for whom?' asked Mary, flustered.

Mrs Winters closed her eyes again and spoke out to her spirit. 'Tell me, young lady, why must Mary and Walter seek justice?' Her face began to show a resigned look of disappointment. 'I'm sorry, Mary but the spirit leaves me now.'

'No please,' cried Mary in despair.

'She's gone…I'm sorry.'

'What does all this mean?' Mary asked in sheer frustration and allowed her head to fall.

Lifting up Mary's chin, Mrs Winters gave her a look of sympathy, showing she did understand how things must appear, and just how confusing it all was to her. She tried to explain. 'Sometimes all is not immediately apparent, my dear, but things will reveal themselves in time and then you will make sense of your experiences. If the spirits mean well, they will guide you.'

'If they mean well!' cried out Mary, most disturbed at the suggestion they might not.

Mrs Winters clarified her comments. 'There is a belief that in the spirit world, strong feelings and emotions between two people create energy, power that a troubled soul will use to seek closure of something.' She hesitated for a moment, before also offering an alternative theory,

'However, it is also believed a restless soul can wish purely to play games. I'm afraid such a spirit will tease your mind and draw you into the most passionate and unsuitable of relationships, and often with disastrous consequences.'

'I see,' Mary acknowledged, 'and you think perhaps…'

Mrs Winters's finger gently pressed Mary's lips to stop her talking. 'Mary, I dare say that your experiences won't have such consequences. But just be cautious.' She produced a small card from her purse and handed it over. 'My address, if you feel I can help you in the future. I'm sure you'll find my rates quite reasonable.'

Mrs Winters bade Mary farewell and left her to contemplate her words. Not surprisingly, Mary felt uneasy and tried to make sense of the brief encounter. Was the woman genuine? Did she truly know of her dreams? Or was she merely seeking to deceive, hoping to secure money by private consultations? Mary wondered just when her strange experiences would end.

After a successful show, Mrs Winters brushed against Mr Elliott as they passed on her way out of the hall. She stopped and turned back to address him.

'Mr Elliott, isn't it?'

'Yes, indeed,' replied a courteous Elliott.

'Do look beyond the memories of the locket, Mr Elliott. Behind the velvet, that's where a past has to be studied.'

With that, she was on her way out of the building, and all before Elliott had time to assimilate her words.

That evening, in his study, he took out Walter's locket once more. Gently teasing back the velvet lining, he was surprised to discover a thin piece of paper. It was concertina folded and quite heavily stained from being glued to the locket. Once the paper was open, it was clear the writing had not stood the test of time and was badly faded, as well as being covered with brown spots. Holding the paper up to the light, he could just about make out some words written in pencil. They made no real sense and read:

My darlings,
If the dear Lord has mercy,
Mother has fallen, my sweet an
protect you. Now I live in
when Hart and the ma
will take you both
Street. I so pray you will
over evil. I beg that one
learn the truth. Seek
May the Lord always.

Elliott copied the words onto a piece of paper and began to ponder what they meant; and what the medium, Mrs Winters, meant by, 'a past has to be studied.' He thought long and hard but, as all the words had not survived, it was just a jumble. As for Mrs Winters, he was perplexed as to how she knew anything about him having Walter's locket, and even more so about how she knew of the note behind the velvet lining.

Whereas most people would have been impressed by the woman's supposed powers, Elliott was a sceptic where spiritualism was concerned. He believed all mediums were tricksters of one kind or another, and it would take a very strong argument for him to be convinced her words were anything other than a clever deception.

'Of course!' he called out and smiled smugly at his realisation. He had remembered his wife had organised a meeting of local women at their house recently. And who should be a guest at the meeting? None other than Mrs Winters. He further recalled he had left the locket on his desk when ushered out of the study. 'The crafty woman,' he said, presuming Mrs Winters had seen it there, and then, that night in the mission hall, had made her comment about a note behind the lining. Was it not a good ploy for a medium to risk suggesting that any locket could hide a note? he thought, And if it did, then what mystical powers she could profess to have.

Regarding the words of the note, he concluded they were probably no more than a verse or passage in a book, which had meaning only to Lucinda and were something she wanted to pass down to Walter as a poignant memento.

Elliott looked over to the clock and realised he had been pondering the problem for a good hour. It probably would have been longer but for the family dog, who came over and rested his head upon his master's knees. Those stoical eyes looked up at him in the hope that Elliott hadn't forgotten his last walk of the day.

CHAPTER 8

A Judge's Opinion

In the Judge's Chambers, Elliott watched Judge Wilson flick through the pages of his report. He could see that the man wasn't impressed. In truth, he knew himself that, whichever way he chose to dress it up, the fact remained that Walter was a criminal. Judge Wilson thought so too and was less than sympathetic in his appraisal. 'You've gone to some trouble, Robert,' he said from behind his large desk, adding, 'but I see nothing here that would call for any leniency.'

'I was merely hoping that details of the lad's past might help you understand his character,' Elliott explained, with a hint of contempt.

The Judge rebuffed him. 'Understanding someone's character doesn't change the law, Robert.'

A further fifteen minutes' talk between the men served no real purpose and ended with Elliott leaving the chambers once more frustrated. He had dealt with hundreds of confirmed criminals in his time, and found most turned to crime by accident rather than on purpose. This was a view, however, not shared by the judge, who appeared to have no appetite for even the smallest of scratches below the surface of a case, even when presented with overwhelming evidence that a further prison sentence would likely do more harm than good. Consequently, Elliott reluctantly accepted that, barring a miracle, Walter would receive a custodial sentence when he appeared before Judge Wilson in court.

Elliott would not let the meeting bother him for long, however. He was not someone who brooded over what he could not change. He was convinced of the advantages of probation over custodial punishment; and his philanthropic tendencies were firmly rooted in his religious beliefs; but he was never one to see his profession as merely saving offenders' souls by divine grace, and was the first to acknowledge that Christian faith and Temperance beliefs alone could not steer the future of probation work.

When Tuesday came round, Walter waited patiently for Mr Elliott in a little office Matron Hanson had agreed could be used for their meeting. At 3 o'clock, Elliott duly arrived and, unlike their first meeting, Walter stood up as a mark of respect. 'Please take a seat,' Elliott said, impressed with the change in the lad, not just in attitude but also in appearance. So great was the change that he could hardly believe he was looking at the same man.

Now he could clearly see his mother in him, not just in looks but also in mannerisms. He gave a wry smile, as Walter flicked at the fringe of his hair and twitched his nose like a rabbit. It was a habit that Elliott connected with, and which rolled back the years for him. Had he not gone to college that September, how different things might have been, he reflected!

'Well, I understand you're fully recovered…and looking all the better for it, I have to say,' he finally commented.

'Yes, I am, thank you, sir, and mainly due to Nurse O'Driscoll's help. Without her, happen things would have been different,' Walter replied.

'Yes, she is a good sort,' remarked Elliott, this being the extent of his praise. Not that the praise wasn't genuine. In fact, he had deep admiration for Mary and her work, but somehow he always fell short with compliments, for fear of sounding too ingratiating.

'We'd better look at this predicament of yours then, Walter,' Elliott said, ending the pleasantries. 'I shall arrange for you to have some counsel and…'

'No!' Walter interrupted. 'There's no need, Mr Elliott. Thank you all the same, but I'd rather not.'

'Not having legal representation seldom, in my view, provides for a beneficial outcome,' Elliott offered.

'Counsel costs money and they'll go after my folks for it and I think I've caused them enough heartache. Let's face facts, sir. I'm as guilty as ever I could be. No, I'll take what's coming to me, without involving others.'

Even if he didn't entirely agree with Walter, Elliott had to admire the lad's pragmatic appraisal of the situation and, therefore, didn't oppose him further.

Elliott had put aside half an hour for preparing Walter, but there was no more to be done after ten minutes, and the remaining time was spent discussing cricket and, bizarrely, the many ways to tie knots. Elliott had little interest in either, but he was enthralled by Walter's knowledge and enthusiasm about both subjects, in particular his demonstration of a hangman's noose. He did, however, conclude that it perhaps was not wise, when in court, for Walter to bring his pastimes to the notice of the judge.

Finally, the arrival of two police constables outside the door signalled their meeting needed to come to a conclusion, and Elliott realised he had not mentioned the chain and locket. He took the small tissue-wrapped package from his pocket and handed it over to Walter. 'I believe this may belong to you?'

Walter was visibly moved at seeing the jewellery again and caressed it. 'Oh, sir, you've no idea what this means to me. I thought I had lost it for good.' He finally kissed the locket. 'You see, it was a gift from my mother.'

'Yes, so I understand,' Elliott replied, remembering the conversation he had had with Walter's old friend Mills. He wanted to tell Walter all about its origin, but he realised that he could be wrong and it might not be the one that he had given to Lucinda. If he was wrong, how stupid he would look telling a romantic tale of his youth. He therefore decided not to enlighten Walter as to what he suspected, at least, not until he was absolutely sure. He did, however, quiz him on the other half of the locket, and also asked if he knew of the piece of paper behind the velvet.

'It's rather unusual to have just half a locket,' remarked Elliott.

'Yes, the other half belonged to my sister, but she's dead, sir.'

'Of course, I do remember your old friend Mills telling me,' said Elliott, with sympathy.

'George Mills. How is the old sport?' Walter laughed with affection, as the conversation focused on his old school mate.

'Very well. He sends you his regards.'

Walter gave Elliott a resigned look. 'Yes I believe he would, sir, and I don't know why, because I hardly treated him very fairly.'

'True friendship holds no malice, Walter.'

'Yes, I dare say,' replied Walter with melancholy. 'Well, if you've spoken with George, happen there's little left you don't know about me.'

Elliott returned to the matter of the locket.

'I have to ask, Walter. Are you aware of a piece of paper behind the velvet?'

'I see nothing gets past you,' said Walter.

Elliott offered only a pleasant grin in recognition of the fact.

'Yes, I am aware of the paper, Mr Elliott. I discovered it some time ago.'

'Does it mean anything?'

'No. it's just words. I do wish the whole thing was complete.'

'Indeed,' muttered Elliott, who would equally have loved to learn more about Walter's mother's writing.

Their conversation was suddenly ended when a policeman knocked on the glass window of the door.

'Please, may I ask one last act of kindness, Mr Elliott?' pleaded Walter. 'Will you look after it for me? It will be safer with you than where I'm going.'

Elliott happily agreed to take the locket, now feeling a pleasing connection with the lad through Lucinda and a duty of care beyond that of a court missionary. He looked forward to the day he could perhaps help Walter be reconciled with her and his father.

Walter exited the room, only to be unceremoniously handcuffed, in full view of a group of nurses now watching events, their faces showing their disappointment at the imminent departure of their favourite patient. None was more upset than Mary, who looked on forlornly from a distance. But Walter was resigned to his fate. He stood there, patiently, as the constable read him the formalities of returning to custody and gave the watching nurses a warm smile. Jovially he called out, 'I'm afraid it looks like I'm being asked to leave, girls.' His quip brought a giggle from a couple of the student nurses. However, the sight of Matron Hanson suddenly approaching soon brought back straight faces.

'Ladies!' she cried, clapping her hands forcefully. 'Might I remind you this is a hospital not a playhouse. To your duties!' The nurses dispersed obediently.

'Ah, Matron,' chirped Walter, 'you've been a most genial host and I will heartily recommend your place to folks.'

'Goodbye, Mr Stanford,' she said curtly, then turned her back on him and strutted away. Whilst it was hard to imagine the Matron showing any degree of jollity, a close observer might just have seen the faintest of smirks, signifying a fondness for Walter.

Eventually, Walter was led away, but not before he had turned to Elliott and shouted, 'When I return, sir, send me somewhere out of the country, to sea for choice. I should be out of temptation on a sailing ship. I could climb the rigging and do no harm to anybody. Or an Indian wigwam village might do. Perhaps even a Bedouin encampment – no attics there, I understand.'

He managed to slow down his escorts as he passed Mary. 'Goodbye then, Mary, and thank you. Not many people have afforded me such kindness in these recent times.' His words were warm and gentle. As he walked on, the sorrow in her eyes was so apparent that even Elliott could not help but notice there was something between them.

Walter's trial, when it came, three days later, was a brief affair. Judge Wilson took off his glasses and finally concluded, 'You are an habitual criminal, Mr Stanford.' Looking towards Walter, he continued, 'I am minded to bring the full force of the law to bear and sentence you to one year in prison.'

Walter looked over to Elliott in horror.

'However,' said the Judge, 'I am convinced otherwise by Mr Elliott here, who believes he can make good of you!' Then, throwing down his gavel, he passed sentence: 'Three months penal servitude with hard labour, after which you must report to Mr Elliott and take heed of his advice.' Then, to the court officers, he declared, 'Take him down!'

Elliott gave the Judge a look of appreciation, as the defendant was led away to prison. He knew this was a fair sentence and an unexpected compromise. As promised, Elliott had done what he could for Walter, who was not, to his mind, a wicked person; but he had to admit that the lad was a creature of habit.

The newly convicted Walter stood at the prison cell door, holding a blanket and an enamel mug and plate. As the prison officer opened the door, a shaft of light revealed the stark conditions. He slowly walked in and took a deep breath of resignation as the large steel door slammed shut behind him.

Mary, in the hospital, felt a shudder down her spine.

~~~

During Walter's imprisonment, Mary felt herself on a roller-coaster of emotions. One day she was bright, breezy and happy with all that Tom had explained; the next day she found herself deeply saddened by her experiences and thought only of what the clairvoyant, Mrs Winters, had told her. She hadn't dreamt anything as vivid about Walter as previously, but he was always on her mind, lingering in the background, ready to rise to the forefront of her thoughts. It was almost as if somebody was deliberately turning on a switch and sending her into a trance – often at the most inappropriate moments, such as the time she was in the butcher's shop, lost in reflection, watching the butcher pound down his cleaver onto a carcass. 'Utterly ridiculous task,' she inappropriately said, experiencing a vision of Walter in prison, pounding down and crushing rocks for six hours a day. Breaking out of her trance, she could only say in embarrassment to the perplexed butcher, 'I'm sorry, I was miles away.'

Her dreaming was soon to take a dangerous twist, however.

One evening, after a long hard shift, she allowed herself to soak in a hot bath and closed her eyes to relax. Without any reason, she let her head slowly drift under the water. Suddenly she could hear muffled voices calling out to her. 'Victoria, no! Victoria!' they shouted. She opened her eyes and felt paralysed. As her pupils began to dilate, she could see Walter's face, full of distress, peering down at her, through the water.

'No, no, noooo!' he cried in slow motion. Then, bizarrely, she found herself standing in the corner of the bathroom, watching as Walter leant over his sister, Victoria, who now lay submerged in the water. He plunged his hands into the water to pull Victoria's head up, and Mary was suddenly once again beneath the water herself. She felt his hand lift her neck and, finally, she surfaced, spluttering and gasping for breath. The look on her face was one of absolute terror as she fought to regulate her breathing. Terrified and trembling, she clambered out of the bath and stood there, clasping her towel to her mouth. She was not to know that she had just re-enacted a scene in which Victoria had had a seizure in the bath some years earlier.

From the corner of her eye, Mary caught a glimpse of someone and, when she turned, she saw the same young woman as in her previous vision: the one who watched her dancing with Walter.

'Who are you?' Mary asked, anxiously. But the woman gave her a sorrowful look and simply faded away.

For the first time, Mary honestly believed she might be ill, that her visions were sending her mad; and what worried her more than anything was that she could not control them. Mrs Winter's alternative theory about spirits playing tricks with her mind also came flooding back and frightened her even more.

CHAPTER 9

Solace

One solace in Mary's troubled world was her work in the deaf school, to which she escaped whenever she could. Each Thursday night found her amongst the small group of mothers in the mission hall, offering help and demonstrating techniques to help them communicate. To teach a devoted mother and her deaf child to sign, and watch them 'talk' to each other, brought her immense joy and put her own problems into perspective.

On one such Thursday evening, Mary welcomed a new mother and her young daughter, a fresh-faced little girl of about four or five years, with tight curls of ginger hair and what looked like a smart new dress. On first sight, an observer would have not have noticed anything amiss with her, until she opened her eyelids to reveal one normal eye and one that was a little cloudy, with no iris colour at all. Her mother stood nervously at the door, clutching her child hard into her legs.

'Hello, you must be Mrs Walker,' said Mary in a warm, friendly voice, stretching out a hand to greet her. Mrs Walker took hold of the hand, grateful for anything to dispel her fear of a strange new place and meeting new people. 'Please, do come on in and join us,' Mary continued, trying to alleviate the woman's anxiety.

'Thank you,' said Mrs Walker, relaxing somewhat.

'I'm Mary O'Driscoll, we've exchanged letters.'

'Of course, yes, hello, I'm Catherine Walker.'

Mary bent down to the little girl. 'And this must be little Emily.' She took hold of the child's hand and said, 'Hello, Emily, I'm Mary, a friend of your mother's. I hope that we can be friends too.' Of course she knew the little girl couldn't hear a word, but wanted to gain her trust and, more importantly, that of her mother.

Emily pushed back into her mother and looked up for reassurance. Catherine picked up her daughter and held her close.

'Yes, we'd like that, wouldn't we, Emily?' she said, nodding, until Emily finally joined in.

'Well, welcome. Let me show you around and introduce you,' Mary said. She led the way over to a small group of mothers and began to explain how the classes worked. After what seemed an endless round of 'Hellos' and 'Nice to meet yous', followed by the mothers' varied descriptions of their children's deafness, Catherine was rather relieved when Mary suggested, 'Perhaps we should make a start.' The two women sat down on some chairs tucked away in a quieter corner of the hall.

Mary learned that Emily was not only born totally deaf but was also blind in one eye. Communication between mother and daughter had been hard thus far, and consisted only of the basics of sign language, or rather, pointing to objects and giving simple nods of approval or rejection. This, combined with some crude mime actions, had helped establish a basic form of communication between them.

'It was my brother who suggested your school,' explained Catherine, holding Emily on her knee.

'Put Emily's fingers gently to your mouth as we talk. Let her feel the movement,' Mary directed. A dialogue of brief questions and answers followed, whilst Emily explored the movement of her mother's mouth, initially with enthusiasm at the apparent new game, but soon with waning interest.

'Stand her to face you. Let her touch your lips again. Now, repeat after me,' Mary said, positioning herself behind Catherine and in view of Emily. She kept saying 'Mother,' encouraging Catherine to keep repeating it, and then slowly she began signing the word, over and over. Mary smiled broadly when, finally, the little girl mimicked the signing. There was nothing more heartening for her mother to see, and it brought tears to her eyes.

'Very impressive,' came a man's voice. Mary instantly recognised it and looked up. 'Mr Sharpe!' she exclaimed in surprise.

'Tom!' Catherine said, as she leant over to kiss him. 'It appears you already know each other,' she continued, looking over to Mary.

'Indeed we do,' replied Tom, as Emily jumped into his arms.

'Well, er…yes,' Mary said, finally. 'We work at the same hospital.'

'Then you'll know all about my brother!' Catherine said with humour.

'My dear, your impression of me is all wrong,' Tom jokingly replied.

Emily, seeing drinks being poured, pointed and struggled to be let down. 'Would she like a drink?' Mary asked.

'Yes, that would be nice…I'll take her over,' replied Catherine, her daughter already leading her away. Tom and Mary were left to talk together.

'Sorry, I assumed you were…,' Mary started to say.

'Married?' he interrupted. Mary looked slightly embarrassed by her assumption.

'No, Emily is merely my niece,' Tom clarified. 'Her father died four years ago,' he went on to explain.

'I'm sorry.'

'These things happen,' he replied pragmatically.

'Catherine and Emily came to stay with me for a couple of weeks, two years ago and…well, never went back; and I don't mind really.'

Mary looked over to Emily, now busy drinking home-made lemonade with glee. 'What happened to her eye, Mr Sharpe?'

'Please, I would prefer it if you called me Tom…at least when we're not at work. Can we agree that much?'

'Very well,' Mary conceded, with hesitation.

Tom smiled in gratitude and continued, 'Corneal infection and ulceration, not long after birth, I'm afraid.'

'Poor mite…and there's nothing can be done?'

'No, sadly,' he replied and then changed the subject swiftly. 'So, have you had any more dreams or visions? I'm always here, if you want to talk about things again,' he said, with genuine concern, but perhaps also in hope of seeing her again.

Mary felt uncomfortable and fell silent. She so wanted to talk about her most recent experiences, but knew now was neither the time nor the place. Apart from which, she feared Tom would begin to think her silly and neurotic.

In the ensuing silence he gawped at her like a little boy lost. He was truly smitten.

'Shall we get a drink too?' Mary at last said and gestured to him to lead the way.

Tom agreed, although still unable to take his gaze off

her. This was the first time he had seen her hair down and he was suitably impressed. Eventually, he appeared less mesmerised and asked, 'So, this is another of your skills?'

Mary looked a little puzzled.

'Teaching signing,' he explained.

'Oh, I see. Yes, I've been doing it for some years now.'

'You have relatives who are deaf?'

'No…it's just something that took my interest when I saw a poster asking for help.'

They pulled up by the table where Mrs Elliott was serving drinks. '…and Mrs Elliott here encouraged me to get qualifications in the subject. Ann, may I introduce you to Mr Sharpe?'

'Tom,' he corrected her.

'Sorry, Tom Sharpe. He's a surgeon at the hospital and here with his niece for the first time tonight.'

Ann Elliott greeted Tom with her usual hospitality, shaking his hand, and then thrust a cup of lemonade into it.

'You're lucky to have such a talented teacher in the school, Mrs Elliott,' Tom said, much to Mary's embarrassment. Although the only qualified sign teacher, she wasn't comfortable about taking credit alone.

'Like a hospital, the success of the school is down to the efforts of a lot of dedicated, Christian people,' she reminded Tom.

A sudden interjection by Mr Elliott made them all turn around. 'Indeed we are lucky to have her, and so too is the court system, I might add.'

'Oh, please, Mr Elliott!' Mary said, now acutely embarrassed by all the admiration.

Ann came to her rescue and jokingly teased her husband, 'Ah, my dear. It wasn't a rumour. You are helping me tonight!'

He smiled cheekily, knowing he was always guilty of getting sidetracked.

'My husband is very good at offering me help, Mr Sharpe, but somehow forgets he has to give it!' Ann playfully mentioned, giving Elliott a firm rap on the hand as he went to pick up a drink. She had the measure of her spouse.

Ann Elliott was a popular and admired member of the local community: a person of drive and determination. Even with two small boys, she still found time to get involved in a multitude of activities, from fund raising to singing in the mission choral group, all of which sometimes caused her husband frustration when he found himself roped in to do things in which he didn't have much interest and certainly didn't remember volunteering for. Nonetheless, theirs was a solid and happy marriage, despite the fact that she was ten years his junior, a fact she would always remind him of as he moaned and slumped into an armchair after the long family walk on a Sunday afternoon.

Ann was always a supportive wife and as opinionated as her spouse on matters relating to court missionary work. He wouldn't willingly admit it, but he invariably followed her suggestions, particularly when faced with a seemingly impossible challenge.

'This is Tom Sharpe, a surgeon at my hospital, Mr Elliott,' said Mary, introducing Tom again. The two men shook hands firmly. 'He was the man who operated on Walter,' she told Elliott.

'Ah, yes,' Elliott acknowledged.

'How is the rogue?' Tom enquired.

Elliott explained Walter's sentence and reported that, by all accounts, he was doing well. Mary listened intently. The mere mention of his name made her flush with warmth, and why still mystified her. Yes, Walter was intriguing, intelligent, good-looking and, without doubt, charming, but then so were many other men she knew, not least Tom, whom if she was honest she could easily fall for. Nonetheless, Walter was the one who wouldn't leave her thoughts. She had wanted to ask Elliott about his welfare many times, and had even agonised over whether to visit him in prison. But she would have needed Elliott's help to find out in which prison he was held. She couldn't do that. How would it appear?

As Tom watched Mary, the look on her face told its story. He knew she was desperate to see Walter once more and, if jealousy were expressed in colours, then Tom would have appeared as green as a pea. Despite all his fascination with, and great knowledge of, psychology, he suffered from one great flaw in his personality: a romantically jealous nature, something he could rationalise, but never fully control.

Tom's jealousy of Walter had been further stoked by a conversation he had had with Professor Michaels, Head of Neurology, not long after Mary's first visit to him. He confided the problem as that of a private patient troubled by visions of a man.

The Professor's experienced view of such matters wasn't quite what Tom wanted to hear. He suggested that the patient could simply be attracted to someone who didn't fit her mind's ideal and moral upbringing, but who provided her with a thrill she desperately sought. 'Crudely put, dear fellow, his testosterone screams very loudly at her and she damn well wants him. Her emotions will be constantly fighting each other. You see, outward emotions provoke a response like a bear: run! But, inwardly, she'll experience wonder, love, sexual desire and joy.'

Tom's face was a picture of disappointment, which he hopelessly failed to disguise to the Professor, who could easily see the truth of the surgeon's yearning. He gave an understanding shrug of his shoulders. 'The other lover of this patient of yours, Tom. He might just have to accept he's not her chosen one!'

Tom couldn't help but remember that final sentence as he forlornly looked at Mary, who continued to talk to Elliott about Walter. However, he wouldn't give in without a fight.

'So, shall we see you at the church festival, Mary?' Elliott asked, after the conversation about Walter came to an end. 'Any help is always appreciated.'

'Of course,' Mary replied.

'And perhaps I could offer you some help, Mr Elliott,' interrupted Tom, seizing the opportunity to meet Mary again out of work. He certainly intended to prove the Professor wrong. To Tom, Mary's dreaming problem stemmed from the fact that she was seeking love, and he was determined to be the one she fell for.

Elliott didn't need asking twice: volunteers were always needed, especially ones of Tom's size and strength. No sooner had he asked the question than Elliott had whisked him off to confirm where he would be needed.

'Oh, poor man!' Ann exclaimed, with sympathy, knowing her husband's persuasive nature. She then raised her eyebrows and gave Mary a smirk, 'Quite a handsome catch, Mary, don't you think?'

'Ann, really, he's a surgeon!' Mary exclaimed.

'And?' came the simple reply.

Through all her naivety, it was finally dawning on Mary that she had a serious admirer.

CHAPTER 10

A CHURCH FESTIVAL

The annual church festival in the grounds of St Mary's was set to be another great success, with the sun beating down and record crowds predicted for the fifth year running. In truth, these days it had become more of a carnival, with stalls, events and livestock. Much of the success could be attributed to the efforts of Mr Elliott, elected chair of the organising committee. His work for the church mission was unrivalled. This year he'd set several young delinquents in his care to work making a variety of wooden board games and an impressive cradle and multi-seated swing.

Tom, as predicted by Mrs Elliott, was certainly much in demand as a volunteer. He'd lost count of how many poles he'd carried, tent pegs he'd hammered in and makeshift stalls he'd helped erect. Not at all bad, for a man with no real skill as a handyman. Finally, he was done and it was time for a well-earned rest. He sat on an upturned water butt, mopped away the sweat from his brow and rolled his sleeves even further up his impressive biceps.

'Tha best be gettin' thee sen spruced up, lad,' called out Jack Williams, the ironmonger, in his broad South Yorkshire dialect.

Tom wasn't altogether sure, but thought the man had suggested he should get cleaned up. Although originally from Yorkshire, Tom hadn't really experienced the gritty language of working communities, having spent the early part of his childhood in privileged surroundings. His father was a wealthy merchant from York who had settled his family in nearby Richmond. By the age of eleven, his father had chosen his career and Tom was sent to boarding school, in preparation for future training as a doctor. Luckily for the father, his son took to medicine naturally and excelled throughout his time at medical school in London. By the age of twenty-eight, he already had a good reputation as a surgeon, a reputation that had led to his being asked to consider a lead surgeon position in Sheffield's City Hospital in 1910.

Tom's brisk approach and often eccentric personality could sometimes be interpreted as arrogance; but really, he was far from arrogant, albeit a little too abrupt at times. He cared deeply for the welfare of less fortunate people and those in distress. This was the main reason he had remained at the hospital once Walter had arrived on that fateful evening. Some surgeons of his standing would have chosen to leave matters entirely to their junior staff, whilst they departed for an evening of fine dining.

He pushed back his head, closed his eyes for a moment and let the strong sun beat down onto his face. Totally exhausted, he allowed himself to drift. Suddenly a giggle made him start.

'Well, somebody looks like they've been hard at it,' said Ann Elliott, who was accompanied by Mary, both of them suitably dressed for the festival.

Tom realised he had been oblivious to anything or anyone around him. 'Oh, hello Mrs Elliott.' He then bowed his head in acknowledgement to Mary, 'Mary.'

She smiled and courteously said, 'Hello.'

'We should have warned you!' Ann joked, referring to the fact that her husband would have a volunteer doing all manner of things.

'Oh, I don't mind, really,' he replied, brushing back his hair.

Mary had not seen Tom dressed casually before and was somewhat surprised to see him in a collarless shirt with his braces hanging loosely. She also could not help noticing just how masculine he was: his ample chest and well sculpted muscles showed clearly through his shirt, which was open virtually to his waist, a state he had no intention of remedying.

Tom had had his fair share of female admirers over the years, with many attempts made by well-to-do parents to introduce him to their daughters, in the hope that romance would blossom. But Tom had not really pursued any relationship seriously, considering his work and career far more important, although he had shown some interest in Lady Greaves, daughter of the Earl of Brampton. However, as a doctor, he was considered unsuitable by her family, and any further acquaintance was discouraged. Tom quickly learnt the fickleness of high society and the way they valued social position above suitability or even true love.

So why, suddenly, did he have a yearning to pursue Mary? For all her sweetness and beauty, she would be judged by people in his social circle as hardly suitable to be considered as a future wife. Tom knew all too well the problems caused by inappropriate relationships, both socially and in people's careers. He had known many a fine doctor whose career had faltered following an ill-considered liaison. His own brother, a lawyer who had fallen in love and married an assistant in a women's outfitters, was considered by his family to have lowered himself and had been ostracised in the most cruel way.

Quite simply, Tom didn't care. His heart had been captured, he desired only Mary, and he longed for the day he could tell her so. As for a career, his future was assured; he had made himself self-sufficient, and he had no need of money from his family. If his path at this hospital should be barred, then so be it. He knew his skills would be in demand elsewhere in the country. A change of scenery might even be beneficial. He cared nothing for what society people thought of his personal life, and as for their friendship, he could count on one hand the times when he had truly enjoyed being in their company.

'Well, we ought to leave you to it. Don't let Mr Elliott work you to the bone. Go and enjoy the entertainments,' said Ann, knowing that if he did not go, he would soon be allocated some more tasks.

'I have every intention, Mrs Elliott, just as soon as I'm washed and changed.'

'Then we shall bid you good day, for now.'

Tom could not let the opportunity pass, and he turned to Mary and asked quite openly, 'Perhaps you would allow me to accompany you around the stalls later, Mary?'

'Er…well…yes, that would be nice, if you're sure, thank you,' Mary responded, not really able to give any other answer without appearing ungrateful for what was, after all, only an offer to wander around the stalls.

Ann tucked her arm into Mary's, 'Come, Mary, let us try to find that husband of mine…and perhaps have a sneak at the cake tent before the masses arrive. Bye Tom.'

'Yes, goodbye, ladies,' replied Tom, tipping an imaginary hat.

Ann gave Mary a big smile as they wandered off.

'What?' Mary said. 'I've told you, he's a surgeon.'

'And I remember saying…and?' retorted Ann.

'Oh, stop it, Ann. It's not allowed. Besides, who says I like him anyway?'

Ann gave her another coy smile. 'We'll see.'

Mary pushed Ann's arm in slight embarrassment.

Meanwhile, Mr Elliott was sitting in a shaded area of the grounds with Canon Brockwell, whiling away the time in light conversation.

Herbert Garner, selling tombola tickets, interrupted them. 'Ah, gentlemen, might I interest you in the tombola? There's some lovely prizes again this year, including some fine port, Reverend,' he said, showing him a bottle. Herbert knew the mere mention of port was enough to gain the Canon's interest.

'Then we'd better be having a few shillings' worth of tickets,' was Brockwell's reply, as he looked eagerly at the label. Elliott gave Herbert a wink, then handed over his money for tickets.

'So, Robert. One hears young Walter Stanford was sentenced to prison again,' volunteered an inquisitive Brockwell.

'Regrettably so.'

'Well, I dare say had he come to you earlier you could have stayed his criminal ways.'

'Perhaps,' responded an unassuming Elliott.

'What of him now?'

'Oh, I'm hopeful the mission will support me putting him to sea.'

'To sea!' said Brockwell, very enthusiastic at the thought Walter would no longer be on the scene.

'I'm convinced he'll do well there. For me, it should have been plain enough from the beginning: he himself is as a ship adrift with nobody at the helm to set its course. And the pity of it!'

'A brilliant idea, Robert! And we may hope that he will relinquish any further wrong doing,' Brockwell concluded.

Elliott saw a glint of cunning in his friend's eyes that, just for a moment, made him think of Alice Harper's comments about the Canon when he interviewed her in the police station cells. However, his line of thought broke off as he caught sight of Mary approaching. He slowly raised his big frame out of the chair. 'Ah, Mary, do come and join us,' he said, positioning a chair so she could sit down.

'Canon, this is Mary, the young nurse I was telling you about,' Elliott said.

Mary's eyes opened wide in fear. For a brief moment, a dark vision came across her mind, a blurred image of someone walking around in a small room, although she couldn't make out who. She started as a baby gave out a hungry cry. The blurred image then came into focus and she saw a harsh-looking woman stirring a large bowl of liquid. 'Oh, baby wants some food!' the woman said in a malicious voice. Suddenly, Mary's vision was gone, and she was again looking at the Canon, who was staring at her. It was only when Elliott gave him a strange look that he realised that everyone could see he was unnerving her.

Brockwell broke into a one of his insincere smiles before gushing, 'Ah, Nurse, a pleasure to meet you again.'

'Oh! You've met before,' commented Elliott in surprise.

'Indeed we have, Robert. How are you, my dear?' responded Brockwell.

Mary was still flummoxed as to what had just happened, but gave a polite reply. 'I'm well, thank you, Canon.'

She sat down as Elliott poured her a drink. 'You're enjoying the festival, Mary?'

'I'm so impressed. Yet another success, Mr Elliott.'

Elliott just smiled appreciatively.

'So how long have you worked in Sheffield, Miss…?' Brockwell asked, and waited for her surname. He appeared to be innocently conversing, but he had his agenda, and sought to clarify his suspicions.

'O'Driscoll, Mary O'Driscoll,' she confirmed. 'I came over to England in 1910, first to Wiltshire, and then last summer I moved up to Sheffield.'

It was as he thought. Since last meeting her, it had bothered him where he'd seen her before. Finally, he knew.

'And from the Emerald Isle, obviously?' he continued.

'Yes, Limerick.'

'I see. And do you enjoy your nursing here?'

'Really, Charles,' Elliott interjected. 'The poor girl will think she's at an interview!'

'You're right, Robert. I'm so sorry, my dear.'

Mary was confused as to why the Canon was showing such an interest in her but tried to be courteous and answered, 'It's quite all right. Yes, I do very much enjoy nursing. It must run in the family: my mother was a nurse and my father a doctor.'

Elliott sensed a change of subject was perhaps needed, so mentioned, 'Mary has been helping me find a property for the mission, somewhere we can place ex-offenders, until they get back on the right path – a sort of stepping-stone.'

'Very admirable, and have you had any success?' Brockwell enquired.

'I think so, a small terrace on Newsome Street, number 24,' Elliott answered.

Brockwell froze: his face went white within an instant. Just how was he to respond to this news?

'Oh dear!' he sighed, with a hint of cunning.

'What is it, Charles?'

'Well, it's an altogether bizarre situation. You see I'm aiming to conclude an agreement to rent the very same property next week, on behalf of the diocese, for hardship cases.' It was a convincing explanation which neither Elliott or Mary had any reason to doubt.

Although it would cost Brockwell a handsome amount in weekly rent, this was a small price to pay to stop Elliott being around the place, particularly as Brockwell knew his passion for researching the history of a house. How long would it then take for his name to surface in its past? he thought. Whilst his old friend was no real detective, he knew that prolonged rummaging often got the pig a truffle.

'Oh, I see... Well, I guess we need to begin our search again, Mary,' Elliott said, with some disappointment.

'Hello, Mr Elliott! I thought it was you,' Tom declared as he strolled up and broke into the conversation.

'Aah, Tom! Join us, please.' Elliott then introduced him to Brockwell. 'This is Tom Sharpe, a surgeon from the hospital.'

Brockwell stood up to shake his hand before stating, 'Another from the medical profession. Are you trying to tell me something, Robert?' His quip brought a titter of laughter.

'Listen, let me leave you three to chat. I really ought to be heading to the flower judging or I shall be in trouble. It's been a delight to meet you again, Miss O'Driscoll. You will help yourself to the flower displays after the show, won't you? I'm sure your hospital wards will look all the lovelier for them.'

'That's very kind, Canon. They're all so beautiful and will be very welcome, I'm sure,' she felt obliged to say; but somehow she sensed his gesture was more to show his generosity to other people than it was a genuine charitable offer.

'Good, that's settled then. Well, good day to you and nice to meet you too, Mr Sharpe,' Brockwell finished, tipping his straw boater to Tom, who courteously reciprocated. He then began to walk away, but not before turning back to take another look at Mary.

The dark vision again came over Mary. It was night-time, and she saw the same woman as before in the dark, dingy room, spooning powder into a bowl of what looked like milk. On the table were numerous empty baby bottles. A male figure entered, although she could not see his face because of the shadows, only that he accompanied a young mother holding her baby wrapped in a dirty shawl. The woman appeared out of the darkness, her harsh face nodding to the man to take the bundle off the reluctant mother. Eventually, the mother agreed to give up her baby and then wept sorrowfully as the man led her away. The austere woman simply laid the infant on the table and promptly carried on stirring at the milk mixture. Mary quite jumped out of her skin, as the young paper boy she remembered suddenly appeared beside her. He looked at her and said quite acceptingly, 'That was me.'

Mary gave him a very puzzled look.

'We can only grow up so much afterwards, you see. Then we need closure. You will help us, won't you Mary? You and Walter, you will stay together and help bring him to justice?' urged the boy, before the familiar young woman of her previous visions appeared and took hold of his hand to gently guide him away. Mary then found herself standing, in daylight, looking towards a river, where policemen were dredging with long poles. There was a flurry of activity as a young constable pulled out a wrapped bundle, tied up with twine and seemingly the body of a baby. A rook suddenly flew onto the branch of a tree nearby and began furiously to flap its large wings. Its piercing shrill noise made her immediately snap out of her trance.

'Mary, is everything all right?' asked Elliott.

She looked around bewildered. Although she had only been elsewhere for a few seconds, it felt to her like she had been there for a lot longer. The blood had all but gone from her face and to Elliott she looked somewhat disturbed.

'Yes, sorry…I'm fine. I don't know quite what came over me. If you don't mind, I'll perhaps just sit here for a moment,' she answered.

Of course, Tom knew she had had another out-of-body experience and he gave her a reassuring smile. 'Let me get you a drink, Mary,' he said sympathetically, then turned to Elliott. 'You carry on Mr Elliott. I'll keep an eye on her. Doubtless, it's the heat that's made her feel a little queasy, that's all.'

Elliott, happy to see that Mary had returned to something like her normal self, took the hint and made his exit so the pair could chat. He certainly had no intention of being a gooseberry.

With Elliott gone, Tom wasted no time in asking the question: 'You had another vision, didn't you?'

Mary answered honestly, 'Yes I did.'

'And was it with him, Walter?' The inflection he gave to the name couldn't disguise his frustration at the idea of the man.

'No, it wasn't.' She paused in thought and then said, 'But I'm sure it's all connected to him, just like Mrs Winters said.'

'And who is Mrs Winters?'

Mary was slightly embarrassed and hesitated before giving him an answer. 'She's a spiritual medium,' she finally said, knowing exactly what Tom's response would be.

'Oh! Mary, why on earth would you want to seek out one of those and have them fill your head with nonsense?'

'I didn't go seeking her, Tom. She just came up to me in the mission hall and started telling me why I was dreaming and visualising as I do.'

Tom let out a sigh of frustration. 'These people are just tricksters. It's all mumbo jumbo, Mary, designed to get you to spread the word, so other people will pay good money to go and see them.'

'Perhaps, but some things she couldn't have known.'

'It's called hot and cold reading – trying to get information in a very clever way.'

'Maybe Walter and I are meant to be together for good reason,' she said unexpectedly.

The look Tom gave her was not one of his best. He decided it was time to tackle the problem of Walter, head on.

CHAPTER 11

AN UNEXPECTED VISIT

Walter was not used to having visitors, except the prison chaplain, who would visit him at least once a fortnight. On each visit, he suffered the Reverend's offer of prayers and redemption from sin politely, not wishing to offend.

It was, therefore, a surprise when, one day, he was pulled out from the line in the exercise yard, and told to go and see a visitor.

'You're wanted, Stanford,' said the prison officer, taking him by the arm.

'Me! By whom?' replied a hesitant Walter.

'I don't ask questions, lad. I just follow instructions.'

Walter was duly escorted down a corridor and towards the medical block.

'Why are we coming here?' asked Walter, realising where he was.

'That's what you'll soon find out,' concluded the officer

and opened the door, gesturing Walter to enter. Walter did so rather nervously and was shocked when he saw who was waiting for him inside.

'Mr Sharpe!'

'Hello, Mr Stanford, come on in, please. Close the door, won't you.'

'Well, I certainly wasn't expecting to see you of all people,' said Walter and felt around his operation scar. 'Don't tell me you've left one of your instruments inside me,' he joked.

Tom smiled. Despite his problem with Walter, he did quite like the man and could appreciate his wit. 'No, I'm here to pass on your notes to the prison doctor and I thought that, while I was here, I'd take a look at how things are going. Please lift up your jacket and lie on the table there.' He then turned to address his escort, who was dutifully standing guarding the door, 'Perhaps you wouldn't mind waiting outside, officer.'

Walter unbuttoned his jacket and sat on the table. 'The doctor here reckons you did a good job.'

'Only good, Mr Stanford! I would say a damn fine job, myself. Lie back please.'

He proceeded to inspect Walter's scar. 'Nothing amiss here.'

'Well, that's reassuring,' responded Walter before ending the pleasantries. 'All right, Mr Sharpe, as touched as I am by your concern for me, I'm sure you haven't come all this way to check on my scar.'

Tom pulled down Walter's jacket and walked to the sink to wash his hands. 'No, you're right, Mr Stanford.'

'Walter, please. Mr Stanford always makes me feel like I'm before a judge.'

'Very well, Walter, no I haven't come all this way for your welfare. Seeing you this way means I can speak with you alone.'

'I see. Well, I don't often get chance to talk so...' He spread his hands out. 'Please, as you will.'

'It's about Mary.'

'A lovely girl,' Walter offered his opinion.

'Yes, and one I wish to see remain so.'

'Please, we're grown men. Let's not dance around each other. What's on your mind?'

Tom was happy with that and got to the point. 'When you're released, Walter, I don't want you to try and see her.'

'Why not?'

'Because Mary is...well, let's just say impressionable in her current state of mind.'

'Are we dancing again?' asked Walter, giving a frown of confusion.

'Very well, she sees you as a substitute for her true feelings.'

Walter gave Tom's statement some consideration before

answering, 'Aren't substitutes what get us through life?'

'Mary's mind is playing tricks, confusing infatuation with something else.'

'Desire perhaps?' Walter answered with conviction.

Tom gave him a cold glare. Walter, in turn, gave back a shrug of his shoulders, showing he was more than ready to continue in this fashion.

'I warn you, I will not stand by and watch Mary ruin herself with you.'

'And I assure you, I won't let people continue to tell me what I can and can't do, or how to feel and think anymore,' replied Walter with defiance. 'So what if there is some chemistry between Mary and me? Why shouldn't there be? And more, why shouldn't I seek out those feelings?'

'You're a criminal, an undesirable!'

Walter gave a laugh. 'And you think desire and feelings know social boundaries?'

'Keep away from her, Walter,' Tom reiterated, showing a pointed finger.

'If that's what Mary wishes, then so be it. But a word of warning to you, Mr Sharpe.' Walter went to open the door and stood in the doorway. 'Don't underestimate the power of fate where feelings are concerned.'

CHAPTER 12

24 NEWSOME STREET

Brockwell sat in his chair staring out of the French windows and drank his umpteenth glass of port. Seeing Mary's response to his presence had unsettled him and he knew he needed to be on his guard with her in future. He thought back to Newsome Street.

The house was ordinary enough, in fact quite pretty. It was an end-of-terrace in a good state of repair and with an abundance of flowers at the front, growing in tubs inside the small walled yard. High on the house wall was the street name sign, which was always cleaned whenever the windows were and, to any observer, it seemed a house lovingly cared for. However, inside, no love could be found; only an intense sadness that betrayed its awful secret.

The property was owned by Ellie Hart, a rather quiet woman of mature years, who could look very severe one moment and yet so gentle the next. It was a trait she had perfected in the course of her trade. Hart was a widow and went about her daily business without attracting much attention, despite the fact that there would always be at least three babies in the house. Not that they ever made much noise with their crying; and therein lay the miserable truth about her activities.

Mrs Hart was known to locals as 'Mrs Hart with a heart,' for she was the kind, older woman who would take in and care for babies, mainly those of desperate or fallen women, and always seemingly wanted to help the poor souls. The truth was, however, that her only motive was money, which she gained in the most ruthless way, and latterly with the aid of a young vicar, Charles Brockwell.

Hart had practised her vile trade of baby farming for the last fifteen years, and always conveniently moved on whenever suspicion of her activities was aroused. Her most recent relocation had brought her to Sheffield eight months earlier and, soon after her arrival, she began to run advertisements in local newspapers. They were brief, sympathetic but always appealing to desperate, young or disgraced mothers:

'NURSE CHILD WANTED, OR TO ADOPT – Caring widow would be happy to accept the charge of a young child. Age no object. If sickly, would receive a parent's care. Terms: fifteen shillings a month or would adopt entirely if under two months for the small sum of twelve pounds.'

Of course, for an inexperienced, unwed mother, rejected by her family, Hart's advertisement was a godsend. The more astute and callous mothers would read the coded message and know that their child would never be adopted and an unexpected death was a certainty. For twelve pounds, their problem was gone, with no questions asked. The fee would invariably be paid by the father, seeking a quick solution. Such men were often the husband or son of the family where the mother worked as a domestic servant. Naive mothers, on the other hand, would struggle to pay the monthly fee, only to find their child falling sick and wasting away. It was a heart-wrenching cycle of despair, as they tried to provide extra money for medicine, never suspecting Mrs Hart of slowly and deliberately starving their baby in order to maximise her profits.

It was a murderous trick Mrs Hart had learnt years earlier and now practised with unemotional precision. By adding lime and cornflour to watered-down milk, she could ensure that the babies would die of thrush and malnutrition, the awful outcome invariably being hastened by water on the brain, induced by the laudanum used to keep the babies quiet.

Hart's evil nature knew no bounds, and neither did her thirst for money; but inevitably, placing advertisements had its limit of responses. An equally sordid and profitable activity was soon found. Some thirteen or so miles away she secured the rental of a large detached property and used it as a lying-in house where young girls could give birth, discreetly and away from their families. To soothe the misery and trauma of their situation, Hart would offer them drinks laced with opium-based narcotics; soon the women became addicted and unwittingly drifted into a life of prostitution, in order to maintain their new habit of drugs.

The only problem for Hart was what to do with the babies after they were born, but she again used the predicament to her advantage. She knew that mothers new to the sordid business of prostitution would be more productive if they saw their children were being well-cared for; and even more willing to take extra clients if their child was slowly to become sick and need costly medicines. Consequently, Newsome Street was assured its steady stream of babies and its future profitability.

It was at the lying-in house that Hart first met Brockwell and discovered his insatiable desire for sexual gratification. In the company of her drug-dependent young women, he fulfilled his cravings ceaselessly.

However, Brockwell was soon to pay a higher price for his pleasure than just fees for Hart's girls. Hart needed more desperate girls with babies and she found a far more successful way to attract them than advertisements. Within weeks, Brockwell was being blackmailed into luring young mothers and their babies away from work-houses; for who better to find unfortunate women than a man of the church with unquestioned access to these institutions of gloom.

On the promise of domestic work at Brockwell's house, desperate mothers would willingly leave their babies with Hart. Soon, however, they were dragged down into a world of drugs and realised that the only real work on offer was selling their bodies.

It was on a visit to the lying-in house that Brockwell saw a newcomer – a young, heavily pregnant and disillusioned Lucinda, accompanied by a gypsy man of strikingly hand-some appearance, yet with a brazen and uncouth manner. The frightened girl was pushed in front of Mrs Hart.

'Give the cow a bed,' the man demanded, thrusting a bundle of notes into Hart's hand. He then walked away, without so much as a glance towards Lucinda.

The young vicar was mesmerised by Lucinda's beauty but kept his distance at first. However, it wasn't long before he made his move, in readiness for the time when the girl would give birth, and he began to gain her confidence with talk of how he might help her in her unfortunate situation. The inevitable offers of strengthening drinks were soon being made and, within a matter of weeks, the girl was begging for more and more laudanum. She ulti-mately gave birth to twins under the influence of the drug, and was seldom stable enough afterwards to experience the joy of motherhood.

One evening, Brockwell laced Lucinda's drink heavily and watched her drift into her private hell before pitilessly defiling her lovely body. It was a fantasy he had waited long to fulfil. Mercifully for Lucinda, she knew little about it. Further weekly visits ensued, as Brockwell took his pleasure in return for drugs. Always he would insist she lie naked, with only her locket around her neck, then, perversely, he'd slowly tighten the chain as he moved towards his climax. It was a horrible business. Each time he quietly opened her door and stood there, leering like a wolf, she recoiled with revulsion. But her thirst for laudanum was unstoppable; and the use of her body was the price she had to pay for it.

Brockwell made sure his victims were always thoroughly addicted to drugs and unable to fight back before he made his advances, and he was very clever at hiding his terrible secret under the guise of being a kindly vicar helping fallen women. If challenged, he was able to rebuff any accusation of wrong doing with ease. After all, who would listen to the word of a whore, barely able to string two words together because of narcotics, besmirching a wholesome and charitable man of the cloth?

Lucinda, on the rare occasions when she wasn't drugged, tried her best to care for her twins. But she soon learnt the awful truth about where her babies were destined to go. With each passing day she feared Newsome Street more and more, knowing just what it meant for her babies. As for Brockwell, she loathed everything about him – the vile hypocrite whose desire for her was becoming insatiable.

One day, in a lucid moment, she took her locket and split it in two. Finding some thin paper, she folded it, concertina-style, before carefully cutting it into the shape of the half locket. She opened it out again, then wrote down a message or more aptly, a plea to her children, to one day seek out Brockwell and expose him for what he was. Gently, she teased back the velvet lining of the locket half and placed the note underneath before sticking the lining back down. The whole process was then repeated with the same message in the other half. She then hid the lockets amongst her children's few items of clothing, in the simple hope that they would be found. Hope was all Lucinda had left.

'Where is your locket?' asked Brockwell on his next visit, moving his wet, slimy lips around her neck.

Lucinda made no answer, but he insisted. 'Does my sweet not enjoy our little game?'

Still she didn't answer and could only flinch as he continued his loathsome kissing. Suddenly he flew into a temper and shouted, 'Where is it?'

'I've given it away,' she answered.

'But why?' he said, calming down.

'For drugs. What else?'

'Does the kind Reverend Brockwell not give you all you need?'

'I was desperate.'

'I trust the locket was the only payment,' he urged, with morbid jealousy.

She looked at him submissively. 'Of course.'

Brockwell suddenly bellowed out, 'Liar!' and slapped her hard across the face. She lay on the bed holding her cheek, fearing his next move, which was not long coming. She struggled as he straddled her trembling body. Finally, he pulled out a hip flask containing his mixture of spirits and laudanum and forced it into her mouth. She gagged and spluttered until the job was done. Only then did he relax his grip, and he sat on her, laughing and waiting for the drink to take effect.

'May the note in that locket see you rot in hell!' she spat out.

He glared at her in astonishment and anger, although he had little reason to be surprised that a girl so abused should want to reveal the truth about him. 'What note?' he shouted and began to shake her.

But Lucinda's eyes just rolled over and, once more, she entered a world of hallucination and unconsciousness. When she finally awoke, she found herself bruised, bitten and bleeding, having been brutally ravaged by Brockwell. She also found that her babies had gone. They had been taken to Newsome Street. It was the last straw for a young woman who could take no more misery, her fragile state of mind finally dissolving in a nervous breakdown.

Four days later, Hart and Brockwell's arrangement, which had lasted nearly twelve months, finally came to an end. A neighbour near the lying-in house had long suspected it was nothing more than a front for illicit activity and, finally, persuaded police to investigate the place. The tissue of lies quickly began to unravel, and then it was only a matter of time before 24 Newsome Street was also revealed as the tragic and sinister place it was. Hart was duly arrested on charges of suspected child murder. During her time at the house, it was believed that 86 babies had died as a result of her neglect and brutality, and it was thought that, over the previous fifteen years, upwards of four hundred babies had suffered at her hands, a fact she never denied, even at the gallows. During her trial Hart did implicate Brockwell as having provided her with young mothers and their babies, but no reliable witnesses were put forward to testify to her claim. Lucinda could certainly have testified to the truth of the accusation, but she was now locked up in the local asylum.

Brockwell was interviewed by the police; but because of their misplaced respect and his position in the church, any investigation was soon dropped, if indeed one ever really started. For twenty six years afterwards, he lived the normal, respectable life of a vicar, and his wretched secret and past sins remained hidden.

As for Lucinda's twins, it was their good fortune to be the last babies taken into Newsome Street. Four days in Hart's house was thankfully not enough time for them to succumb fully to her starvation treatment. Two other babies, however, were not so fortunate and died shortly after their rescue.

The twins were eventually placed with a childless couple, Mr and Mrs Stanford, and so too were their belongings. Hidden inside a shawl were the two halves of their mother's locket.

CHAPTER 13

WALTER'S SOLUTION
AND FAREWELL

Eventually, Walter was discharged from prison to the care of the mission and to supervision by Mr Elliott, who had urged him to visit him at his home upon his release. Walking towards the path, Walter looked a dejected soul, thin, and once again unkempt, consistent with a spell of hard labour and poor conditions. He rapped on the door with the large brass knocker and waited, taking in the pleasant view over the well-maintained garden, with shrubs in the borders and a large tree in full blossom. Eventually, the door was opened and the housemaid, Lily, greeted him or, more accurately, frowned at him.

'Am I at the right house to find Mr Elliott?' asked Walter, courteously, lifting his hat.

Looking him over with disdain, Lily's reply was less than friendly. 'You'd better wait there.' Then she promptly closed the door on him. Lily found it hard to show respect to visitors like Walter and the many other wayward types Mr Elliott invited for consultation. In her previous employment, Lily had been required to send 'begging vagabonds', as her master had called them, away with a flea in their ear.

The door opened again. 'Walter! It is good to see you. Please do come in,' called the much friendlier voice of Elliott. 'Thank you for coming,' he continued, leading Walter to his study. 'Well, how are you?'

'As well as can be expected, sir,' Walter replied, somewhat taken aback by Elliott's hospitality.

'Ah dear…' Elliott broke off his conversation as his wife walked into the room. 'This is Walter Stanford, the young man I was telling you about. I'm hoping the mission can help him.'

Ann Elliott gave Walter a pleasant smile. 'Pleased to meet you, Mr Stanford.'

'And I'm very pleased to meet you too,' Walter replied, rising out of his seat, still not quite accustomed to being spoken to again with civility. For the last three months he had been treated barely better than a dog.

'Would you like a cup of tea, young man?' Ann asked.

'That's most kind, thank you, Mrs Elliott,' Walter acknowledged.

'I'll get Lily to bring some in,' she said and left Elliott and Walter to continue their discussion.

They sat at either side of Elliott's desk. 'I've been giving your situation some thought, Walter, during your time away.'

In truth, Elliott had given a lot of thought to Walter's future during the last couple of months. In particular, he was sad to think of the young man having nothing more to do with his parents. Moreover, he often wondered just how Lucinda, Walter's mother, was. Did she know of her son's most recent plight? How would she view him now? The one thing he did know was that, through his intervention, he could ensure a completely new start for Walter, one that would help him build a future that might mean Lucinda and his father could be justly proud of him again.

'Perhaps there is some good which can come of your proposal,' Elliott said.

'My proposal?' Walter answered, totally baffled.

'For a new beginning and fulfilment.'

Walter was still puzzled.

'I can't offer you an Indian wigwam village or a Bedouin encampment, but I can put you to sea,' Elliott explained. Finally, Walter grasped his mentor's meaning.

'I've managed to get you work on a sailing ship bound for trading in the Middle East, as you desired,' explained Elliott, before pausing as Lily arrived carrying a tray. The maid began to lay out the crockery, her looks all the while towards Walter indicating her resentment at having to serve someone such as him.

'That's all right, I can manage,' Elliott said. She needed

no further encouragement to leave.

'I know a captain who has need of good deck hands,' Elliott said, drawing Walter's attention to the milk jug. 'Milk?' He leant over and offered the jug.

'This offer of work is very gracious of you, sir,' replied Walter.

Elliott knew there was no reason why Walter should not easily adapt to a new sphere. 'There's room for you at sea, and I'm of a mind you're likely to do nothing but good there. That much is clear to me.'

Walter was genuinely touched by Elliott's suggestion, remarking, 'It's more than I deserve, Mr Elliott.' He took a sip of his tea. 'I won't let you down, sir.'

'Very well, that's all arranged then,' Elliott concluded, and he went over to his desk. He picked up an envelope and a small parcel and handed these to Walter. 'There, a gesture of six shillings and some clothing from the mission, and your instructions for the ship.'

He explained that Walter should find lodgings for the night near to the train station and be on the 8.15 am to Southampton, where Captain Smith was expecting him.

'I can't thank you enough,' Walter said, accepting the parcel. 'Truly, thank you.'

'Oh, before I forget,' Elliott remembered, 'your locket and chain.' He took out a small tissue from his drawer and handed it over. As before, he desperately wanted to tell

Walter how he had given it as a present to his mother, but he realised it might raise questions that could distract Walter from starting a new life at sea. Besides, did it really matter if the lad never learned that he had known his mother, long ago? Therefore, he simply offered his hand. 'Well, good luck, Walter, and God's protection.'

Walter stood up and firmly shook his hand. 'Thank you again, for everything. I'll look you up on my return and I'll write with my news.'

Elliott sincerely hoped he would, just as many other youngsters in whose lives he'd played a part had. However, something deep down inside him told him that Walter would find his true calling overseas, and that he would not see him on these shores again.

~~~

Walter looked around his room in the Dog and Partridge tavern with little enthusiasm. It was smelly, dirty and the bed could only just qualify as such: a mattress supported on wooden crates. He turned back the filthy sheets to expose a lumpy threadbare mess, stained with God knows what, but the stench gave him a clue! It was a far cry from what he had expected, considering he'd spent four shillings. Even in prison, he'd had a clean blanket, most of the time. He took comfort in the fact that he was only to stay for one night and decided to abandon the bed, in favour of lying on the wooden floor, with his bag as a pillow. Not that he would get much sleep anyway, due to the constant din from the bar below. In addition, the shouts and occasional muffled moans from the adjoining rooms confirmed Walter was lodging not so much in a tavern but more in a brothel.

He walked over to the window, which offered only minimal light, due to the accumulated mold, and wondered how he should spend the evening. Certainly, he had little appetite for a night in the room. Rubbing at the glass, he made enough of a hole in the dirt to show a bright summer sky, with a red hue, as far as the eye could see. He tried to open the sash but found it was firmly jammed shut, confirming that the room had not been visited by any fresh air for a long time, perhaps years. His mind was made up. He would take a walk, returning as late as was possible. He even contemplated sleeping rough on the street, as the weather was good, although he realised that staying out late at night and alone in this vicinity might not be such a good idea.

The trip along the hallway back to the stairs was an obstacle course of empty bottles and litter. Ahead of him, a man was fondling a young prostitute. He had to smile at the irony of the faded picture above them of the Holy Father. Walter walked past them with his head down, trying his best to be inconspicuous, not that the man took any notice of him; he just carried on groping the girl's buttocks. Then, on the stairs, he was presented with another couple, this time further into the activities that had been paid for. He quickly passed round them and through the door at the bottom, which led to the bar.

Somewhere, through the mass of bodies, was the exit, but where it was Walter couldn't exactly make out. The place was packed. What he had failed to realise when renting a room was that the tavern was frequented by Irish navvies, and today was pay day, which meant a long night of gambling, drinking and raucous behaviour. The groups of pretty young women present, showing ample amounts of cleavage, told him there would be more unsavoury scenes to witness as the night progressed.

Walter tried to push through the immediate crowd, only to find his way blocked by two men sitting at a table. Both were strapping men, clad in dirty work wear. One wore a slouch hat and sucked on a small clay pipe. The other had very obvious deep dark rings around his eyes, and sat cutting pieces off an apple with his bowie knife, and then carefully licking the juice from the blade. On the table was a pile of money, hands of playing cards and enough bottled beer to quench the most ardent drinker's thirst.

Declan Killgallon gave a lustful look at the serving girl's large breasts heaving over the top of her blouse, as she placed yet more bottles on the table. Staring her straight in the eye, he proceeded to lick his knife blade, his tongue flicking off the tip suggestively then dropping to show mushed-up apple. He sniggered. She simply took an empty bottle and ran her tongue around the rim, before curling it into a point, and pushing it firmly in the hole. Raucous laughter rang out from those standing close to the table. Declan gave a wry smile and nodded his head in recognition of the girl's cheeky response.

Walter looked over to Sean Roche, who pushed up his hat. Sean was not impressed with his opponent's showmanship and snorted down his nostrils, whilst curling his lip slightly. He turned over his cards without looking at them. Instead, he confidently stared at Declan who, by contrast, took forever to peep at each card before flipping them over, intentionally not putting them in numerical order. Only when he turned the final card did it confirm a flush of diamonds, against the three queens Sean had. Declan took another slice of apple and then started to scoop up his pile of winnings. That was until Sean's hand came down over that of his opponent. 'Not so fast now,' he said calmly. 'If I'm not mistaken, the nine of diamonds has been played.'

Declan fixed his fierce eyes on Sean's, then called out over his shoulder, 'Did you hear that, Cian? He thinks I'm cheating. Me a cheat, a sloper! How evil a reputation would he have cling to a man!'

'I'm telling you the nine of diamonds has gone,' Sean firmly repeated.

Silence came over the crowd of onlookers, which soon doubled in size. Walter's slight frame was easily jostled, until he could barely see the two gamblers now locking horns. He chirped out innocently to a man who was pulling him further away, 'Just a minute!' his accent making it plain he was not a native Irishman.

'English shit,' was the not-very-pleasant response.

Declan leaned over into Sean's face to declare, 'In Dublin, accusing a man of cheating is like calling his mother a whore!'

Sean retorted, 'And in Derry, a cheat is the son of a whore!' as he leant further into Declan's face, so they were almost touching.

Incensed at the insult, Declan swiftly took his knife and stabbed it straight through the back of Sean's hand, pinning it to the table. He followed with a head butt and shouted, 'Have that, you orange bastard!'

Sean clasped his hand and screamed in pain but that wasn't the end of his suffering, for Declan pulled up at the table to flip it over. The knife handle pushed back hard onto Sean's forearm, making the blade tear further into his hand, until finally it snapped out of the wood, leaving a three-inch tip showing through his palm. He screamed in agony. One of his friends immediately leapt over to attack

Declan, grabbing him by the throat. Within minutes, a full-blown brawl was under way, the like of which Sheffield had never seen before. Certainly, the tavern was no stranger to drink-fuelled fights, but this was suddenly at a different and far more dangerous level.

Walter felt the thud of a fist on his jaw and saw little white flashes before his eyes. Who threw the punch he had no idea. Dazed, he felt his lip, which had burst open at the corner. He looked up to see a ginger-haired man smiling broadly at him and he knew what was coming if he didn't move. The big fist came straight at his face but only scuffed his head as he ducked. All but crawling, he found his way to an opening in the sprawl of bodies, some now covered in blood. A beer bottle narrowly missed him before it smashed onto the floor, emptying its contents and projecting glass in all directions. He knew he had to get out. It was fight or flight, but in his situation, he had no intention of meeting the law again, so opted for the latter.

Finally arriving within sight of the door, Walter stood up and ran, bumping against bodies all the while. A hand suddenly pulled at his shoulder, 'And where you going, chicken?'

Walter turned and pleaded, 'Please, I don't want any trouble.'

'Then go, English coward,' the man said, forcefully kicking Walter in his back and pushing him forward.

Walter grimaced as he smacked into the big brass door-plate and handle.

~~~

The hullabaloo coming from outside made Mary go over to the window to look out. What she saw on the street opposite was a fighting mass outside the tavern doors. 'No, not again!' she sighed to herself. She suddenly gasped in shock, seeing a man come crashing backwards through a window, taking half the frame with him. A moment later, he was back on his feet, shaking off pieces of glass and looking for the next available man to fight.

It didn't matter that she was still dressed in her uniform, Mary had to go down and help the injured, as she had done on several previous occasions. She stepped out onto the street, which was now heaving with fighters and spectators alike, and pushed past Mrs Johnson, one of her neighbours. Alarmed that no one was intervening, Mary shouted, 'Is nobody going to do anything?' but nobody wanted to get involved in a brawl which was fast becoming very nasty.

Walter's body flew through the door along with several others. Unable to stop themselves, they ended up in a pile. Punches and expletives were soon being distributed in equal measure.

Walter finally got to his feet and watched in horror as a hand came over his shoulder and smashed a bottle into the back of the head of a man in front of him. He looked on in amazement, waiting for the man to collapse. But he didn't. Instead, he turned around and gave a bewildered and exhausted Walter, the most horrible, vengeful stare. 'That wasn't me! Honestly, that wasn't me!' he cried, but his pleas were in vain and a large fist went straight across his cheek. Walter slumped to the ground. However, his attacker wasn't finished, and promptly started raining down punches on him. Walter could do no more than to curl up into a ball and hope for deliverance.

Mary pushed her way through the fighting crowd, totally unconcerned for her own safety, shouting, 'In the Lord's name, will you stop!'

There was no chance of that and fighting continued unabated. She eventually saw the curled-up ball take more and more kicks. 'Good heavens, no! What are you doing? Get off! Leave him alone, please! Will you stop it? You're like animals!' she cried. 'Have you no regard for anything, knocking each other senseless. Go home!'

Some would say it was brave of her, others that it was foolhardy, but either way Mary put herself in front of Walter to stop the beating. She had no idea that it was Walter and was merely acting out of mercy.

'In the name of the Lord, stop! Please. Can't you see the

poor man can no longer defend himself? You'll end up killing him.'

One of the navvies gave her a glare, like a frenzied wolf pulled away from his kill.

'Well? Is that what you want? To kill the man? Leave him be! Go home... Just go home!' she tearfully finished.

In the far distance, a faint whistle could be heard and finally the fighting stopped. Some of the men started to disperse whilst others stood and nursed their wounds.

Having no idea who it was, Mary crouched down to the injured Walter and rolled him over. 'Oh, will you look at the state of him! Have none of you any humanity?' she said, looking at his heavily bloodied face. She began to wipe it with her handkerchief, 'Oh no, Walter. Tell me it's not you!'

But it soon became all too obvious whom she was holding. He had grown his hair again and was a lot thinner than she remembered, but there was no mistaking him. 'It is you. Oh, Walter!' she cried, cradling him in her arms.

The sound of police whistles became more audible, which immediately caused the remaining navvies to flee. None of them intended being there when the police arrived. Mary's neighbours too were unwilling to be found on the scene. They had learnt through bitter experience to avoid being a witness to trouble. Not only were they fearful of reprisal attacks, but being a witness would invariably mean a day in court, without pay. Before long, Mary and Walter were alone, except for a couple of men who were simply too drunk to care. Walter, although hurt and dazed, knew he also had to flee the scene and tried to get up.

'Be still now. The police will soon be here,' Mary explained innocently. Not for one moment did it register with her that, because Walter was a criminal, recently released from prison, it would look bad for him if he were discovered in this situation. Walter was acutely aware of the possibility, though, and once more tried to move.

'No, Mary, the law cannot find me,' he muttered with a grimace.

'Don't be silly, you're hurt,' Mary responded, trying to hold him down.

'Please Mary, I beg of you, I cannot stay,' he stated, listening to the police whistles get louder as they got nearer. Finally, he made it to his feet. Mary looked at him in disbelief.

'Walter, your wounds need looking at.'

'I have to go, Mary.'

'Go where?'

'I don't know, anywhere! I just can't let the police find me. They'll take me in again, back to that hell. Please…I couldn't bear it,' he explained and began to stagger off.

Mary called after him. 'Walter. Stop! Look, you can stay with me for a while, at least until everything has calmed down. I lodge just over there,' she said, pointing to the terraced house.

Walter took her hand to thank her. 'Mary, thank you. If ever there was a virtuous one, it's surely you.'

'Yes, well. Let's hope Mrs Walsh sees me that way. Taking a man to my room. Oh dear, I think not!' she replied with a sigh.

Walter held onto Mary for support as they finally reached the door, and just in time, for rounding the corner were at least a dozen police constables, brandishing their truncheons and blowing their whistles wildly. With the door shut, Walter leant his head against the wall, exhausted. 'Thank you,' he murmured to Mary, casting his sorrowful eyes on her and realising just how close they'd been to being caught.

'Come on, we'd better get you to my rooms,' she said, offering her hand to steady him. He looked up at the flights of stairs and puffed out his cheeks.

They staggered up the final few stairs, with Walter now only able to drag his leg. Try as he would to be quiet, he made a thumping sound with each step.

'Sssh!' implored Mary, as she saw Mrs Walsh's door open below. She was surprised her landlady hadn't been out sooner to see what was causing the noise. 'Thank goodness we just missed her,' she sighed, as they eventually got to her door.

Mrs Walsh shouted up, 'Will that be you there, Mary?'

Opening her door, she let Walter in, then shouted back, 'Yes it's me, Mrs Walsh.'

'You'll not be having any company up there now, Mary?'

'No, everything is just fine, Mrs Walsh. Just moving some, erm…er…goodnight!' she said and slammed the door shut.

Mrs Walsh looked up the stairs and said to herself, 'Strange girl, if ever I saw one.'

Walter cast his eyes around the room, impressed with the order of it all.

'Sit here,' Mary called, taking a shawl off the couch. She pushed her hair back and, finally, caught her breath.

Walter did as instructed and flopped onto the couch, thankful to be safe and able to rest.

'We'd better get you cleaned up,' she said and moved the screen to one side to enter the sink area in the corner of the room.

'I'm putting you to some trouble,' he declared, as she returned with a kettle of water, placed it in a cradle, and rested it in the flames of the fire.

'Well, it's not exactly what I had planned for this evening, that's for sure.'

'I'm sorry,' was all he could offer in reply.

'Ah, it's no bother.' Then carefully, she inspected the cuts on his face. 'How on earth did you come to get involved in all that?'

'It's a long story.'

Mary gave him a smile. 'Isn't everything with you, Walter!'

He could only give her a coy smile back, knowing that of course she was right.

She began to tear up some strips of cloth to bathe his wounds. 'I thought you were…well, it's just that, Mr Elliott mentioned you had been sent to prison for…'

'Three months,' he confirmed. 'Yes, I was released a couple of days ago.'

'Oh, so you've managed to keep out of mischief a while then,' she exclaimed more in jest, but Walter looked away, embarrassed all the same.

'I know it doesn't look good. I won't pretend otherwise. But really, Mary, I had no hand in any of it. I just got pushed along, that's all,' Walter said, wanting to explain his innocence. 'But what chance would I have, the word of a criminal, just out of prison!' He looked over to her and watched her soak the cloth in the warm water. 'You do understand, Mary?

Mary said nothing; instead, she just shook her head in playful agreement. 'Here, keep still.' She gently began to wipe the blood from his face. 'Well, they've given you a beating all right. You're going to be sore for a few days.'

He winced as she put some iodine to the corner of his mouth.

'What on earth were you doing in the tavern?' she enquired. 'Have you not heard of its reputation?'

'I needed lodgings and it was the cheapest room I could find.'

'And now you can see why. It's a home, or should I say a den of iniquity, for navvies.' She looked down at his bloodstained shirt. 'You'd better take off your shirt. Let me take a look at those cuts.'

Walter looked down at the patch of blood on his torn shirt. 'It's fine, honestly,' he said modestly.

'I am a nurse and besides I have seen your chest before, remember!

Walter conceded the fact and began to strip off his shirt, as Mary went to get more cloth. On her return, she was shocked to see his lean torso covered in cuts and bruises of all sizes. She stared in concern towards the side of his rib cage and a set of half-healed cigarette burn scars. 'Walter, how did you get those? They're certainly not all from tonight.'

'One of the joys of prison. It's what you're favoured with on occasion,' Walter could only say, indicating resignation at the humiliating treatment handed out to him by bullying officials.

'That's altogether disgusting. I'll be having words with Mr Elliott about this, see if I don't,' Mary replied assertively.

Walter just smiled, appreciating her indignation but realising she had no real idea about the reality of prison life.

Mary carried on gently cleansing his wounds, with the tenderness of a mother nursing an injured child. He eventually placed his hand over hers and she looked up into his eyes, eyes that drew her into his world, that tantalised and made her heart skip a beat.

'Thank you for helping me tonight. It's a good deal better than I deserve,' he muttered to her, whilst squeezing her hand.

She wanted so much to clasp his hand and pull it close, to kiss it, but her reserve wouldn't allow her to do this. Once more, she found she could only joke with him to lighten the moment. 'I've said it's no bother. Just don't be making a habit of it now, do you hear?' she said and finally checked over the area where he had his operation months earlier. 'Well, everything looks all right here. I'll give you some liniment to rub on those cuts.'

He attempted to put his shirt back on but she stopped him. 'Let me wash it through. It will dry off quick enough by the fire,' she offered, and took his shirt to the sink.

Walter called over to her, 'There will be no danger of making a habit of this.'

'I'm pleased to hear it,' she called back.

'You see, I'll be on my way to sea tomorrow, on a merchant ship, and as pleased as ever a man could be.'

His words cut straight through her and echoed back in her head: 'On my way to sea tomorrow.'

'You're going to sea?' she eventually replied, inflecting her voice to show interest, whilst she struggled to hide her disappointment.

'Yes, Mr Elliott has arranged it with the church mission. They've given me a new start. I owe Mr Elliott a great deal...As of course, I do you, Mary.'

Mary felt wretched inside but couldn't show it. Instead she again chose to be flippant. 'Aye you do, so don't you be forgetting that, Walter Stanford, when you return with foreign silks or the like.'

Walter walked over to the screen and watched, as Mary wrung out his shirt. 'I really shouldn't impose on you anymore, Mary. I ought to be making tracks.'

'You're in no fit state to go anywhere at the moment,' replied Mary, and made her way past him to hang his shirt on a chair by the fire, 'and I haven't tried to clean this for nothing.' She hesitated and then concluded, 'Look...you can sleep on the couch, for tonight.'

'No, I couldn't possibly. What if your landlady were to find out? How would you explain things to her?'

'With great difficulty, I shouldn't wonder.'

The next two hours were the most joyous Mary could remember. As she sat with Walter by the fire, she couldn't help but delight at their conversation. They discussed everything from politics to the arts. She felt so at ease with him, so natural, so right! Then, like an attentive child, she finally leaned her head against the arm of the sofa and listened to his stories of how, when he was translating letters sent from abroad to old Mr Mills, his friend's father, he would change the wording. Out of sheer devilment, he liked to see the old master rage and he recounted the time when he took an innocent letter of enquiry from a high-ranking Dutch official and made it seem to deal with another matter entirely. 'Mr Mills, I fear you lack the intellect to comprehend the gravity of our country's economic situation. It seems so useless for you to ignore basic commercial facts and simply demand we pay your prices. Your views on business are but a century behind the time.'

Mary looked at Walter aghast, then laughed and tapped his nose with her finger, 'You mischievous devil.'

As usual, he offered only his charmed look of guilt as his defence. He reached out to grab her finger and kissed it. She was surprised, but didn't draw back. Instead, she seemed to lose any inhibitions and took hold of his hand and held it close to her.

'You're going to think me silly,' she said out of the blue, to which he raised his eyebrow in playful anticipation. 'Oh, Walter, I don't know what it is, it's just…well, I feel…I feel…'

She couldn't finish because, in truth, she didn't actually know what it was she was feeling. Did she want to say it was a feeling of love? Or simply attraction, or even infatuation? What also went through her mind were the words of the spiritualist: that Walter and she were being thrust together for a reason. All she knew for certain was that her heart was telling her something.

She released his hand and let her head sink onto the arm of the sofa. 'You think I'm silly?' she asked awkwardly.

Walter spoke softly and lifted his hand to stroke her hair. 'No, Mary, I don't think you're silly.' He knew there was something happening between them, some chemistry he'd never experienced before. Lifting her chin, he bent down to kiss her. She closed her eyes and willingly let their lips finally touch. It was a gentle sensation that triggered feelings inside her that she didn't understand. Her heart raced and her breath was quite taken away. She knew what she was doing was wrong, against all the morals she had been taught, yet she was powerless to resist. There was an overriding thrill as he ran his hand over her shoulders and then pulled her up towards him, pressing ever harder on her lips. She sighed discreetly as his hands tenderly moved over her body.

'No we mustn't,' she moaned, watching him undo a button on her blouse. Mary was beside herself with trepidation, a multitude of thoughts going through her head. What on earth was she doing? Was she no better than a cheap whore?

Her desire for him was finally to prove too strong, and she allowed herself to be laid back, half-naked, her soft breasts pushing firmly against his bruised chest. If he felt any pain, he didn't show it. He ran a finger down her back, sending a pulse of pleasure to her legs. The sense of doing wrong no longer inhibited her and her legs naturally wrapped around him. He showered her neck with kisses. Another pulse of joy went through her. Mary was at the point of no return, and return she had no intention of doing. As his thighs pushed against hers, she flinched, not knowing what to expect or how to react. Finally, she relaxed and let nature take its course. Her hands gripped tightly on the back of the sofa and she pushed against him, all the while feeling his warm breath moving across her breastbone.

'Oh God,' she cried as he entered deep. 'Oh, dear God,' again she murmured when he slowly moved in and out. She felt no pain, just a moment's discomfort, which gave way to an experience of sheer delight. Then, without warning, she felt her inner muscles tighten, her thighs shudder, and she cried out as the flush of orgasm burst through her body.

~~~

The knocks on the door became louder and more

frequent. 'Hello, are you there, Mary?' shouted Mrs Walsh. There was another knock. Mary finally stirred and then awoke, her pupils dilated with terror. She panted uncontrollably, unable to register quite what was happening. Immediately she thought of what had just occurred – she had made love!

'No, no I can't have!' she told herself. 'No, it was surely yet another dream. Yes, it had to be…of course it was, silly,' she convinced herself, realising she didn't feel sore. Unceremoniously, she felt between her legs. She was wet and there were signs of a little blood. She breathed in and out wildly, to get air into her lungs.

Another knock on the door made her start. Mrs Walsh again called out, 'Hello, Mary. Will you open the door? I have the police here.'

Mary was totally disorientated and pushed the palms of her hands against the sides of her head.

'I'd just like a few words about tonight, if I could, miss?' shouted a male voice.

Mary instinctively replied, 'Yes, I'm here.' She began to try and reconcile events. Had she been dreaming or not? No, it was too real, she thought. Then she was disturbed by her thinking: Where was Walter? Finally, she concluded it must have all have been a dream: the whole night's events simply didn't happen. In reality, she must have returned from work and fallen asleep on the sofa. Then she saw the bloodied cloths in the water bowl. She covered her mouth and gasped, desperate and thoroughly confused.

Once more Mrs Walsh banged at the door, 'Mary!'

Mary gathered her thoughts enough to know she had to open the door.

'Yes, I'm coming. Please, just wait a moment,' she responded, as she picked up the bowl and took it to the sink. Glancing over to the fire, she noticed Walter's shirt had gone. Also, the skylight was half-open. She could only assume he'd exited through it and fled over the rooftops.

'I shan't be a moment,' she shouted, picking up her dressing gown. She took one last look around her room and then a glance in the mirror. Her hair was tousled and, again, this forced her to wonder whether something had actually taken place or not. Perhaps it had, and they had simply fallen asleep afterwards. Then Walter might have been awoken straight away by the knocks on the doors and just fled in panic.

Mary couldn't keep her visitors at bay any longer, and she opened the door.

'Ah, finally,' said Mrs Walsh. 'We've been knocking for an age!'

Mary was in no mood to be chastised. 'Yes, finally, here I am, Mrs Walsh. I was asleep!' she retorted, as tartly as she could manage.

'There's no need for that tone, young lady!' Mrs Walsh responded in her strong Irish accent, fully intending to carry on telling Mary off, until Constable Lansdale interjected politely.

'Might I come in and have a word, miss?'

'About what?' Mary asked.

'Yes, it's all right, officer. Go ahead, they're my rooms,' chipped in Mrs Walsh.

And don't I know it! thought Mary.

Lansdale realised that if he was to get anywhere he needed to speak with Mary alone. 'Well, that's very kind of you, Mrs Walsh,' he said, expecting her to take the hint and leave, but she wasn't dissuaded so easily. It was only when Mary blocked her entry into her room that she conceded.

'Will there be anything else, Mrs Walsh?

'Well er…no I suppose not,' replied a perturbed Mrs Walsh.

'Then perhaps you'd leave us to talk,' Mary said, curtly.

'Yes, well. I'll be…' But the landlady didn't have time to finish before the door had closed on her, much to her annoyance.

'So, officer, how may I help you?' Mary enquired, pulling her shawl tighter around her shoulders.

Lansdale opened his little notebook, ready to note down anything of importance, and stated, 'There was some trouble tonight in the tavern opposite.'

Finally, Mary had confirmation that at least some of the evening was real.

'Yes, I know, I was there,' she responded.

'Was you now?'

'Yes, as was half the street. We were all disturbed by the commotion. There was a huge brawl and I went out to try to break it up.'

Lansdale began to look around the room, making mental notes. Finally, he peered through to Mary's bedroom.

'Are you looking for somebody, officer?' she asked.

Lansdale gave her a cautious smile. 'This brawl… Rather brave of a young woman to intervene, was it not?'

'Look, they were like animals tearing each other apart. I couldn't just stand there whilst they tried to kill each other. A man was badly beaten and needed help, so I helped. I'm a nurse, that's what we do, help injured people.'

'Quite,' he answered. 'And were you aware of a man being stabbed tonight?'

'No.'

'Well, someone was. This man that you helped. Where did he go?'

'I don't know. I walked him to the alley; he said he was all right and then he went.

'Went! Just like that?'

'Yes.'

Lansdale wandered over to the part-opened skylight

and looked out over the roof. 'Rather chilly to have your window open this time of night, isn't it, miss?' he quizzed, pulling his head back in from the window.

Mary was suddenly as sharp as a razor. 'I suffer from asthma. It gets very stuffy up here in summer. I need a flow of air. I don't mean to be rude, but are there any other questions, officer? It really is late and I need to be resting before my duty in the morning.'

'No, I think that's all for now, miss. You will let us know if you think of anything else, won't you?'

'Of course,' replied Mary, 'although I don't think I can add anything further to what I've already told you.'

'You never know. Perhaps after some sleep you'll remember more. Tends to happen… Well, goodnight then, miss.'

'Yes, goodnight to you, officer,' she said and opened the door, only to find Mrs Walsh falling inwards as she tried to listen in. 'And would you be hearing everything you wanted to now, Mrs Walsh?'

Lansdale gave a wry smile and proceeded to put his helmet back on and walk down the stairs, whilst the landlady scrabbled back to her feet and followed him abjectly, eager to learn what had been said. Mary closed the door, thankful to be finally left alone. She ran to her bed and burst into tears. What was left of the night was going to be long and soul-searching.

~~~

Walter had fled Mary's flat in panic and made his way to the only person he knew would help him – Mr Elliott. He stood at his front door in half-wet, bloodstained clothes and banged hard with the knocker. It was finally opened by the domestic servant, Lily, who gave him a long look of disgust. 'Oh, it's you,' she simply said.

Walter implored, 'I need to speak to Mr Elliott.'

'Have you any idea of the time?'

'I know it's rather late but I must speak to Mr Elliott,' he reiterated.

The commotion soon woke the household and Elliott called down from the top of the stairs, 'Who is it, Lily?'

'It's the man that was 'ere this morning, Mr Elliott, says he needs to speak with you.'

'What? Walter?' Elliott asked, as he made his way to the door.

'I believe that's his name,' pronounced Lily, unimpressed with the man in front of her, who was disturbing everybody's sleep.

Elliott opened the door to see. 'Walter, it is you. Dear God, man, whatever happened?'

'I've met with a bit of trouble!' was all Walter could say.

'So I can see. You and trouble seem to have become very well acquainted! You'd better come in,' Elliott invited,

167

much to Lily's annoyance, for she feared she would have to stay up until the so-called guest had gone.

Walter entered the hallway and offered Elliott some explanation. 'Sir, I don't mean to impose. It's just that, well, with the police all over I really didn't know where else to go.'

Having fled Mary's room, he knew he couldn't go back to the tavern, so had made haste over the rooftops of numerous terraced rows until, finally, he had slipped down a drainpipe and wandered the streets.

'I thought you'd be able to help, somehow. I don't want any more trouble with the law, Mr Elliott.'

'That's fine, Walter. Calm down. You did the most sensible thing. Come! Let us talk in my study. Perhaps, Lily, you would be good enough to make a pot of tea.'

Lily's worst fears of extra duties were confirmed. She acknowledged Elliott's instructions with a bow and went to the kitchen, but not before giving Walter a look of utter disdain. Both men walked into the study, where Walter explained what had happened earlier that evening.

'Does Mary know you're here?' asked Elliott.

'No. I do hope she's all right. It disturbs me if I have brought a burden on her with the police. I should be of a mind to go back and check on her.'

Elliott simply suggested, 'Perhaps not the best idea, considering the circumstances! Whatever the police want,

I'm sure it will be nothing Mary can't deal with.'

Walter gave Elliott's analysis a moment's thought and concluded, 'Yes, I'm sure you're right. She is such an angel, Mary.'

'You seem quite fond of her,' Elliott suggested. He was not the most astute person at spotting two people's attraction for each other, but he couldn't help but notice Walter's affection for the girl.

'Well, yes, I am.'

'Possibly as a suitor?' Elliott jumped straight to the point, with his usual subtlety.

'That's quite a frank question, Mr Elliott.'

'Indeed! But one to which I should like to know the answer.'

'Forgive me, but why the sudden interest in my association with Mary?'

'Walter. I've known Mary a while now. She's almost family. It's not unreasonable for a man in my position to want to be protective.' His thoughts drifted back to a difficult time, which he had now come to terms with, but the memory of which would always be with him. It was almost eighteen years to the week that Robert and Ann Elliott had lost their precious little daughter, Amy, a week after her birth. Even with the subsequent gift of two beautiful baby boys, his pride and joy, Elliott would still imagine how his little girl would have turned out, as the years rolled by. Not surprising then that Mary had become his vision of Amy, and hence the daughter he had never had.

'And would the prospect of my being a suitor offend you? Or do you merely wish to know if I have designs on her virtue?'

Elliott was not a violent man, but he could be quite menacing when distressed; and where Mary was concerned, he was not ready to hear any crude talk. He grabbed at Walter and held him by the collar. 'I see prison has made you vulgar.'

Walter knew his flippancy was a step too far. 'I'm sorry. I spoke out of turn. Be assured, sir, I have no desire to hurt anyone, least of all Mary,' he was forced to respond. Slowly, Elliott released his grip on him.

Lily entered the room with the tea, intent on getting back to bed as soon as possible. 'Will there be anything else, Mr Elliott?'

To her disappointment, Elliott replied, 'Yes, if you would make up the guest room.' He turned to Walter and unexpectedly said, 'It is best if you stay with us for what's left of the night. A comfy mattress and clean sheets will undoubtedly aid some much-needed sleep. I have no desire to see you once again on the streets, the victim or, worse, the perpetrator of yet further trouble!'

By 8.15 the following morning Walter was on the train bound for Southampton and a new life at sea.

CHAPTER 14

WRONG ASSUMPTIONS

'Will you be more careful!' Sister Lester hollered at a probationer, as the tray crashed to the floor. The young girl scurried to pick it up.

'I'm so sorry, Sister.'

'Patients need peace and quiet, not frightening half to death.'

'Yes, Sister,' the girl humbly replied and curtsied.

'I am not Matron, there's no need to curtsy,' Sister hissed, giving a glare of disapproval. 'That tray must be thoroughly scrubbed. Do I make myself clear?'

Again, the girl gave a curtsy in acknowledgement.

'What have I just said?'

'That I'm to scrub the tray thoroughly, Sister Lester.'

'No!' Sister threw her hands up in exasperation. 'About curtsying? Oh, no matter. Be on your way, Miss Thompson,' she sighed and walked away down the corridor.

Rounding the corner, she was surprised to see Mary

waiting outside the operating room doors. 'Nurse O'Driscoll, what are you doing here? Didn't your shift finish an hour ago?' she asked.

Mary looked rather pensive and offered only a vague response. 'Yes, I'm waiting for someone.'

'Are you now. And who might that be?'

'It really isn't of importance, Sister.'

Sister Lester was not impressed. 'On my watch, everything is of importance, Nurse…like who sees whom, and when. Is that understood?' Mary knew she had little option but to be more forthcoming.

'I'm waiting to see Mr Sharpe.'

'Really! And is he expecting you?' Sister demanded to know.

'Well, no, not exactly.'

With authority, Sister challenged Mary, 'Not exactly! It's either yes or no, Nurse.'

'Then no,' Mary had to concede, with tears in her eyes.

'Is everything all right, Nurse?' Sister asked, more out of duty than genuine concern.

'I'm fine, thank you…'

Just then, the doors to the operating rooms were flung open and out walked Tom Sharpe with another doctor. 'Ah, ladies!' he said, with his usual welcoming tone. 'And what brings you to theatre?'

'Nurse O'Driscoll and I were just chatting on our way

down to the wards, Mr Sharpe.' Sister Lester was determined that Mary would only see the surgeon when she had approved and arranged it. Equally, Mary was adamant she would speak with Tom, whatever the consequences.

'I see. Well, don't let me stop you,' said Tom, beginning to walk on.

'Might I speak with you, Mr Sharpe?' Mary called after him.

Furious that her authority had been challenged, Sister Lester gave Mary a glare that left her in no doubt there would be repercussions. Mary, however, was not really bothered about consequences at work any more. She worried only about things that were happening in her personal life, and she knew only Tom could really help with her troubles.

'Of course, Mary,' Tom replied.

Sister raised an eyebrow in surprise at the doctor calling a nurse by her Christian name. There were rules of etiquette and this was highly irregular, even for Tom, who never really did things conventionally. Her suspicions were aroused. She gave Tom the smallest of forced smiles and left Mary and him to talk undisturbed and unheard, or so they thought.

Turning onto the next corridor Sister noticed that the store cupboard door was open, which was unusual. Her suspicious nature once more got the better of her, and she decided she must look inside. As she glanced over the stock of towels and sheets, she heard footsteps and then the voices of Tom and Mary. By sheer chance, they stopped just outside the store cupboard, its door just slightly ajar. Sister Lester could hear every word and was most alarmed to hear Mary say, weeping, 'I'm sorry, but I could be pregnant.'

Behind the door, Sister's eyes opened wide in amazement. She held her breath and listened intently, not daring to move a muscle for fear of being discovered.

'Listen, Mary, I just need to drop these notes off to the ward, then we can talk properly. Why don't you go and wait in my rooms and I'll be back as quickly as I can,' suggested Tom.

Through the gap in the door, Sister watched as Tom held his hand over Mary's. She was almost paralysed with shock at the thought. Tom Sharpe had got a nurse pregnant. The scandal of it all! But how wrong she was. As people often do, Sister was going by first appearances. Within minutes she had run down to Matron's office as fast as her legs could carry her, in order to break her news.

In her office, Matron Hanson nearly choked on her lemon tea as Sister Lester recounted her version of the situation. She rose in horror from her chair and took her cup and saucer to the window. 'You're absolutely sure you didn't mishear things, Sister?'

'I heard as plain as I hear you now, ma'am,' maintained Sister Lester.

Matron took a sip of tea and thought for a moment, before turning back to speak. 'You realise such grave accusations could have repercussions far beyond anything I can deal with. This has to be a matter for the hospital's board of governors.'

Matron had dealt decisively and severely with many a fledging romance among her staff of nurses, but she was particularly uncomfortable at the thought of this situation.

'It's my duty to report such matters,' Sister Lester stated.

'If you're wrong, Sister!' Matron replied, not wanting to contemplate the consequences.

'I only tell you what I heard, ma'am.'

Matron took a deep sigh and thought again until Sister broke her concentration. 'She's in his rooms right now... No doubt doing something unsavoury.'

The muscles in Matron's forehead tightened into a scowl. 'Let's stick to facts, shall we, and not let an over-active mind run away with itself.'

Sister took the reprimand and cast her eyes downwards, 'Yes, ma'am.'

'Very well. Follow me,' said Matron decisively and walked over to open her door. 'What will be, will be,' she concluded and strutted up the corridor, with Sister Lester in tow, towards Tom's rooms.

Mary was sitting in his room when Tom returned. He gave her a warm smile, but she looked devastated, and bowed her head. 'I don't want to burden you, Tom, but I can't turn to anyone else.'

'Mary, look at me,' he said and pulled over a chair. 'Listen, whatever the problem, it can be sorted out. Why don't you start at the very beginning.'

Mary took a deep breath and began to re-live her night with Walter, describing to Tom everything in as much detail as she dared without being indelicate. She finished in tears and muttered, '…and I have to know if I'm pregnant.'

Tom had listened intently, not interrupting or passing comment, and he tried not to give any indication of his emotions, which in truth were near to bubbling over. The mere mention of Walter was bad enough for him; but hearing details of Walter and Mary together, whether a dream or not, was unendurable and left him with a hollow feeling inside.

He told himself to simply analyse the facts. As always, there would be a rational explanation. His dream theory was what he wanted to cling to; but his heart was aching at the possibility that this had not been a dream and that Mary had actually made love with Walter. Tom had fallen head over heels in love, and the last thing he wanted to contemplate was the thought of Mary's love being given to someone else. It was too much for him to bear.

Whatever the explanation, ultimately, he had to decide what would win – his jealousy of Walter or his desire for Mary. If it was the former, he would allow the green monster to slowly let her drift away; and if the latter, he had to be pragmatic, to get Mary to accept the theory that she was still being tortured by her dreams.

'Mary, these experiences are just dreams! The root cause still lies in your desire to find love,' he said, pushing the jealous monster in him back down – at least for now.

'So why was there blood?' she wept.

Tom offered, 'Do you really want to know?'

'Yes, of course,' Mary sobbed and waited for his words of wisdom.

If she was to believe his theory, then he was going to have to make it damned convincing. 'You simply got aroused in your dream and, well…started to stimulate yourself, probably quite lustfully,' he said, without batting an eyelid.

Mary nearly fell off her chair with astonishment at what he had just said. 'I beg your pardon. Did I actually hear you right?'

Tom laughed, 'It's perfectly normal.'

'It may well be to you! But I assure you – certainly not to me.'

Tom continued, 'You see, girls sometimes…'

Mary held her hand up and squeaked like a mouse. 'Tom please! I think I'd rather not learn more.'

Tom laughed again at her naivety but all the same he found it endearing.

'Is there no way you can tell now...whether I'm pregnant, that is?' she asked desperately.

'You're not pregnant, Mary. It was a dream!'

She gave him another desperate smile. 'I so want to believe your theory, Tom, honestly I do. But can't you see, I just won't rest until I know for sure... Are there no tests?'

'I'm afraid not,' Tom said, shaking his head, much to her disappointment.

'Not even...well...you know through those women?' Mary referred to the elderly women she knew, who professed to call themselves 'helpers', when in truth they were nothing more than back-street abortionists.

'Mary, you must promise me to put any notion of visiting those women out of your head. Promise me.' He held up her chin. 'Listen, doctors have been trying since Egyptian times to foretell pregnancy but still the only way to know is through missing menstruation, and even then, it's not certain.'

Mary looked forlorn but managed to give him a weepy smile. 'But if it isn't a dream!'

'Then you won't menstruate. Most likely, you will be pregnant. My theory will have been all wrong and, between us, we'll have a problem,' he joked.

Mary couldn't help but see the funny side and began to laugh through her tears. He opened up his arms to offer her a reassuring hug, which she accepted. Tom suddenly felt his whole body warm as he held her tight. She could not help but feel the intensity of his embrace and released herself slightly to look into his eyes. 'You're a kind man, Tom. Thank you for listening to me,' and then she allowed herself back into his embrace. She felt her heart begin to race. If his theory was right and she was simply longing for the love of the right man, then there wasn't a more attractive and desirable man than Tom.

'Listen. Why don't you visit us for dinner, one evening? Catherine would welcome the company, and I'm sure Emily would love to see you,' he said.

'Yes, I might just do that,' she responded, feeling him squeeze her a little tighter.

'Everything is going to be just fine, Mary, just fine.'

With only a brief knock, Matron flung open the door saying, 'Mr Sharpe, I'm sorry to disturb you but...' She stopped in her tracks, seeing Tom and Mary in an embrace. 'Oh!' was all she could splutter, and she chose to turn her head away.

Mary immediately pulled away and went bright red in embarrassment. Oh dear, how does this look? she thought. Tom, on the other hand, was quite unperturbed.

'Come on in, Matron, why don't you.'

'I did knock, Mr Sharpe.'

'And waited?' Tom batted back.

'Yes, well…I wasn't expecting…' She turned to look at them both and finished with a hiss, 'This!'

'Nurse O'Driscoll and I were simply discussing a private matter.'

'Evidently!' she scoffed, pushing her nose so far into the air that Tom fully expected rods of damnation to rain down on him.

'So, what is it you want, Matron?'

Matron huffed, before finally composing herself. 'I should like to speak with you. Alone!'

No sooner had she spoken her last word than Mary was half out of the door. She dared not look her superior in the face: that piercing glare of disgust was simply too much for her to bear.

'Sister Lester, please escort Nurse O'Driscoll to my office,' Matron instructed. With that, the door closed and she was left alone with Tom.

'So, Matron,' Tom said, inviting her to carry on.

'Mr Sharpe, I surely need not remind you of the rules of this, or indeed any, hospital.'

'Rules regarding?' Tom enquired, trying to be as difficult as possible.

'You're an intelligent man, Mr Sharpe. I don't think I need spell things out.'

'Matron, what you've seen, I can assure you, is nothing inappropriate.'

'Were you or were you not in a passionate embrace with my staff?'

Tom couldn't resist a flippant reply. 'I wouldn't call it passionate.'

She gave him a look that could have curdled milk. Matron Hanson was an old-fashioned disciplinarian in the Nightingale tradition. There was no place for broadmindedness, tolerance or liberal thinking. Black was black and white was white. More importantly, rules were not to be debated but to be upheld, sometimes with great severity.

'And was Nurse O'Driscoll not heard to remark, in the course of a conversation with you, that she might be pregnant?'

'The trouble with eavesdropping is that reasons are seldom understood, Matron!'

Matron stared straight at Tom and calmly stated, 'I have no intention of listening to sordid reasons in which I have no interest, Mr Sharpe. My report will be submitted to the Board of Governors first thing in the morning and, until then, by the authority invested in me as Matron, I shall ask you to leave these premises.'

Tom would normally have argued the point vigorously, but he realised how wrong everything appeared, and he wasn't prepared to give Matron a chance to reject the truth. 'Very well,' he said and began to walk out. However, at the door he stopped and gave Matron his parting shot.

'Steadfastly upholding discipline is a skill that makes a worthy matron; but, when combined with a firm belief in people's wickedness, it hardly makes a great one!'

Mary walked in silence with Sister Lester until they reached Matron's office, but then she chose to walk straight on.

'Nurse O'Driscoll, what are you doing? Come back! I insist you return, this instant,' Sister shouted.

But Mary did not. She had decided she would not be subjected to the indignity of Matron's investigation, and the ruthless character assassination that would undoubtedly follow. She knew that simply being in Tom Sharpe's room was enough to warrant instant dismissal. Instead, she would return home and write her resignation. Either way, Sheffield City Hospital would lose a good nurse, albeit one in crisis.

In her bedroom, she took her parents' letters from the little casket at the top of the tallboy and pulled at the ribbon. Then she read each one in turn from beginning to end. 'Oh father, what is happening to me?' she wept. In the space of just three short months, her world had been turned upside down and all by a man who was now far away at sea.

Later that night Mary felt her usual monthly stomach cramps, brought on early no doubt by the stress of the day. Never before had she welcomed her period with joy, but then never before had she thought she might be pregnant. She curled up by her fire and slowly closed her eyes in exhaustion.

~~~

Elliott's career had taken a positive turn when he had been elected to become the first probation officer for the city, a pioneering role which at last offered him hope of influencing for the better what he saw as a failing court system. What it also brought him, though, was an ever-increasing postbag, full of documents for comment and papers about legislative changes that had to be read. Opening his post one morning, he was intrigued by the postmark on an envelope: it was posted in Tenerife some two months earlier. The letter was in fact from Walter and, although brief, it was infinitely precious to Elliott.

Dear Mr Elliott,

The copyist in that commercial house was not unhappy in his work: only shut out from the joys of life. Yet this lad always had hope and sought his adventure. But alas, he was much misunderstood and paid the price with his freedom.

The gates then burst open, and a generous friend decided to give him liberty and the chance to breathe these fresh Atlantic breezes. He looks back to his barred and gloomy cell, horrified and amazed as he reflects how once his soul was satisfied to endure involuntary captivity. He knows it would kill him now!

What an inspiration, sir, that brilliant decision to nurse a sick soul to health in an ocean cradle! Accept the everlasting gratitude of a mute restored, a captive released.

Yours,
Walter

Elliott had often wanted to take news of Walter to his parents, and he was curious to see where Lucinda, his dancing butterfly of long ago, had finally landed and closed her wings. But his experience had told him it was better to wait for convincing proof of a final successful outcome before raising hopes. Now, armed with Walter's letter, he decided to take the news he had post-haste to his parents, in the hope they would rejoice in their son at last following a straight course.

Elliott made his way across the street and rounded the corner, until there in front of him was the small chemist's shop: a rather drab little place, with its large frontage showing only the faintest resemblance to anything that could be considered an attractively dressed window. Still, it was appropriate for its purpose and had brought Walter's father a modest income over the years, as the local pharmacist.

The small hand-written sign on the door advised him the shop was closed for lunch and Elliott, therefore, followed the instructions to, "Knock on the adjoining house door for enquiries". He was somewhat apprehensive as to whether Lucinda would be the one to open the door. If she did, exactly how should he introduce himself, he suddenly thought. The anxiety began to build up in him. After all, it was over thirty years since he had last seen her. He felt a tug in his stomach, just like the first time he called on her at that little caravan long ago. It took several knocks before the door slowly opened. He was a little relieved when a male voice politely said, 'Hello! Can I help you?'

'Aah, yes, good morning, sir,' said Elliott.

The little man before him took a look at his watch, which prompted Elliott to realise it was actually afternoon.

'Sorry, afternoon,' Elliott corrected himself, before continuing, 'Mr Stanford?'

'Yes.'

He was rather surprised to find the husband of his once young love was not as he had imagined – a tall, strong, dashing man, with the looks of a screen idol. Instead, the man before him was a small gentle man, bespectacled, with thinning grey hair and wearing a shabby, ill-fitting suit.

Elliott duly introduced himself and asked, 'I was hoping to be able to have a word with you and Mrs Stanford.'

'I'm afraid Mrs Stanford is no longer with us, Mr Elliott:

she died last year,' replied the husband, quite matter-of-fact about his statement, and he continued without emotion, 'Pneumonia, sir.'

How deep the dagger went into Elliott, as he suddenly learned of his butterfly's demise.

'Oh!' he responded, crushed by the news. 'I'm so sorry.'

'Can I not be of assistance to you?'

Elliott took a while to answer. 'Erm! Well, yes, of course. I've come to talk about Walter, Mr Stanford.'

'I see,' said the father in a resigned tone. 'Then I suppose you'd better come in.'

They went through to the parlour: a little room in which, seemingly, nothing was out of place and yet, curiously, nothing seemed to want to belong to its place. Everything appeared to cry out for a woman's touch: the sofa to be positioned just so again, the table turned the other way round, and the lampshade moved so that there did not seem to be a divorce pending between it and the armchair.

'My son is in trouble again, I take it?'

Elliott patiently explained the situation and tried to paint an optimistic picture of the son's new life. Walter's father, however, had been here many times before and gave only a cautious welcome to Elliott's news. Still, Elliott plugged away, trying to draw out anything that might prolong the conversation; but it proved difficult for him to learn much of the father and son's relationship. The only thing he could surmise was that Walter had deeply hurt and disappointed his parents with his behaviour over recent times.

Elliott thought he might perhaps have to be content with the fact that Arthur Stanford was a man of dignity and strong moral virtues, a man who felt that anything that fell short in his family should be dealt with privately and without drama. However, the father did provide him with more information. Indeed, he had sent money and brief letters to his son during his term of imprisonment, albeit letters more of rebuke rather than encouragement. As for Walter's mother, she had become increasing ill until, finally, when bedridden, they had given her better news of her son than was strictly true: a further reason why he should keep away till his manner of life justified the picture painted of him for her comfort. At the sixth time of incarceration, the father had lost all hope for his son returning to a straight course and, consequently, their paths were, sadly, not to cross again.

'Walter was given everything my status would allow, Mr Elliott: a good education and possessions few others from these parts could attain to,' commented the father.

Elliott felt he would not disagree; but he was at a loss to understand why the man could not also see that his son had a spirit that needed nurturing and controlling with more than mere material things. It was obvious Walter had inherited what Elliott remembered of his mother's character and her desire for life's enjoyment, fullness and fun. Walter was no more than a kitten seeking mischief and unable to appreciate the difference between fun and foolishness. But like any kitten left to its own devices, it had started to grow into a wild cat!

As Mr Stanford went through to the kitchen to put the kettle on, Elliott took more notice of the brass picture frames on the mantelpiece. He picked up and studied the photo of Walter as a young lad, a charming picture in which the eyes were alive and trouble-free. Next to that was the photo of a young girl whom he surmised must have been Victoria, Walter's sister. She was certainly pretty, with a pleasing smile, yet her face couldn't altogether hide the anguish of her condition: the consumption that was to bring her life to an end. At the end of the mantelpiece was a picture of a woman sitting on a chair, her husband, Arthur Stanford, standing next to her like a statue. Both held a peculiarly rigid pose, and had an expression one would have expected any professional photographer to suggest should be relaxed somewhat. Elliott took a closer look, then a closer look still.

Surely this was never Lucinda, he thought in horror. His butterfly had turned into a dowdy old moth!

Elliott was so engrossed he hadn't even noticed his host's return to the room. Eventually, he sensed he was being watched.

'Those pictures and memories are all that's left now,' the subdued voice announced.

'I can see where the pair get their good looks from,' was the best Elliott could think of, to make the moment a little lighter.

'Hardly, Mr Elliott.'

'Oh come now!'

'No, you misunderstand. You see, Walter and Victoria were adopted, so you'll hardly see a resemblance to me or Beryl.'

Elliott could count on the fingers of one hand the number of times he had been lost for words, but this was to become one of them. He was genuinely shocked. Finally, he found his tongue.

'You must forgive me, I had no idea... I was under the impression that your wife was called Lucinda, Mr Stanford,' remarked Elliott, reeling in confusion.

'No! Whoever told you that?'

'Well...I...I can't honestly remember,' Elliott babbled, now realising that for all this time he'd simply added two and two together and made five.

Mr Stanford could see Elliott was totally bewildered, so began to offer him an explanation. 'I suppose it's an obvious assumption to make, that both of them would be ours; but, unfortunately, my wife and I couldn't have children.'

'I'm sorry,' replied a compassionate Elliott.

'I did know of Lucinda, though, Mr Elliott, and you would be right to connect her to Walter,' the man went on to confirm, 'because she is his mother.'

'I knew it,' Elliott called out in excitement.

'I take it you knew her too?'

'Yes, but many years ago, we were, well…' Elliott paused to choose the right words. 'Well, let's say friends, when we were no more than sixteen or so, after which we lost contact, I'm afraid.'

'I see.'

'May I be so bold as to ask what happened. I mean, how did Walter and his sister come to be adopted, Mr Stanford?'

'Take a seat, Mr Elliott, and join me for a cup of tea, please.'

Elliott was more than happy to do so and helped by setting out two china cups and pouring the milk.

'I'm afraid Lucinda didn't quite maintain the innocence you perhaps knew in her when you were younger, sir,' continued Mr Stanford.

Elliott didn't say anything, but his look of disappointment said more than any words could.

'My wife and I were told she took up with some man, a heathen by all accounts, from a travelling group, who enticed her into wild ways. Although their union was short lived, it did nonetheless leave her pregnant.'

He went on to further explain that Lucinda's father, once so caring and loving, had rejected her totally and soon moved away in shame. Thereafter, the confused and desperate girl eventually found the door of Ellie Hart's sad place.

'Such a horrible episode with that Mrs Hart.'

Elliott listened with interest, but frowned with confusion.

'She was responsible for that baby farming scandal, Mr Elliott.'

'Aah yes, I do vaguely remember hearing something about her.'

'What she did to those poor babies!' He sat and gazed into space with a look of distaste and then gave his opinion. 'Hanging was too quick for the wicked woman. If I'd had my way... Well, never mind. Anyway, when the police raided the place, they found four babies: two died; but a pair of twins survived and Beryl and I, we were asked if we'd take them in, with a view to adopting them. Of course, we jumped at the chance, Mr Elliott.'

'Of course and very admirable of you both,' Elliott responded, taking a sip of his tea. He winced and grimaced.

'Is something wrong?'

'You don't have a little sugar?' replied Elliott, as his face returned to normal.

'Yes of course, I'm sorry.'

Returning with the sugar bowl, Mr Stanford watched agog as his guest proceeded to put five spoonfuls into his small cup and stirred furiously, before beginning to drink it. Elliott was oblivious to this being anything but normal and simply sighed, 'That's better,' then continued with his questions. 'If I could ask, what can you remember of a locket? When you took the babies, did they have a half locket with them?'

The father smiled. 'Yes, I remember them very well. Lucinda must have hidden them amongst their clothing. We gave the lockets to them both at an early age, as a keepsake, you know, as a memory of their mother in future years.'

'And Lucinda?' said Elliott, wanting to know what ultimately became of his fallen butterfly.

Mr Stanford's head dropped. 'All we learnt, sir, was that the poor girl was ravaged by drugs and abuse. People tried to help in providing for her, but she was eventually institutionalised. Then one day, she just upped and disappeared. I fear it wouldn't have been long before she was beyond help. We never heard of her after that.'

'I see,' replied a sorrowful Elliott. However, he was content that Lucinda had at least tried, in one of her clearer moments, to make sure her babies had a token to one day remember her by.

Just then, their conversation was broken by a loud tapping on the window. It was a customer, Mrs Fothersgill.

'Hello! Are you there, Mr Stanford? It's gone two o'clock you know,' she shouted.

'I do apologise, Mr Elliott, but I really must be re-opening the shop. You will let me have further news of Walter? I do so want him to do well, despite how things may appear. I'm sure our differences will be reconciled one day.'

There was another tap on the window. 'Mr Stanford! Mr Stanford!' cried the impatient woman.

'I'm afraid dispensing Mrs Fothersgill's prescription will wait for no one!' he joked.

'Indeed,' Elliott agreed with a smile.

'And I'm sorry I couldn't give you better news of Lucinda.'

'The facts of life, sir, the sad facts of life,' replied Elliott with a sigh.

Walking back home, he finally accepted that the plight of Lucinda might just have to remain a mystery, and that his memory of her should be one of happier times.

CHAPTER 15

MOVING ON

Tom, like Mary, had chosen to resign from his post at the City Hospital, having the foresight to realise that a misconduct hearing would inevitably become a public affair and that a resulting dismissal would not help his future career. More important to him, though, was that he had no desire to drag Mary's name through the mud of an official investigation. It wasn't long, however, before he was offered a surgeon's position at the Derby Royal Infirmary. Although he lived in, he managed to get back to Sheffield most weekends to see his sister and niece – and of course Mary, who was really the main reason for his frequent returns.

Mary had often thought of Walter since his departure, wondering where he was and how he was doing. However, the traumatic visions and experiences had gone and in their place were only tender thoughts; memories of a relationship from which she had moved on. Although sometimes it felt as though the void in her life could only be filled by him, she was pragmatic enough to realise her infatuation was based purely on the mystery of the man, a character so intriguing and stimulating, yet so vulnerable and unpredictable. She realised that she wanted to make more of Walter than he actually was.

Also gone were Mary's thoughts of the spirit world having any part to play in her past experiences. However bizarre an occurrence had seemed, Tom always had a rational explanation for things and ensured that Mary had plenty of papers and books on the subject of visions and dreaming. Conveniently, these all reaffirmed his theory that she was satisfying her desire for love with a fantasy about Walter. It was a theory she slowly started to accept, and she therefore began to store dreams of Walter simply as references to what she was seeking in life: a loving, caring man who could excite her, dance with her heart, and take her to a place in her mind where she could find completeness.

Mary now put all her efforts into working full-time in the deaf school. She was still intent on returning to nursing but, for now, was happy to give her time to afflicted children and young people who otherwise would receive no help. However, the church mission was only able to pay her a very small wage and the time was fast approaching when she would need to consider her financial situation. The company administering the trust fund set up for her by her father had now been liquidated and all legal dealings were at best confused. It was ironic that the thing her father had used to secure her future was now her burden.

Mary's affection for Tom soon began to turn into true love and their relationship quickly consumed her every thought. Tom had finally won over her heart and now desired only to lead Mary to the altar.

Choosing a Sunday afternoon in the park, he asked his friend to meet him and to bring his two Dalmatian dogs, along with their adorable litter of eight puppies. Mary loved the breed of dog: 'We'll have at least three when we're married,' she had joked. So, instructions were given: at precisely twelve noon, the parade of hounds would appear, one of them carrying around its neck a braid of emerald green ribbon with a velvet ring box attached. Simple enough, one would have thought; but an unruly puppy can scupper the best-laid plans.

Picnicking on the grass, Tom teased Mary with his piece of sponge cake, first offering her a bite, then withdrawing it. Finally, he dabbed her nose with jam. 'Oh, Nurse, I do hope you're a prettier maid under all this cake,' he joked and dabbed her nose again, before finally letting her have a bite.

She hit him playfully. 'You horrible thing, you.' They

both laughed at her trying to speak with her mouth full.

'The wondrous draw of a girl, her pretty face covered in jam,' Tom said, gently wiping away the crumbs from her face. 'I do love you, Mary. Kiss me.' He playfully leant over, only to be pushed back.

'Tom, stop it! We're in public!' she laughed.

'Who cares?'

'Me. I'm a lady, if you hadn't noticed…and ladies do not kiss in public.'

He took a look at his watch. It was approaching midday. 'When we're married then?'

She lifted her eyebrows and opened her gorgeous eyes wide. 'Married, indeed! Tom Sharpe, is that a proposal?'

Tom just smiled, as the boathouse clock struck twelve o'clock. Right on cue, the little puppies and their parents started to appear around the corner.

'Aagh, look! Aren't they just adorable?' she called out in delight, not having the faintest idea of his ploy, until, eventually, she saw the designated puppy toddling about with the ring box around its neck and realised what was happening. She held her hand to her mouth and gasped, 'Oh, Tom. I don't believe this!'

Tom bent down to try and retrieve the box, only for the puppy to snap and yap at him. This in turn caused the protective mother to bound over and snarl. The next moment there was a hilarious scene with Tom being chased off, followed by the parade of pups, all yapping in excitement. Mary stood there, howling with laughter.

Eventually Tom returned, none the worse for his experience. He opened the jewel box to present a delicate ring set with diamonds. 'Mary, will you marry me?'

How could she refuse such a theatrical proposal? She flung her arms around him and looked longingly into his eyes. 'Yes, Tom Sharpe, I will marry you,' she whispered, and promptly gave him a gentle peck on the lips. He gave her a jovial look of surprise. Mary just had to say in return, 'Well, we are to be wed!'

For all Tom's romantic fancy, he had no real understanding of just what the big day entailed.

Mary stated calmly, 'No my dear, it's not just about a simple exchange of vows, the passing of rings and that's it – man and wife!' She then insisted he listen to her plans for a perfect white wedding.

Tom looked genuinely surprised to learn that the napkins needed to match the tablecloths and, moreover, there was a horrible dilemma: should they be folded like a fan or in a rectangle? Then, of course, there was the importance of the centrepiece – should it be tall or short? Tom slumped back on the grass, smiled generously and allowed Mary to educate him further.

~~~

There is something indescribably pleasing about receiving a personal letter, and even more so when it brings joyous news. Elliott felt as much delight as it was possible for a mortal to feel, as he read Mary's letter announcing her engagement. He looked upward and drew in a deep breath to control his emotions. Inside his pocket, he clenched his hand around a little knitted baby's bootie and imagined how the letter could have been from his daughter, Amy, had she survived. The joy he would have got, as a father, seeing his daughter become engaged. He read Mary's letter again and tears welled up. 'How then could I think of anybody else, Robert. Please will you do me the great honour of giving me away,' the letter read. He could not have felt more pride than at that moment.

The happy couple had been invited to stay with the Elliotts in the days leading up to the wedding. Ann had been a rock in helping the bride-to-be organise things, whilst her husband proved a welcome distraction to Tom, who was clearly more at home debating Elliott's day-to-day court proceedings than ever he would be discussing seating arrangements in the mission hall. Mary was eternally grateful to Robert and Ann for all their love and support. On the eve of her wedding day, with all plans prepared and Tom dispatched to stay with his sister, she could finally rest with the two people she considered true friends.

As she slept that night, Mary's thoughts of Walter, which had all but disappeared when Tom became her only focus, suddenly came back to her in a most vivid dream.

It was a dusk so evocative, a sunset so beautiful, a time so peaceful. Never before had Walter witnessed such a glorious sight. The golden ball of fire slowly melted into a perfectly still sea. Above was a dark pink sky, washed with shades of yellow and crimson, threaded with blue clouds. In the far distance, the mountains were finally released from the sun's scorching grip and fell into shadow, a myriad of grey-green hues. In the stifling warm air, crickets chorused relentlessly, amid the chant of prayers coming from the minaret. This was Yemen, his new blessed land.

Walter had spotted this place, at Zinjibar, whilst sailing up the Arabian Sea to the port in Aden. Through a spyglass, he looked in fascination at a small, near-derelict dwelling, surrounded by a grove of date palms and a plantation of coarse grasses. 'I'll fix it up, Tosh, and make my home there,' he had said to the monkey, which was sitting beside him. The little creature gave a grin and chattered its teeth. 'You see every man has to finally have a place.' Tosh listened intently to his master, moving his head from side to side like a dog. How odd it would have seemed to anyone watching: a man talking to a monkey, and the monkey seemingly revering every word, its eyes ablaze. 'Yes, a man has to ultimately lay down his hat,

Tosh,' the master continued, producing an orange and starting to peel it. The little furry head bounced back and forth, looking at Walter one moment then fervently at the orange the next. Finally, after the fruit was divided, Tosh again cocked his head to listen, whilst eagerly nibbling away at his prize. Of course, one eye was always watching to see if there was perhaps one last segment coming his way! How beloved the master; how fickle his friend.

'Well, little fella, it's time to say farewell,' said Walter, opening up the sling bag containing his meagre possessions. He took out a small package and unwrapped it, watched eagerly by Tosh. Inside, was a beautiful silk scarf which he rolled up and made into a neckerchief for the monkey. 'It was meant as a gift for someone special, but I doubt I shall see her again, so you might as well have it, old lad,' he said, watching Tosh leap up and down with excitement.

Mary became unsettled, her head beginning to thrash from side to side on her pillow. She held out her hand, desperate for Walter to take hold. She called out, 'No! please, I'm here. Walter, please! We can see each other again.' But this time, her dream didn't allow any interaction between them, and she had to watch him step onto the gangplank, before the picture slowly faded and he was gone.

The scene suddenly changed and Mary once more saw the familiar woman seated in the chair opposite her bed, smiling at her. As always the woman never spoke. She just breathed in deeply, as if she were taking in the energy from Mary's encounter with Walter. Then she too faded, and the chair was empty.

When Mary awoke in the morning, lovely sunshine flooded through the curtains in her room. She got up and went to open them and looked out onto the light-filled garden below. Standing there, she pushed back her long, silky hair, closed her eyes and allowed the warmth of the sun to bathe her face. She recollected her dream, which had felt so real. Mary couldn't yet realise it, but the events in her dream were not just her imagination.

What she was also unaware of was that at the time of writing to Mr Elliott, months earlier, Walter had also written to her, suggesting they should meet when his ship finally docked in Southampton. However, he had addressed the envelope to her at the City Hospital, which, of course, she had left on bad terms. Not surprising then that she never saw his letter, and was unable to respond. Having received no return mail from her, Walter took it to mean that she did not share his enthusiasm for a reunion.

Once again her emotions were highly confused. Here she was on her wedding day, thinking not of Tom, but of a man far away. Any feelings of guilt, however, were dispelled by her common sense, which told her that, whatever the reasons for her dreams of Walter, they were only dreams. In reality, she adored Tom and knew he would make her happy. She had to believe in his theory. But theories were just theories.

Ann and Mary busied themselves preparing for the big moment that afternoon, much to Elliott's amusement, as he watched the two women in his life fret over the smallest detail. His comments weren't helping matters at all. '…Yes my dear, the taxi cab is booked for two o'clock. Or is it three?' Ann's glare told him it would perhaps be wiser if he were to take the dog for a walk.

Eventually alone, Mary stood in her room and looked out towards the garden. The one sorrow on her big day was that her parents could not share her happiness. She cast her eyes skywards and softly said, 'I do so love you.'

She walked over to the full-length mirror, twirling from side to side, admiring her dress. Suddenly, she saw a reflection of a man standing at the door, or at least she thought she did. The figure, dressed in Bedouin costume, bestowed on her a smile she immediately recognised. It was Walter! She spun around in shock and shouted out, 'Walter,' but there was nobody there. Her eyes were wide open in confusion, her throbbing heart raced like an engine. Turning slowly back to the mirror, she gasped in disbelief; the reflection she saw was not that of herself in a flowing white gown but instead one of a Bedouin woman adorned in traditional wedding costume, her robe a riot of colourful and intricate patterns on a black ground and her hijab decorated with the most fascinating beads, threads and coins. The little Arab woman's dark eyes stared out at her.

Mary was in a trance. She fixed her eyes on Walter, as he reappeared and walked towards her. They stood, simply staring at each other through the mirror. Finally, she watched his hand gently squeeze her shoulder and she let out a sigh, slowly closing her eyelids. 'You look beautiful,' he called out. She moved her hand over his and opened her eyes. They dilated in shock. Behind her stood Mr Elliott.

'I said you look beautiful,' he reiterated.

Poor Mary was totally bemused and looked so, her eyes still wide open, yet expressionless. All colour drained away from her cheeks, and her face was as white as a sheet. It was now nearly a year since she had had any such vivid visions of Walter. So why, now of all days, should he reappear in her mind, and in such a strange way?

'Mary, my dear, is everything all right? Mary!' continued a concerned Elliott.

It took a further moment for her to register reality. She burst into tears and fell into his arms, holding him so tight for comfort. 'Oh, Robert,' she whimpered.

Elliott pulled away and made her look at him. 'What on earth is it?

Mary took out her handkerchief and finally stopped crying. 'Don't worry!' she told him and breathed deeply before explaining, 'Sometimes I just drift away and think strange things, Robert, that's all.' She began to look more her old self and smiled at him. 'Ignore me, I'm just a little emotional.'

Elliott simply offered his hands in sympathy, which she held and gently squeezed in appreciation.

'Will you look at the time!' she said, changing the subject abruptly, and began to fuss about herself in the mirror. 'I'd better get a move on or there'll be a doctor who'll think I've changed my mind.'

CHAPTER 16

BLACK WALT AND HIS BLESSED LAND

Captain Smith, the skipper of The Swan, who had taken Walter into his employ, would visit Elliott whenever he was back in England. He was a staunch supporter of the church mission's aim to rehabilitate wayward men and, over the years, had taken upward of twenty lads on as deck hands. Not always with success, it had to be said; but he had nothing but praise for Walter and told Elliott so. The two men sat in the study talking for a good two hours. Thirteen months at sea meant the Captain had much to tell and, once more, Elliott became an avid listener.

'As good a sailor as ever stepped on my deck, that's for sure, and a demon for work. What floors me is why he was there. Of course, he must have a past. I know that. But a man like him has no need to beg for a job anywhere,' Smith insisted.

Elliott made no comment. In his line of work, there was

a well-known rule forbidding those who helped a man to his feet from revealing his past mistakes or misdemeanours.

'You never told me what a marvel he is at languages. Happen you didn't know yourself,' Smith added.

Of course, Elliott did know; but he raised his eyebrows to show some surprise, not wishing to steal the Captain's thunder.

The Captain continued, 'I don't believe he'd be in the company of any foreigner a week without getting to know his lingo well enough to make him understand. I've found him useful, I can tell you, many a time.'

Elliott listened with interest as the skipper recounted his observations of Walter, all of which bore out the lad's eccentric nature. 'A rare, merry sort, full of devilment, Mr Elliott…and as for his knowledge of seamanship… Well, there's few I know that could surpass him. Certainly there's nothing much I could have taught him,' Smith observed.

Walter had indeed settled well on board, becoming a well-liked crew member, always up to his tricks but, equally, taking a ducking or two for his cheek, like the time the men returned aboard laden with gifts and he encouraged the ship's monkey, Tosh, to sneak away a sailor's present of a silk scarf. 'Here, Tosh, I think we can have a bit of fun with this,' he'd said, and then set about making it into a little turban for the grinning creature.

Later that afternoon the furry little rascal could be seen

parading around the deck attired in his headgear. 'Hang on a minute, that's my silk. How's it made it up into a turban? I'll kill the little bugger. Come 'ere!' shouted the mystified sailor, Bryn, chasing after the shrieking primate.

'It's not the monkey that's done it, you idiot! It's Black Walt taking the rise!' said another sailor.

The whole crew howled with laughter as the huge frame of Bryn awkwardly chased Black Walt, as he had affectionately become known. Eventually, Bryn grasped hold of the prankster and promptly tossed him overboard. But Walter would not let things end there, and the following morning Tosh was strutting around deck, proud as punch, wearing a broad white collar with the words: Turban Maker to the Crew of The Swan.

At last, it seemed, Walter was alive again, free to indulge himself in his love of climbing and his passion for sailing. Many was the time he would happily volunteer to scramble up the rigging and sit in the crow's nest during the severest storm, when all other sensible men were on deck below him.

'We all waited for him to earn a white feather, but damn me, the rogue never did,' Smith recalled, likening Walter to Jekyll and Hyde. 'Sometimes though, the lad would be the quietest of men, off in his own little world, stroking that chain and locket of his.'

Elliott couldn't help but notice that Captain Smith always referred to Walter in the past tense and asked, 'You say "was"… "Walter was", as though he were no longer with you.'

Smith gave him a rather puzzled look, then realised, 'You didn't receive my letter?'

'No!' replied Elliott, fearing dreadful news.

'I'm afraid Walter jumped ship, Robert, some two months ago, in Aden.' He went on to explain how, after six months on board, Walter just disappeared one day and simply didn't return. 'I waited another 24 hours before setting sail, far more than any right-minded skipper would do!'

Elliott could only give a wry smile of appreciation.

'I just can't figure the lad out: one minute he's fine; then, out of the blue, he's gone!' concluded Captain Smith.

Elliott didn't say so but he knew this was very much in keeping with Walter's character. Nonetheless, he couldn't help but feel the young man's desertion from Smith's ship keenly.

~~~

Walter had gained a good knowledge of the Arab language during The Swan's trading in the Middle East: certainly enough to get by with on a daily basis. Some weeks on, with a fully grown beard on his tanned, swarthy face, and dressed in a caftan, he became indistinguishable from a native Arab. Although he was not afraid of being seen as an obvious foreigner, he knew he would be more trusted if he embraced the local looks and customs. As time went by, he became immersed in every part of the culture and found his heart given over totally to his new land and its people, people who would willingly help him create his new life.

With the little money he had saved from his wages on ship, Walter managed to negotiate a down payment on the old house in the date grove, with the promise of more cash once he could find suitable work. Whether the house's owners actually meant to sell it to him or were simply duping him, only time would tell. Meantime, he made good one room of the house, enough for him to live in, and then he set about finding work. The little village of Zinjibar was but a short way from the port of Aden and it was there he tried first.

Even with his native looks and good grasp of the local tongue, Walter was still treated with some suspicion amongst the local 'fixers' and, consequently, struggled to find any work, even the most menial. Each day he would queue with the other men, hoping to get scraps of unloading work with the dhow traders but, alas, he was always shunned. That was until the day Sheikh Ibraham pulled into port with his large trading vessel. Walter immediately recognised the dhow and its owner. He had interpreted for Captain Smith when he traded with the Sheikh. Considering himself a trusted ally of the man, Walter was sure, if he could get to speak with him, he would secure work. However, getting to speak with the man would not be easy.

The small, grey-haired elder was a successful and respected trader; and, whilst not as wealthy as it was assumed a Sheikh would be, he did have enough prestige to employ a small group to look after his interests on the dockside. For a few small coins, they would willingly turn away any beggars, as well as the dangerous and unpredictable opium smokers who, without a second thought, would run a knife through a man to settle a score. The minders immediately challenged Walter, as soon as he tried to make himself known. He spoke in Arabic, but wasn't recognised.

Finally, he tried a different tack and called out in English, 'Would the Sheikh shun me if I were the Englishman from The Swan?'

It worked. The Sheikh stopped and turned to study the strange man before him. 'Walter?' he asked curiously.

'The very same,' said Walter, removing his keffiyeh.

Suddenly, Walter was the star attraction and received two kisses on each cheek from the Sheikh, who then proceeded to present him to the crowd. 'Walter Swan…Walter Swan,' he called out repeatedly, proud of his pigeon English.

Walter just smiled and placed the keffiyeh back on his head, as the Sheikh continued to embrace him. Finally, he led the way to his dhow. On board, Walter sat drinking something he assumed had its origins in coffee but he couldn't be sure. In his developing Arabic tongue, he explained his circumstances.

The Sheikh listened with interest, then made his offer. 'Then you shall sail with me, and teach my men your English ways on the seas.' For the man had witnessed first hand, Walter's impressive nautical skills.

Two days later he was once more at sea, travelling extensively along the Red Sea, into the Gulf of Aden and onwards into Mesopotamia. Again, the eccentric Englishman would prove popular on board ship and, within weeks, had the crew playing the quintessential game – cricket! It wasn't long before he was almost second in command to the Sheikh.

On occasion, Sheikh Ibraham would take his family on board, particularly when visiting Basra. In addition to his wife and only daughter, his family included a small tribe of brothers, uncles and cousins, all laden with goods for trading. Walter would help the women on board and ensure they had all the provisions they needed below decks. Most of them proved poor sailors and seldom ventured on deck. On the rare occasion they did, Walter would see in their eyes the sheer misery of their journey. The exception was the Sheikh's daughter, Iza, who would always be on deck and, each morning, would carry up her little box of charcoal and vellum paper, treasured gifts that her father had bought her from Dutch traders. How she loved to sketch the sea and capture the light skipping across the water.

Walter watched fascinated as, at dawn each day, the little frame would appear, always dressed in a black robe and burqa. She would carefully set down a linen cloth and tenderly line up her charcoal and pastel sticks in order of hue. Then, with paper pinned to a board, she would sketch away until midday, after which she would disappear below deck and not re-surface until the next day. The small woman captured Walter's imagination, if indeed she was a woman and not a girl, for he had only seen her eyes. Even so, he guessed she was probably about twenty. Was she pretty though? Or was she ugly? he wondered. It would be a while before he found out.

In the summer, the dhow was once more prepared for the long journey to Basra, and Walter would again see 'the little cherub' as he imagined her to be. This time he had a gift for her: an art book he had purchased from a sailor in Muscat. During a glorious sunrise, he waited patiently until, finally, she arrived and set about her usual routine of preparing her materials. Standing a discreet distance away, he watched as she outlined her picture.

'It is a beautiful morning for drawing,' he said casually in Arabic.

Taken quite by surprise, she looked around to see him staring at the paper. Not sure how to react, she decided to ignore him and carried on drawing. Never before had a crew member dared to try and engage her in conversation, for fear of what the Sheikh would do. The unwritten rule was that no man was to show interest in, or strike up a conversation with, the Sheikh's beloved daughter.

But Walter had spirit. 'Your drawing is good…very good.'

Iza scanned the deck to see if anyone was watching. She eventually responded, 'You should not speak with me.'

'Why?'

'Because it's not permitted.'

'Not permitted? By whom?' he insisted.

'Please! My father will be furious. I have no desire to see you banished.'

'Then, if it worries you so, I shall seek your father's permission.'

With that, he headed off, book in hand, to find the Sheikh.

Below deck, Sheikh Ibraham was studying a map; in the corner of the room his wife folded clothes. Walter suddenly burst in.

'Please, sir, forgive my intrusion but I need your permission,' he said without hesitation.

Somewhat surprised at Walter's boldness, the Sheikh asked, 'Permission? For what?'

'It's a matter of wanting to speak with your daughter… about her drawing, and to present her with the gift of this book,' Walter explained and opened the book to show him.

The Sheikh's wife simply bowed her head and waited for the full force of her husband's terrible authority to descend on Walter. Unusually, it didn't. Although the Sheikh was taken aback, he reacted to Walter's request with calmness. With a flick of his head he signalled to his wife. She knew what it meant: to fetch their daughter.

Iza walked into the little room with her head bowed. She had once before spoken to a boy without permission, so knew what was coming. She looked up at her father with dread, but she saw there was no solemn face, no anger in his eyes. Instead, her father calmly rolled up his map and invited Walter to place the book on the table.

'Iza, my good Englishman friend would like to present you with a gift.'

She stared down at the book, then at Walter, moved on to her mother and, finally, rested her eyes on her father's. A raised eyebrow and slight nod of his head told her it was all right to pick the book up. She opened it and gently thumbed through the pages, occasionally stopping at a full-page picture.

'It is most beautiful, thank you,' she said to Walter from under her burqa.

'A Monet study of the effect of light on water,' Walter said, quite cocksure; that is, until Iza giggled at his incorrect choice of words. Loosely translated he'd actually said, 'A Monet study of the backside of light on water.'

Not that it all meant anything to her puzzled parents, who had no idea who Monet was anyway.

'So, I have your blessing…to speak with your daughter in future?' Walter enquired of the Sheikh.

'If Iza desires, then Macca shan't object.'

Macca was the name that close friends used to address the Sheikh and Walter was indeed highly honoured to be received into the Arab's circle of friendship. Moreover, the die was now cast for a fledging relationship!

Two months went by, and Iza's visits to the ship had become more frequent. She was always accompanied by her mother, who kept firmly to the side of her daughter when Iza was in the company of Walter. Only once did she show a softer side and discretely walk on slightly and allow the pair to talk more freely. How Walter detested the custom that forbade Iza appearing unveiled before a man. He would, however, finally get to see his cherub whilst returning from a trading visit to the Fao Peninsula.

As the dhow set sail, Sheikh Ibraham's spirits were high. He stood on top of the grain sacks to address his assembled crew and gave them news of how successful trading had been. This visit had been particularly good, with the purchase of 15 tons of grain secured at a rock-bottom price due to the failure of a merchant ship to collect the goods.

'Praise be to Allah,' he shouted, and sank his scimitar

into the sack, so that the grain ran out like a waterfall. He stood laughing at the men below him trying to catch the grain in their mouths, as if it were ale.

What he hadn't noticed was what had moved behind him; an Egyptian cobra flexed its muscles and slithered over a sack and down into a gap in the pile of hessian. Its forked tongue flicked the air. Finally, the head appeared. Macca heard the distinctive hiss break through his continued laughter. He turned quickly. The reptile's head danced from side to side, its hood fully flared, then, like a whiplash, it struck out. He felt its deadly fangs enter his leg.

Letting out a piercing wail, he leapt into the air. The men below immediately fell silent as the Sheikh regained his position on the sack, scimitar in hand. He faced the dancing reptile, which was ready to pounce once again, and slowly raised his sword. The snake flicked at it several times in warning. Then, with a flip of his wrist, Macca swiftly sliced the blade straight through the creature. The headless body dropped like a stone. Clambering down from the sacks, Macca finally collapsed in front of Walter.

'Quickly, help me get him below,' Walter shouted to the crew. There was no shortage of volunteers to assist in carrying their master.

Iza and her mother jumped up in shock, as Walter and three men burst through the door to the cabin. Mother and daughter instinctively pulled their burqas over their faces.

'What on earth is it?' Iza called out hysterically, as she watched her father being gently laid on a pile of cushions.

Walter looked up at her. 'It's all right. Please don't worry,' he said. But Iza would not be calmed so easily.

'It's not all right! What has happened?' she insisted.

'He's been bitten,' Walter admitted.

'Bitten! By what?'

'I'm afraid a…' Walter paused for a moment, knowing the sheer terror the word conveyed, '…cobra.'

Iza sank into her mother's arms for comfort. She knew only too well that a cobra bite was, most often, a guarantee of death!

Walter pulled up her father's thawb and exposed his leg. A knife in its metal sheath was strapped to his thigh, for Macca had learnt from experience that, in this dangerous land, carrying a hidden dagger was good practice. Examining the length of the leg carefully, Walter looked for the bite. Eventually he saw a lump at the side of the sheath. Gently he untied the leather strap and put it across Macca's mouth. The man's piercing black pupils fixed him firmly – his only hope was an Englishman! Macca bit down hard on the leather as the dagger made its incision. Walter then closed his lips around the wound and sucked hard. Finally, he released his grip and spat out. In this land, sucking poison out of a snakebite wound was still considered the only way to try to prevent death. However, people were unaware that this treatment was useless, and that Walter in fact ran a great risk of bacterial infection.

Although Walter was ultimately hailed as a hero and the saviour of the master, in truth, what actually saved Macca's life was the fact that the cobra's fangs had partly struck the metal sheath surrounding the dagger, causing the reptile to withdraw quickly, leaving only the smallest of punctures and thus only a minimum of venom. However, there was still enough to make Macca quite poorly, and he ran a terrible fever.

For three days, Iza and her mother dutifully cared for Macca. Never was a pair so anxious and so devoted. Day and night, they kept vigil at his bedside, mopping his fevered brow and cleansing his wound with poultices and potions. Iza crouched down by her father to pray and then, exhausted, finally slumped down to sleep. On the third day, all prayers were answered and Macca's fever broke. Within hours, he was taking water unaided and again able to move his previously paralysed body. The venom had done its worst but mercifully hadn't been sufficient to attack any vital organs.

In the early hours, thinking her father was in a slumber, Iza took her little box of pastels and paper and nestled down beside him to draw. Glancing over to check that he was definitely asleep, she began to do what was expressly forbidden to her – to draw the human form. Her skilful hand traced an image she held in her head and delicately she outlined a figure, strong and masterful, holding onto the ship's rigging. Her feverish strokes captured his face, cheerful and windswept. Tenderly, she worked on his features and created his look, so real, so full of life and passion. Of course, it was Walter.

'So, the Englishman finds himself the hero of your studies,' Macca said quietly, taking his daughter totally by surprise. She quickly slid the picture under her board, fearing what punishment would be declared.

'Father, I didn't realise you were awake!'

'Evidently,' replied Macca, glancing down to her board.

'Please forgive me, father, it was just foolish scribbling.'

'Scribbling indeed. My child, I may be ignorant in matters of art but I know enough to see more than scribbles in your studies. Let me look more closely,' he asked. Iza trembled as she gingerly pulled the sketch from behind the board and gave it to him. She bowed her head.

'Father is angry with me?'

He studied the drawing in detail before giving his response. 'My daughter displays such talent, but who teaches you to defy Allah so?'

'Nobody, father. It is only my sin, my imagination.'

'And also perhaps infatuation!'

Iza's head bowed even further. Macca gently lifted her

chin. 'The Englishman has captured your heart?'

'Yes, father,' Iza eventually conceded, her eyes filled with tears.

Macca looked sympathetically at her before answering, 'Then child, you must tell him so.'

'But…but…he is not an infidel to you?'

'No, Walter is not one without faith. His God gives him goodness.'

Iza smiled broadly and hugged her father tightly.

Walter had decided to check on the Sheikh and his family one last time before steering the dhow into the straits for Aden. As normal, he entered the room and this time was heartened to see Macca sitting up and chatting to Iza. Immediately, Iza went to cover her face but was stopped by her father's hand.

'No, my dear…let this Englishman see my daughter's beauty.'

She dropped her hand and stared at Walter. Finally, he could study her face. In all the thousand different ways he'd imagined her, he'd never pictured a young woman with such beauty. Flickers of lamplight danced across her soft cheeks, highlighting her lovely bone structure. Coyly, she cast her eyes downwards. Walter was captivated, his heart lost in desire for the sweet young Arab woman.

'My daughter pleases your heart?' Macca spoke, to break the silence.

Walter could only answer with simple honesty, 'Sir, you judge this Englishman well. A more smitten creature is scarcely possible.'

'Then you shall take her hand, with my blessing.'

'Father!' called out Iza in astonishment.

Macca looked over to Iza. 'My child, is it not the truth that you would give him your whole heart freely?' Then he turned to Walter: 'And you would give yours to her?' He held out his hands to Iza. 'What should a father want better for his only daughter than a husband who loves her perfectly, and desires only her. If that husband should be of the noble British race, then how much more enviable is the father's good fortune!'

CHAPTER 17

SHATTERED LIVES

AUTUMN 1914

Mary and Walter's worlds were far apart and their lives could not have been more different. For over eighteen months, Walter had led an idyllic life in a foreign land, where he felt his heart now belonged, and with a woman he adored, who had borne him twins, a daughter and son, six months earlier. In Zinjibar, he had finally finished repairing his little dwelling and now doted on his family there, beside the small date plantation; although, with the sea always in his blood, he would spend many weeks of the year on his father-in-law's dhow, trading deep into Mesopotamia. While he was away, Iza tended the land, along with the local village women, and brought in the crop. It was a happy existence.

For Mary, married life with Tom had started well, and over the previous year, as their love continued to flourish, so did their careers, which now offered them a steady, affluent lifestyle in London. Tom had been made an offer of a teaching surgeon position at St Thomas's, whilst Mary took a position at Great Ormond Street Hospital to train further in her passion for educating deaf children.

The only missing element of an outwardly perfect life was children. So far, Mary hadn't fallen pregnant, and although they had only been trying for five months, Tom was already seeking advice from their circle of learned medical friends. A myriad of pioneering tests showed that nothing appeared to be amiss, yet conception and the joy of starting a family still eluded them. Their relationship started to become strained, as Tom sought the help of an obstetrician friend whose work in the field of infertility treatment was considered, by many, too maverick and his methods questionable. Mary, now nearly twenty-eight, was becoming resigned to the fact that, if it was God's will for her not to bear children, so be it.

But Mary always had two men in her heart – the physical presence of Tom; and the visions of Walter, which had all but ceased on her marriage, but now recurred almost daily. She continued to be mystified as to her dreams of him; and, when she did experience them, it was almost as if she was happy to enter a mystical world within a world. She kept things secret from Tom, not wishing to open up another debate analysing her visions. Whilst she dearly loved her husband, she now realised his dream theory was completely wrong. It wasn't long before she returned to thinking of the spirit world, and how her dreams were creating energy to enable someone's closure.

Then, without warning, events took place that would change things forever.

In early 1914, Mary found herself pregnant. The joyous news could not have been more celebrated by any couple, and the forthcoming event brought Mary and Tom, once again, closer together. Six months on, Mary was enjoying the bloom of pregnancy and, on the advice of doctors, had taken to gentle daily walks through Hyde Park. On one such day, with lovely sunshine high above, she decided to rest on a bench and watch the horsemen of the Household Cavalry parade up and down the sanded horse track. Before long, the heat of the day took its toll. Feeling tired, she finally closed her eyes and allowed herself to drift away. Within seconds, she was fast asleep and entered into Walter's world of the Yemen. Here, she stood overlooking his plantation near Zinjibar. It had been a good while since Mary had experienced an out-of-body occurrence so vivid.

Although in the Aden Protectorate, and therefore under the protection of the British Empire, Zinjibar was, like many areas, becoming increasingly menaced by Turkish Army 'terror missions', expeditions intended to harass the local Arabs and leave fear in their wake. Mary watched as the grasses of the plantation gently rustled and local women suddenly appeared and pulled at the roots. In the distance, children could be heard laughing and playing. From her vantage point, on a mound, she noticed a plume of dust rise beyond the nearby fields. Squinting in the intense sunlight, she struggled to make out the form until, finally, it became clear as a band of horsemen galloping towards the peaceful scene: some twenty men, wielding swords and flaming torches, were approaching with incredible speed. Within no more than a minute, the field was ablaze and the peace abruptly shattered as laughter turned to screams. Frantically, the women ran about, screaming hysterically to their offspring. Dense smoke began to billow upwards as flames tore through the tinder dry grass. In the distance, Mary saw the plantation dwelling house so lovingly restored by Walter being ravaged by fire.

One by one, the terrified women fled, coughing and spluttering, and desperately holding onto their children. Through the smoke burst the horsemen, screaming chants. Some still wielded swords, others lashed out with staves. Mary looked on horrified, as a poor woman was struck across her back and immediately fell. With the encroaching fire, the mother had no option but to pick herself up and try to run, only to be persecuted by further beating and taunts. Her pretty little girl watched petrified until, finally, she ran out in the open, crying. A tribesman turned his horse towards her and leant over, ready to scoop her up and carry her away to slavery or worse. Mary found herself instinctively running towards the girl and screaming at the horseman. She pulled at his tunic but her hands simply went through him. It was an out-of-body experience where she could have no interaction.

However, in reality, walkers in the park gasped in horror as they watched a heavily pregnant woman get up off a bench and seemingly run straight into the parade of horses, screaming, 'Noooooo!' at the top of her voice. Mary suddenly awoke amongst the military riders, as they struggled to control their frightened horses. Eventually, the riders brought their beasts under control, but it was too late to stop Mary being trampled underfoot. There she lay, motionless, as a crowd gathered around her sand-covered body, fearing the worst.

What Mary had witnessed in her out-of-body experience was not just the product of her imagination, but real-time events happening some five thousand miles away. As she lay helpless in England, Walter turned the dhow once more towards the Gulf of Aden and whistled in buoyant mood, ready for his homecoming after six weeks away at sea. He was totally unaware of what would shortly greet him and change his life forever.

~~~

Tom was taking a quiet moment of reflection before his next operation when he got the news that Mary had been brought into casualty. He flew down the corridor and tumbled down the stairs, taking at least three steps at a time. Had it not been for the handrail, he would almost certainly have tripped and found himself a patient in theatre too. As it was, the only damage was to a tray of instruments that an unfortunate nurse happened to be carrying up the stairs. He finally burst through the operating theatre doors, just as a nurse was drawing a sheet over a face. Tom's heart sank and he clutched his palms tightly to his face in despair. Just then, a firm pair of hands took him by the shoulders and the familiar voice of Jonathan Hayes, a consultant obstetrician and surgeon, said, 'Come on, she's through here.' Tom looked up and, realising his mistake, breathed again. Hayes led the way into the adjoining theatre.

'Right, doctor, tell me what we've done so far,' asked Hayes of the duty junior doctor.

'I've just arrived, sir…I'm still trying to assess,' answered the doctor.

'You have given an injection of saline though?' asked Tom.

'Well no, not yet Mr Sharpe. You see…'

'What! Good God, man,' Tom interrupted and started to roll up his sleeves. He looked around fervently for a drip and stand.

Hayes held out his hand to placate him. 'Please, Tom, let me deal with things.'

'This is my wife, Jonathan!' replied an increasingly emotional Tom.

'And I have every intention of keeping her that way, Tom, but you must let me take charge.'

'I can't just stand by and do nothing. I'll help operate.'

'No!' Hayes immediately responded, rubbing his forefinger up and down his brow, part in exasperation, part in pity for his friend's desperate situation. 'No, sorry, Tom. You're in no fit state and you're too emotionally involved.'

'Then let me administer the anaesthetic!' Tom said, in an attempt at compromise.

Hayes paused and sighed before finally relenting, 'Very well.'

He started to examine Mary and called for a foetal stethoscope. There was absolute silence as he took what seemed an eternity listening for the baby's heartbeat. Tom stood, rubbing his fingers furiously against his thumbs and nibbling at his lip nervously. Eventually, Hayes straightened up and said, 'Just', meaning it was still alive. Lifting up the sheet covering Mary's lower body he saw the pool of blood seeping from between her legs and tried not to show too much of his grimace to Tom. But Tom had dealt with similar injuries before, although he'd never actually operated on a heavily pregnant woman. He knew things weren't good. Hayes gingerly felt around Mary's bump, then towards her side. There, the obvious impact of a horse's hoof was clear to see. He looked towards Tom and said with some hesitation, 'Can I have a word?'

The two men stood beside the big ceramic sink. Hayes again ran his fingers across his brow. 'Look, Tom, you don't need me to tell you the seriousness of things.'

'How bad?' Tom simply asked.

'She's ruptured awfully, most likely in the uterus…and God knows where else until I open her up.'

'Then open her up!'

'There are risks.'

'Of course there are risks; I know that – I'm a bloody surgeon, Jonathan!' Tom shouted, finally showing all his anxiety.

Hayes glanced around at the staff, who were unsure what to do, and simply looked down. He started to speak in a whisper, to encourage Tom to calm down. 'I can't save both,' he said.

Tom was becoming increasingly distressed and clenched his teeth to keep his voice somewhat lower, 'You haven't damned well tried, yet!' he firmly answered.

'Please, Tom. Look, the baby's heartbeat is barely there. If I go in to try and stem the bleeding, it won't cope with the trauma.'

'Then section her,' Tom interrupted.

'There isn't time. Mary will bleed to death.'

'The baby aside, can you save her?' he coldly enquired.

'I don't honestly know,' Hayes had to concede, as Tom looked hard into his eyes.

In truth, they both knew that whatever happened, the risk of post-operative infection to Mary would be the deciding factor as to whether she would survive or not.

'I can only try to save Mary or the baby…I'm sorry.'

Tom just continued to stare.

'I need an answer,' Hayes said, then paused for a reply; but it wasn't forthcoming.

'Mary or the baby, Tom,' Hayes re-iterated.

Tom looked heavenwards and shouted out, 'Damn you!' The next moment he was gently placing the mask over his wife's face and slowly turning on the mixture of ether and chloroform. He nodded at Hayes and said softly, 'Mary.'

~~~

Like Tom, Walter was to have his world suddenly shattered after his long trudge up the track to his village. As he neared the plantation, a sense of foreboding came over him. He knew something sinister lay ahead. No longer was there a cheerful chatter in the air, only an eerie silence. Past the tall wall was his plantation, not yet visible. He rounded the corner to see the devastation: an empty mass of charred vegetation as far as he could see. His eyes then fixed on his house in the distance. Only weeks earlier it had been his joyous homestead. Now it was a burnt-out wreck with no roof and was scarred with black streaks from the furious flames. He fell to his knees in desperation and wept.

Terror at the thought of his family's fate suddenly came over him and he raced towards the house. Like a crazed man, he swept through the bleak and ravaged rooms. Virtually nothing had been spared in the flames and he could barely make out the layout in parts, due to the fallen timbers and crumbled walls. Finally, he staggered out into the open and spun around in circles, continually shouting out, 'Iza! Iza!' But there was no reply. Again, he fell to his knees and held his hands in prayer. 'Allah, merciful…please, not my family!' he shouted skywards. Fearing their deaths, he clasped his hands to his face and wept once more.

He did not hear the footsteps approach from behind him; but he felt the tender little hand of his son rest on his shoulder. 'It's Papa!' rang out the sweet voice of his wife. He slowly turned and looked upwards to see Iza holding their children. The charming little innocent faces peered down at him. Overcome with emotion, he held out his hands and begged to hold them.

'My sweethearts! Praise be to Allah!' he kept repeating, cradling them tight to his chest and showering them, all the while, with kisses.

Eventually, he released them from his loving clasp and stood to face Iza. She looked so exhausted and dishevelled from her ordeal. For two days and nights, she had hidden herself and the children in the small livestock pen, surrounded by the few things she had managed to salvage. Walter watched, as she slowly bowed her head down in shame. He lifted her chin and gazed deep into her eyes. 'My Iza! My dear Iza!' he murmured, then pulled her towards him and clung on to her for dear life, their children nestled into them securely.

He pulled away gently and asked, 'Who did this, Iza? Which men dared to defile our lives so?'

She turned and pointed at the house wall. On it, daubed in burnt charcoal, was a crude image of a crescent moon and star. Walter breathed deeply through his nostrils and spat out, 'Turks! Then they shall pay. With every last ounce of breath I have, I promise you, Iza, I will seek my revenge.'

CHAPTER 18

Soul Mates

Hayes's thirty years of experience and skill as an obstetrician was to be the saving of Mary. Her internal injuries had been so severe that he was barely able to make out all her organs, and he battled for three long hours in theatre in an attempt to save her life. Alas, his prognosis for the baby proved correct and, despite his desperate efforts, the little girl's heart stopped beating an hour into the operation on her mother. Only when Mary was declared stable could Hayes perform a caesarean section. As, finally, he separated child from mother, Tom insisted he hold his treasure. Tears streamed down his cheeks as he cradled her. Then, at last, he gently laid her on Mary's breast. 'Our angel,' he softly wept to his oblivious wife.

The toll on Mary's body was immense and recovery was extremely slow. By the grace of God, she had escaped serious infection to her wounds. However, her physical pain and scars were equalled by the psychological ones;

and, ultimately, these took her to the depths of despair. She could not remember anything at all about the accident that day, and this provoked her worst anxiety. At a military enquiry, eyewitness accounts were given of her running straight into the path of the horses, seemingly without any reason. Although the verdict concluded it was a tragic accident, she carried the burden of blame entirely on her shoulders and could barely look Tom in the eye without feeling guilt and remorse. From her point of view, she alone had denied him the joy of fatherhood.

Six months on, Mary began to experience massive bouts of depression, as still she had no recollection of the accident and could therefore offer no explanation. The ordeal placed her marriage to Tom under enormous pressure and their quarrels became more and more frequent.

Mary's visions of Walter also remained constant, and things finally came to a head one evening on their return home from the theatre. Standing waiting for a taxicab, Mary stared into the reflection of light on a puddle of rainwater and drifted into visualising Walter again. He was standing with his family at a street bazaar when a kitten leapt from the arms of a young girl in the crowd and ran towards a building, eventually clambering up the wall to a high ledge. Seeing the girl's distress, Walter's eccentric nature took over and he simply began to scale a drainpipe to rescue it.

Tom felt Mary pull his arm back as he went to open the cab door. 'Walter, please be careful!' she cried out with concern. He looked at her in surprise, before realising she was having yet another dream experience and, once more, Walter was in it.

Back at home, Tom soon began his cross-examination of Mary and he did not mince his words.

'So he's back,' he said, whilst pouring himself a whisky.

'Who?' replied Mary.

'It's all right, Mary, you don't have to pretend anymore. I know he's back. In fact he never really went away, did he?'

Mary suddenly looked as though she'd been caught red-handed stealing something. Eventually, she answered, 'Not now, Tom, please.'

'Why didn't you tell me?' he insisted, but she didn't respond.

He turned away and walked to the fireplace. 'Has our relationship come to this…that we can't even be truthful with each other?' he said, with his hands stretched out to span the stone mantel and head bowed in frustration and dejection.

'And what good would it have done you, Tom, knowing that your wife, a year after marriage, was still living out visions of another man?'

Tom pushed himself away from the mantel and turned around. 'I'm your husband, Mary, I could have helped.'

'Helped, how? What explanations would you give this time? Am I still seeking love? I thought I'd found that.'

She held out her hand to his, wanting reassurance, but Tom could not take hold of it. For the first time ever, he denied her his sympathy and touch.

'This doesn't just affect you,' he said with coldness.

'And do you honestly believe I don't know that, Tom?' she replied, with tears filling her eyes. 'Every day, do I not see how all this affects you?'

Tom, ever the doctor, was not prepared to accept that his marriage was failing because of what he believed were tricks of the mind and, therefore, ultimately treatable. How easy it was for him simply to compartmentalise the problem, as a surgeon does.

In the days that followed Tom piled on the pressure for Mary to visit a psychiatrist friend to undergo some hypnotherapy. Finally, she gave in to his pleas.

~~~

Mary entered the little waiting room with some trepidation. As she moved towards a chair, she caught sight of herself in a mirror on the wall. She looked hard at herself, and slowly pulled her lank hair through her fingers. Gone was the silky texture she used to constantly brush and nurture. Her complexion too, once glowing with warmth, was now pale and dry, and her eyes, previously alive and inviting, were now underlined in dark shadow. Mary realised she had let herself go and was fast becoming a wreck.

Edward Stapleton opened the door. It was a few months since he'd last seen Mary and he was shocked at how different she looked, but tried not to show it. 'Hello, Mary,' he greeted her, taking hold of her hand and gently kissing her on both cheeks. 'Please do come on through. How are you?' he asked, his voice indicating genuine concern.

Mary gave him only a despondent smile, which confirmed things were not good.

'How are Margaret and the children?' she enquired, bringing up his wife and family out of politeness.

'Yes, good, thank you,' he acknowledged, feeling desperately sad about her situation, 'and they all pass on their love, Mary. You know that?'

'I know, Edward, thank you,' she replied solemnly, and felt another squeeze of his hand.

He helped her off with her coat and offered her a seat on a sofa by the fire.

'I was expecting a long couch!' she declared, attempting a little humour.

'Reserved more for stage plays these days, I'm afraid!'

He smiled back, then took a poker to the fire and rearranged the coal. The resulting flames made the atmosphere a little more cosy and relaxed.

'May I offer you a drink, Mary?'

'No, I'm fine, thank you. If you don't mind, could we just make a start?'

'Of course,' he said and pulled up a chair opposite her.

'Do you think I'm mentally ill, Edward? Because I'm sure Tom does,' she said out of the blue.

Edward was somewhat taken aback by her directness but gave an honest reply, 'You've gone through a traumatic experience, Mary. This is bound to have had an impact.'

'So you think like Tom?'

'No! Look, I simply want to help you in any way that I can. Talking it through while under hypnosis may just help find some answers for you.'

Mary gave him another rather forced smile and accepted he might be right.

'I want you to concentrate on my voice and stare into the fire… Let yourself relax and watch the flames…allow yourself to breathe deeply, in and out… just relax, relax… feel your eyes getting heavier and heavier…and relax…'

Mary's eyelids flickered as she stared deep into the flames of the fire. Edward was surprised at how receptive she was to his voice and how easily she fell into a trance.

'Feel yourself becoming sleepy…and relax,' he continued, and the next moment she was hypnotised.

'I want you to think of a happier time, Mary, a time when you felt safe and free from troubles,' he instructed in a mellow tone, watching as she drew her head up and breathed deeply. A warm smile broke across her face.

'That's good! Tell me, where are you?'

'I'm in my rooms, at Mrs Walsh's.'

'Mrs Walsh being?' he enquired.

Mary gave a disparaging shrug and said, 'My landlady!'

'I see. So this is in…'

'Sheffield,' she finished for him.

'Of course! And were these happy times?'

Mary paused and thought for a moment before answering, 'Yes, they were…they were very happy times.'

'Tell me why?'

'Because…well, I could talk with him for hours.'

'With Tom?' he innocently asked, only to be immediately corrected.

'No, not Tom, he's my husband!'

'Who then?'

'Walter, of course.'

Edward had no idea of who Walter was, and of the fact that Mary had lived so long dreaming of, and visualising, him. He naturally enquired further.

'And Walter is an old friend?'

A broad beaming smile came across her face. 'Oh yes.'

'Do you still see him?'

'All the time. Tom knows. We're open about it.'

Edward looked stunned at the revelation because, of

course, he had no idea that Mary alluded to her dreams. Therefore, he misunderstood entirely, simply assuming she was openly talking to him about a rather liberal relationship. Never would he have suspected Mary and Tom of such an arrangement. He was perplexed. There surely had to be another explanation, he thought, and decided to change the subject and get around to the day of the accident. He wanted to uncover why she'd run into the horses. After all, that was what he had been asked to try to ascertain.

'Let's go back to the day of the accident,' he suggested.

'I can't remember,' she instantly replied.

'You can't remember or you don't want to remember?'

Mary fell silent and expressionless.

'Just relax, Mary. Think. Perhaps it was a hot day?'

She didn't answer.

'Perhaps then…' He tried to finish but was interrupted.

'It's always hot here,' she stated and opened her eyes. Once more, she stared into the fire. There was a pause before she twitched and contorted her face into a grimace and started to throw her head from side to side.

'No! No! Please, Lord, no!' she cried out in desperation. Again, she was reliving the events of the fire on the plantation. Her head thrashed about violently, as she became more and more agitated.

Edward raised his voice above hers. 'What is it you've seen? Tell me, Mary!' he insisted.

'I was there that day, Walter, and I'm sorry…so sorry.'

'For what?' asked Edward, hoping she'd talk to him, as if he were Walter. She did.

'They tried to run! There was smoke everywhere.' She coughed and gasped for air.

'I tried to save a little girl,' she spluttered.

'Who, Mary, who?'

'I tried, Walter! Her mother was stranded, but the horses…'

'Tell me, Mary, where were the horses?' he demanded to know.

'Everywhere!' she cried out.

'Whom were you trying to save?'

Mary was now in a heightened emotional state: sweat beaded on her forehead, her lips were as dry as parchment. She clutched her fists tightly into her skirt and screwed them around.

She wept. 'That little girl from the village… They took her away to God knows what. And I couldn't do anything to help her, Walter.'

Edward watched as, all of a sudden, she slumped back into the chair. He knew he'd taken her to the brink of exhaustion, and he allowed her to rest whilst he took a few moments to analyse things. He eventually realised that Mary must have fallen into a lucid dream that day, the contents of which were so traumatic that they caused her to flee into the path of the parade of horses. This was the only explanation for her behaviour. What he couldn't work out, though, was the significance of the man, Walter, in it all. This was the real mystery and one he'd need to mull over.

Convinced that keeping Mary hypnotised for longer would serve no real good, Edward brought her out of the trance.

'Listen to my voice, Mary. I want you to stop punishing yourself. What happened that day was merely a tragic accident. You're not to blame, do you hear? You're not to blame! Forget everything, feel yourself become sleepy… and relax…'

Eventually her head flopped.

'Tell yourself you're not to blame,' he gently repeated over and over, before concluding, 'On the count of three you're going to awake and you will have forgotten everything. You'll not remember anything other than that you've just had a little sleep. One, two, three!'

Mary opened her eyes and took a moment to recognize her surroundings. Edward smiled at her.

'Do you feel all right?' he asked.

'Yes. How long have I been, well…under?'

'Oh, only a short while,' he reassured her.

She looked over to the clock on the mantelpiece, which confirmed it had in fact only been ten minutes. Mary could not help but want to launch a barrage of questions at him, all of which was normal when a patient came out of hypnosis.

'So, was I able to enlighten you?'

'It's very much as I thought,' he calmly replied. He got up and walked to the door. 'I'll arrange us some tea.'

As they sat drinking, she listened, having no recollection of events. Edward intentionally left out any mention of Walter. He wanted to understand better the relevance of the man before passing any comment to her or Tom. Consequently, he merely explained his belief about her daydreaming. Mary, in turn, was slightly disappointed because she had hoped the hypnosis would help her remember everything and offer some answers. But at least she did now feel some sort of closure, as subliminally she began to accept the message that she should not blame herself.

~~~

Tom poured another couple of glasses of whisky and walked over to the window to Edward. They peered out onto the garden and watched Mary laugh as she walked arm in arm with Edward's wife.

'It's good to see her smile again, Tom,' Edward observed to his friend.

'Yes, isn't it,' Tom replied, longingly looking at his wife. 'Let's hope she can now move on,' he continued and took a sip of his drink.

'And you?' Edward asked.

Tom thought for a moment. 'I'll just be happy if we can get back to normal,' he finally answered philosophically. Edward gave him a reassuring smile.

'Edward, I've been meaning to ask you…' Tom moved away from the window, 'When you hypnostised Mary, did she ever mention someone called Walter?'

Edward froze. 'Ah,' was all he would respond.

'So she did!' Tom surmised.

'Look, Tom, whatever you do in private is your affair.'

Tom glared at him in confusion. 'I'm sorry! Whatever did she say?'

'Is it relevant?'

'You're the psychiatrist, Edward. You tell me!'

'Very well! Yes, Mary did mention him, several times, and I've mused over it ever since.'

'Several times!' Tom huffed in irritation, before adding, 'And?'

'And I can't add any more because I don't know any more. Who is he, Tom? Who is Walter?' Edward asked.

Tom threw back the remaining whisky in his glass and cleared his throat. 'I'm sorry, Edward, but I wasn't entirely honest with you prior to asking you to see Mary. You see, I wanted you to give me an objective view. If I'd mentioned Walter, I thought it might influence things.'

'I see,' replied Edward, but had to ask again, 'Who is Walter, then?'

'Walter is the bane of my bloody life, Edward, that's who he is.'

Edward listened intently as Tom described in detail how they'd all first met and the subsequent start of Mary's dreams. Eventually, he gave Edward his analysis of the problem at the time: that Mary was merely searching for love.

He went and poured himself another drink, as Edward sighed with relief that he had been mistaken about Walter, and he could again look at Tom and Mary without judging their private preferences.

'So when did her dreams start again?' he asked Tom, who studied his wife until she disappeared from view.

Tom turned and told Edward, 'Oh, I'm not sure they ever stopped! But it was after the accident that I knew for sure she was visualising again. You see, I'm not a terribly good sleeper and I often just lie there thinking. What Mary doesn't realise is just how much she talks in her sleep.'

Lying next to her in bed, Tom would listen to every word she spoke and make mental notes. Sometimes she made no sense at all; at other times the events in her dream were so acted out, he could have been listening to a play. To his relief, what was going on never appeared sexual or sensual; but, nonetheless, there was a tenderness of conversation any normal man would feel perturbed by, let alone a man with a keen jealous streak.

'At first I assumed she was having nightmares about the accident. But then I realised she was talking to him – Walter – as clearly as if he were in the room. My training, Edward, is never to accept the unexplained without at least a theory. But I'm beginning to question that.'

'There's invariably a reason for these things,' Edward felt obliged to say.

'I know that much but I'm damned if I can find it anymore,' Tom responded, and he downed the next glass of whisky. He looked at his friend and bluntly asked, 'She's psychotic, isn't she?'

'Let's use the word "delusional", Tom.'

Tom allowed his head to drop. Whatever word Edward chose to use, his diagnosis still meant his wife was mentally ill.

'I've seen similar cases before and, in fact, it isn't that rare. It's about finding what triggers her belief.'

'Belief in what?'

'She thinks Walter is her true soul mate.'

Tom didn't like the comment. The green-headed monster of jealously welled up inside him instantly.

'And me? I'm merely what?' he enquired indignantly.

'You're her lover and companion.'

'Meaning what, exactly, Edward?'

'That you are there for a reason – for intimacy and to help her find her higher self. But you're not her divine counterpart.'

Edward's theory made Tom uncomfortable and Edward knew it.

'Don't look so worried, Tom. True soul mate relationships are seldom sensual,' he explained as compensation, with a hint of wit.

Tom didn't quite appreciate his friend's flippant remark and gave him a grimace. 'Go on.'

'I think Mary is quite rational about Walter in her conscious mind, accepting he was there…is there, to help her grow spiritually. Unconsciously though, she fantasizes about his world, gets absorbed in what she believes is his daily life, and this manifests itself in her dreams and visions.'

'Intriguing. And you believe in this soul mates nonsense?' remarked Tom, with obvious scepticism.

'Yes, I do, Tom. Not everything is explained by science.'

Tom just raised his eyebrows with incredulity.

Edward offered his further opinion: 'There is something in Mary's past that links her feelings with Walter?'

Tom scoffed, 'Perhaps she was Cleopatra and Walter, Mark Antony?'

Edward assumed a droll expression, then stared his friend straight in the eye and calmly told him, 'True soul mates don't part, Tom. And if you try to stop them, you'll not succeed. Find out why there is such a bond, or learn to live with him.'

Just then, the door opened and in walked Mary. 'We thought we'd take tea on the lawn,' she said cheerfully, much more like her old self.

'Absolutely,' Tom replied. He held up an empty glass and added, 'We were just about to have a drink.'

Mary peered down at the whisky bottle, which was a lot emptier than earlier in the day. 'Another one, dear?' she replied, in a tone that got her point across. Then, as quickly as she'd breezed in, she left.

Edward walked over to Tom, who again watched his wife through the window. He placed his hand on his shoulder.

'Listen. Why don't you take Mary back up to Sheffield? Try to rekindle those happier times! It may just help.'

Tom smiled. 'Yes, I might just do that.'

CHAPTER 19

STRANDED

Walter's burning desire to avenge himself on the Turks had to wait. The sort of men who had defiled his home and village so mercilessly would one day pay dearly; but, for now, he had to focus on putting a roof over his family's heads. Day and night, until his hands bled and his body collapsed with exhaustion, he rebuilt his dwelling. Within three weeks, he had restored enough of the house to a standard that could at least offer warmth and shelter for the impending winter.

Father-in-law Macca had made available the dhow's crew to assist in rebuilding the village, such was the devastation. However, the time was fast approaching when his men would be needed back at sea again, to sail up to Basra; for the start of what was to become World War 1 was now all but a certainty, and word had reached the Sheikh that trade was brisk for dhow owners. Foreign merchant ships had little appetite for taking their cargos beyond Muscat, for fear of attacks from Turkish troops stationed along the Fao Peninsula. Dhows, on the other hand, were normally left in peace and took advantage of the handsome financial rewards for transporting goods to the Mesopotamian seaport.

With a heavy heart, Walter knew he must also join the crew, and he sat with his family one last time to eat supper. It was a solemn affair, with only the sound of scraping on plates to break the silence. Afterwards, he sat his children by his side and, in front of a glowing fire, they studied him, as he tenderly carved a small boat out of a piece of wood. Iza finally joined them and nestled into her family, taking each baby to her breast. With full bellies, the babes dozed until, eventually, they fell into a deep sleep in the protection of their mother's loving arms. Carefully, Walter laid them on cushions and took Iza's hand. He kissed her softly on the forehead and led her to the bedroom. That night they made love with a gentleness that few ever have the pleasure of experiencing in a lifetime.

On leaving the next morning, Walter could only take heart from the news that British forces were reinforcing their presence in Aden and that this should offer better protection from the marauding Turks. At least that is how he tried to reassure Iza, as she clung to him one more time, before he made his way up the gangway.

Looking back, he called out in English, 'Count the days,

my cherub! Soon we shall again whisper sweetly together.'

Iza had little knowledge of his mother tongue but her look made it clear she sensed his meaning.

The dhow set sail and drifted into the morning haze, its crew in sombre mood. For several days, there was none of the usual jollity. No more of those makeshift cricket stumps, with Walter teaching eager students his beloved game.

During trading, Macca always took full advantage of the fact that his son-in-law was from the 'noble race' and the dhow owner had built up trust with the English ships' captains, even if many were confused as to how the Sheikh always managed to know exactly what price they'd have to settle at. Never had they suspected any involvement of the strange young Arab man accompanying the Sheikh, teasing them with his poor pigeon English, yet all the while passing on information to Macca about what price was considered rock bottom. How could he be involved? An Arab understanding broad cockney. With negotiations done, Walter would always have one last game before they left ship. How the crews laughed at the Arab's brilliant impersonation of a perfect English gentleman: 'Dear fellows, it has been a delight for one to do business with you.'

This trip, Macca met with a captain looking to secure safe passage to Basra for his cargo, a collection of used foundry machinery: from anvils to complete lathes, there were enough metal parts and tools to keep a workplace productive for years. It was not the usual load for Macca, but, thanks to Walter, a better than fair price was negotiated and the dhow was loaded.

A simple but effective method of payment had been devised in these strange times: captains were to pay their monies to an agent, who then issued a printed and numbered ticket to the dhow owner. When this was presented to the agent in Basra, the agent would consult a codebook and issue a new numbered ticket. When the dhows returned to Muscat, providing the numbers matched the codebook, then payment would be made. However, ticket number 9256 would prove most dangerous for Macca, Walter and their crew.

Normally, the Turks were unconcerned what cargo found its way into port or, indeed, from where it came. Corruption was rife and, for a price, locals were given free rein to continue trading as they liked, that is until the Ottoman general staff took command of operations. The Turkish objective was to seal off the Shatt al-Arab waterway at Fao, thereby controlling access to Basra and, more importantly, to the rich oil fields. As Macca steered around the peninsula, it wasn't long before the dhow was approached by a motor boat, guns pointed in readiness. An officer bellowed instructions for them to pull into dock. At the mooring point, Macca immediately saw the change: there wasn't the normal chaotic activity of traders, only organised unloading supervised by troops.

Macca was below deck with Walter when the dhow was finally boarded. The commotion above them soon got their attention, as army officers shouted at the crew. A cocking of rifles was suddenly heard. Walter tried to listen to the conversation through the grill. Again, his love for learning any foreign language proved invaluable, and his knowledge of Turkish was enough for him to understand the problem.

'There's trouble with the goods,' he said to Macca. Then, he continued trying to make out the conversation. 'Something about arms on board!'

What neither of them had realised, when loading in Muscat, was that several large crates were full of artillery casings and technical drawings giving lathe specifications: an obvious gift meant for the emerging Arab revolt.

'The crew, they're being taken prisoner,' he relayed back to Macca.

Heavy boots suddenly clattered at the top of the stairs.

'In here!' Macca whispered, as he quietly drew back a false panel to the cabin wall. Walter looked at him in surprise. Never had he known there was such a hideaway; but then there was a lot about Macca's cunning he was learning. The two men edged against the hull and slowly closed the panel, and just in time, as seconds later the door was flung open. Two soldiers stood and surveyed the cabin. Finding no one there and nothing of any interest, they joined the other soldiers down in the small cargo hold below.

Walter and Macca spent a further fifteen minutes, in total darkness and not daring to move a muscle, before they took a chance on leaving their cramped hideaway. Gingerly, Walter slid the panel back far enough to peek out. There was no sign of anybody. In fact, the ship was eerily silent, except for the creaking of wood as the dhow strained against its mooring ropes. They both breathed an enormous sigh of relief.

'Trust the experienced, not the learned,' Macca said. On this occasion, Walter had to agree.

Up on deck, Walter slid across a mound of tarpaulins and peered around the corner of the wheelhouse. Only a single soldier appeared to be on guard at the bottom of the gangway. Walter signalled Macca to go starboard and then made his way around to meet him by a big iron press. Ironically, in the jumble of machinery causing all the fuss, there was one piece that was cast with the signature mould: 'Made in Sheffield'.

Walter and Macca stealthily ventured back towards the bow and suddenly saw the dhow crew on the dock, sitting on the floor in two rows, their hands tied and placed on their heads. Guards patrolled amongst them and showed no compassion for the men, totally innocent of any crime but now regarded as 'enemy vermin'. They were continually kicked, spat at and goaded. One man, refusing to relinquish his gold chain, was dragged out of line and brutally beaten with a rifle butt, his fellow men forced to watch and powerless to help him, as was Walter, who looked on in despair. His blood boiled as the crew were rounded up and forcibly led away. Once more, the Turks had dishonoured people he held dear.

Neither of them needed reminding of their predicament, and quite simply they had only one question for each other: 'What on earth are we going to do?' The answer came without warning some twenty minutes later, courtesy of the British Naval fleet. First came a deafening whistle, followed by an almighty explosion, as a shell ripped into a nearby storage building. All then went quiet for a brief moment, until the full force of artillery fire was unleashed offshore and shells rained down all around them. Soon the port was ablaze. The battle to take Fao had begun.

Both men held on for dear life, as the dhow rolled in the thrashing waves. Walter suddenly saw his chance and grabbed Macca's scimitar to slice through the ropes that strained as they held the ship to its dock. Finally, the dhow was free and began to bounce up and down on the sea. It was futile for them to hope for anything more than that the dhow would somehow drift away and towards the open sea.

'Come on lady!' he urged, as the wooden beast began to turn. 'That's it! You can do it! Turn, damn you!'

Then came a thud and a white flash. The quayside shuddered as it took a direct hit. Great lumps of concrete were tossed high into the air like confetti and the vibration was so strong that a metal post was bent. Walter was tossed like a rag doll and dumped hard into the savage water, whilst Macca was thrown at least twenty feet and slammed into the dhow's wheelhouse. It was now in God's hands whether either man would survive.

CHAPTER 20

The Truth Is Told

As suggested by their friend, Edward Stapleton, Tom and Mary decided to make a visit to Sheffield to stay the weekend with the Elliotts. It had been six months since the loss of their baby, and much longer since they'd seen their old friends.

The city still held a kind of excitement for them and they were happy to be back in the chaotic powerhouse of industry. They peered out of the train carriage window and found nothing had changed: the landscape was still harsh, with its coarse factory buildings etched in grime and always belching smoke in their effort to satisfy the nation's desperate wartime need for steel.

Mary eventually caught sight of Ann and Robert Elliott on the platform and pulled down the carriage door window to wave furiously. She was hardly able to contain her delight at seeing her dear friends once more. She had continued to correspond with them by letter, but it was going on a year since they had physically seen each other. As the train finally came to a stop, she flung open the door and ran with all her might into the arms of Ann. They spun around in excitement, clutching each other as if mother and daughter. Both had tears of joy rolling down their cheeks.

'Oh! Ann, I can't tell you how lovely…'

There wasn't time for her to finish, for Ann had again embraced her closely. Eventually, they pulled apart and Ann held Mary out in front of her.

'Just look at you.'

'Beautiful as ever!' came the familiar voice of the man she'd missed so much.

'Robert!' Mary squealed. Elliott just held out his arms for her to fall into.

'My dear girl, it's so good to see you,' he said, squeezing her with delight and kissing her forehead.

Poor Tom could have felt all but forgotten in the excitement of the reunion, but he wasn't and, as he approached them, Ann gave him the broadest of smiles, wiped away her tears and again opened out her arms.

'Tom…how are you?' she said, clutching him close.

For five minutes, the porter waited patiently with his trolley loaded with two suitcases and an attaché box. He watched the greetings continue until, finally, he felt enough was enough and politely coughed. 'Will that be all, or will sir and madam require their luggage taking further?'

'Oh! I'm so sorry! No, that's fine, thank you. I'm sure my husband can manage things from here,' said a slightly embarrassed Mary.

'Why thank you, dear,' Tom joked. As usual, he was oblivious to the fact he should offer a tip and just stood there next to the porter, who was not planning on moving without any monetary gesture.

Ultimately, Mary had to interject. 'Tom, dear!' she said, with eyes opened wide and her head nodding at the porter as a hint.

'Aah, yes.' Finally he caught on and fumbled in his pocket for some loose change.

'Come on then! Let's get you two home and settled in,' Elliott said and stepped in to push the trolley to the taxi-cabs outside the station.

'Bloody hell, luv!' gasped the driver, as he struggled to lift the larger suitcase into the luggage rack, ''As tha brought kitchen sink wi' thee?'

Tom had to laugh, remembering with affection the local folk's forthright honesty, something all too often lost in their lives in London. Finally, with luggage loaded and all passengers on board, they were ready for the off.

'Weer t', then?' the driver asked of Elliott, with all of his best customer service patter.

The journey was no more than a few miles from the station and, despite the cab coughing and spluttering most of the way, they were at the Elliotts' home in no time. Home was a well-proportioned detached house of stone, set in pleasant mature gardens, and in a middle class area of the city. Here, Mary had spent many happy hours, and she had a strong sense of reassurance as the cab turned onto the tree-lined avenue and approached the familiar privet hedge, with its quaint little gate in the middle. She grabbed Ann's hand as they pulled up. It was a while since she had had such feelings of security.

Lily, the housemaid, was there to meet them at the door and inside were the Elliotts' two boys, Henry and Cecil, waiting to greet their guests. Mary hadn't seen them for so long and could hardly believe how much they'd grown, particularly Henry, who at nearly fourteen was becoming the image of his father.

'Well…are you going to say hello, boys?' Ann asked her sons.

'Boys! I rather think they're young men,' Mary observed '…and fine handsome young men at that. So, does Mary get a hug?'

If God had created awkward moments for young lads, then this was a fine example. Henry immediately flushed bright red in embarrassment, desperate that his pimples might miraculously disappear and that he should stop twisting like a shy schoolboy. It didn't need much deduction to work out the boy had a soft spot for

Mary and, in her absence, this had grown to be more of an innocent crush.

'Perhaps we're now too old for all that and a handshake is more appropriate these days,' Mary joked, and held out her hand.

Oh no! How could she possibly think that? Henry thought, and wished with all his heart that she'd change her mind. He reluctantly pushed out a hand.

'Henry Elliott, did you honestly think having not seeing you for a whole year, you could get away with not giving me a hug?' she declared and promptly gave him the biggest embrace possible, with the added bonus of a kiss on his cheek. The young man suddenly felt ten feet tall.

'And as for master Cecil...' She turned her attention to the little brother, all of nine and with a totally different agenda.

'I don't kiss girls,' he said indignantly.

'Don't you now!' teased Mary, turning her lips downwards and letting out a little smirk.

'No! Have you brought me a present from London?' he enquired, with the simple honesty of a nine-year-old.

'Really, Cecil, you are a cheeky rascal,' rebuked his mother.

'I bet Tom has...brought me a present.'

'Cecil, that's enough,' Ann said, with a more serious tone. 'What must Tom and Mary think?'

Tom interjected, 'Come on, you little scamp. Help me

to our room with these suitcases and we'll see what we can find.' Cecil didn't need further encouragement if presents were on offer and started off.

'Ah-em,' coughed Mary and bent down with the side of her face to him, 'a kiss and hug I believe was mentioned.'

Cecil frowned at her and relented, 'I suppose,' he said, and wrapped his arms around her neck. Secretly, he loved every second of it, for he hadn't forgotten Mary, who had been his favourite of all his mother's friends.

With gifts handed over, Tom and Mary could finally settle in their room. It was the same room that Mary had stayed in before their marriage and, although redecorated, was every bit as lovely as she remembered. The fresh new look met with her approval and confirmed that Ann and she shared very similar tastes in decoration. Ironically, it was also the guest room in which Walter had rested, prior to leaving for Southampton. As Mary stood looking out of the window, again the memories of Walter came flooding back.

At dinner, talk of the war was avoided where possible, as much for the children's sake as anything. Young Cecil had already experienced his first taste of the harsh realities of the great conflict: his school friend had suddenly learned that his father was missing in action. Sadly, the boy was to become one of the next fatherless generation. Tom was also becoming familiar with the effects of war and, just three months into the hostilities, he was doing at least ten amputations a week on the returning wounded.

They were all ready and determined to enjoy a weekend free from sadness, or so they thought.

Retiring to the parlour, Tom played slaps with Cecil, though not entirely to Elliott's approval, as he was trying to listen to his music on the gramophone. Mary and Ann sat discussing all manner of women's topics, in which Henry soon lost interest, deciding to read his beloved fishing book instead. Finally, Tom took the hint from Elliott's occasional scowl from over his newspaper and got Cecil interested in the less fraught activity of playing dot-to-dot. Mary kept glancing over to see her contented husband, as the young ball of energy snuggled into his now best adult friend. She felt an awful sense of guilt and longingly looked at the man she knew would have made a good father.

Soon it was time for Ann to shake things up: if nothing else, it would stop her husband from drifting off and snoring behind his newspaper. A game of character charades was prescribed, and before long Elliott was centre of attention and had them in stitches with his inter-pretation of a farmer. Only after a good five minutes did he get around to giving a rendition of milking a cow and, finally, Mary shouted out the correct answer. In turn, she took her card and giggled. How on earth could she act this, she wondered, and stood for a moment deliberating, with a glass of fortified wine clasped in her hand. With her best actor stance, she mimed her character. A volley of suggestions soon rang out, before Henry called out, 'Opera singer?'

Her audience gave a round of applause in recognition of her efforts and she playfully acknowledged this, taking a classical bow to each one in turn. Then, suddenly, she froze, her eyes open wide and her mouth dropping ever so slightly. She stood there as white as a sheet, staring at the vision of the woman standing behind the sofa. Mary's hand went limp and the glass of wine slowly dropped onto the beautiful cream Persian rug. She never flinched, just continued to stare at the woman, who, of course, nobody else could see. Finally, after all this time, the tender voice of the woman spoke to Mary.

'My dear Mary, you've been so brave.'

'Who are you? What is you want with me?' asked Mary, to the alarm of everyone in the room, as they watched her seemingly talking to herself.

Ann called out, 'Mary, whatever...?' but Tom interrupted her by raising his hand.

'It really doesn't matter who I am, only that you know why I'm here,' said the woman, as the young paper boy from Mary's past vision then suddenly appeared and stood next to her. 'We all have so much to thank you for, Mary.'

Tom stood up beside his wife and gently held her arms

as she spoke again: 'Why are you doing this?'

'Please don't be afraid, Mary,' the concerned woman answered.

'But I am afraid, because I don't understand,' replied Mary, anxiously.

'I know it is hard for you. But it will soon make sense. Then we can all have our closure.'

'Tom, what on earth is happening?' Ann asked, as Cecil burrowed deep into her arms in fear.

'It's all right,' he said and looked down to Cecil. 'Mary is just having a dream, that's all.'

'But she isn't asleep,' Cecil answered with logic.

'No, it's a kind of a daydream. She'll awake very soon,' replied Tom, still holding Mary.

The vision of the woman walked around the sofa and held her hand to Mary's face. 'We must leave now, Mary.'

'No, please, I need to know more,' begged Mary.

'Be patient, Mary, just a while longer,' she said, and then all of them had gone.

Tom held Mary tightly as her eyes slowly closed and he guided her to sit on the chair. Kneeling in front of her, he softly spoke, 'Mary…Mary dear,' and stroked back her hair.

A moment later Mary opened her eyes and looked around in confusion. 'Hello,' said Tom and smiled.

Mary took time to appreciate where she was and what

had just happened. She then realised she had been talking out loud and went bright red with embarrassment. 'Oh, dear Lord. I'm so sorry, I must have…'

'You simply drifted, that's all,' Tom interrupted and looked over to Cecil. 'What do we call it, Cecil?'

Cecil looked a little apprehensive but still wanted to impress, 'It's a daydream, Tom.'

'It is indeed, well done.'

Mary felt her foot in the wine spill on the rug and looked down. 'Oh Ann…Robert, I'm so sorry,' she exclaimed, seeing the big stain.

'Don't worry. It was an accident. So long as you are all right,' Ann declared.

'Yes, I'm fine now, thank you.'

Ann looked over to Tom for some sort of explanation. He didn't want to tell the truth and, instead, simply gave a well-practised and non-committal doctor's appraisal, whilst taking hold of Mary's hand and feeling her pulse.

'I'm sure it's nothing more than just a drop in your sugar levels, dear. It's made you dizzy and disorientated.'

Elliott snapped his hands together and ushered the children towards the door. 'Right, boys, time for a trip up the wooden hill. Let Mary have a little rest now.'

Cecil gave out a groan.

'Come on, you'll see her in the morning,' Ann interjected and went to escort them to bed.

'Goodnight, Mary. I do hope you feel better soon,' said a concerned Henry.

Cecil couldn't resist giving her a peck on the cheek. 'Night,' he softly said.

'Yes, goodnight boys,' she offered back with a smile and leant forward to kiss Cecil. Suddenly her chain and locket dropped forward. Little Cecil took hold of it and studied it before commenting, 'Did Tom buy you this?'

'No Cecil, he didn't. But it was from somebody equally as lovely.'

Elliott was rigid with shock. He recognised it immediately and stood staring at it. What was Mary doing with Walter's locket? he wondered.

'Robert. What is it?' said Mary, as Elliott continued to stare.

He eventually got out his words, 'Sorry, ignore me. I'm just a sentimental old fool remembering long ago.'

As he watched Mary tuck away the locket behind her blouse, the realisation dawned on him.

What had started as such a pleasant evening had suddenly fallen flat. However, with the children in bed, the adults talked for a while longer. Mary tried to put on a brave face but didn't really have much inclination to join in.

'Please, forgive me, but I do feel so tired. I think I shall go up to bed. You don't mind?' she said.

'Not at all, my dear,' replied Elliott, seeing she was struggling.

Tom slowly rose from the sofa to follow until Mary placed a hand on his arm and suggested, 'No, you stay and chat for a while. I'm absolutely fine.'

None of them believed that for a minute, especially Tom, who simply wanted to discuss his wife's strange behaviour with her. Finally, he did use the grandfather clock striking the hour as a convenient signal to make his exit.

As he entered the bedroom, he found Mary sitting up in bed, reading a book.

'I thought you would be fast on,' he remarked in surprise.

'I couldn't sleep, so I thought I'd read for a while,' she explained and dropped the book into her lap. 'I'm so sorry, Tom. I don't know what came over me.'

'Don't you?' Tom answered, not exactly sarcastically, more with a tone that meant, 'Well, I think you do.' Mary got the hint.

'Meaning what, Tom?'

He paused, not wanting a fight; but equally he had to get his fears off his chest.

'I asked, meaning what, Tom?' she repeated.

'All right.' He turned to face her. 'Downstairs, I know you had a vision. It's becoming tiresome and, what's more, dangerous. Where does it end, Mary? What would happen if you took young Cecil out, had a vision, and watched him run into a car?'

He knew as soon as he'd said it how much it hurt her.

'Thank you for that, Tom. I didn't realise you were so skilled at cutting deep without a scalpel!'

He turned away, knowing his words weren't fair and realising he was letting his frustration get the better of him. 'I'm sorry, Mary. That was uncalled for.'

'I can't help seeing these things, Tom.'

Tom looked at her with some sympathy, but knew the whole situation had to come to a climax.

'All right, Mary. This vision tonight, was it Walter?'

Mary sighed and flung her hands up in exasperation. 'No! Why does everything have to come back to Walter? It was a woman I saw.'

'A woman! What? A fat one, thin one, old, young... what?' he said, unable to contain his impatience.

Mary just glared at him with disappointment. 'Cynicism doesn't suit you, Tom. Let's just leave it, shall we?'

'You're right, I'm sorry,' he conceded and went over to try and hold her hand. But Mary was in no mood for his sympathy if it wasn't genuine and pulled away.

'I won't allow this to tear us apart, Mary. For the sake of everyone, let's try to make sense of it all,' he suggested. 'The woman, tell me about her. Have you seen her before in your visions?'

Mary eventually dropped her defence but stated her terms for carrying on the conversation. 'If I tell you what I believe, promise me you'll not fly off the handle and just discount it.' She looked at him as he shrugged his faint-hearted acceptance. 'No, promise me, Tom.'

'Very well, I promise.'

'The woman I saw tonight, just like the other people I've been seeing, I think they're spirits. I never wanted to believe it, but now I'm convinced.'

Tom raised his eyebrows in a cynical expression but then remembered his promise.

'I know it sounds ridiculous and I don't expect you to accept it,' she said.

'No, I'm listening.'

'Do you remember me telling you about that medium lady. She came up to me in the Mission Hall that time.'

Tom so wanted to interrupt her, to do exactly as Mary had predicted and discount it all as utter nonsense. But he could play the dutiful listener when needed, and acknowledged her with a nod of his head.

'She told me that troubled spirits need closure to move on, and that my visions of Walter created energy to bring a man to justice.'

Tom struggled to contain himself and bit his tongue to avoid blurting out the words, 'Absolute twaddle.' However, his body language couldn't really disguise his thoughts and Mary sensed as much.

'You wanted to know, Tom. So there, I've told you. I believe the woman just now was telling me my visions are happening so that justice can be done.'

'Justice? To whom?'

Mary cast her eyes downwards. 'I don't honestly know.'

Tom clasped his hands to his face and then pushed back his hair. As a medical man, he was prepared to debate most theories of human behaviour, but talk of spirits was a bridge too far, and he simply couldn't give any credence to such ideas. However, what he could now accept was his psychiatrist friend's theory: that Mary was so wrapped up in her thoughts that she was now forcing visions on herself to play out a story, something that was vivid in her mind and which she subconsciously controlled and developed. He couldn't entertain the theory about soul-mates, but now, finally, had come to the conclusion that his wife was psychotic.

Downstairs, although it was only just past 9.30, Robert and Ann were left to spend the rest of the evening alone.

'Well, it's certainly been eventful, if nothing else, dear,' said Ann. Her husband just gave her one of his 'indeed' smiles.

'I do hope Mary is all right, Robert. She looks so affected by her troubles.'

'I'm sure she'll be just fine, dear.'

Ann stood over the stain and peered down. 'I'd better get Lily to get some soapy water and clean this up before it sets in.'

Robert glanced over to the stain and mused, before offering his expert opinion: 'It would be better to just put some white wine on it first, to neutralise it. Leave it to me and I'll sort it out.'

'And will that be this side of Christmas or next?' Ann joked. She knew her husband only too well and gave him a kiss on his cheek, 'Very well. I'm going up, Robert. See you later.'

Robert sat back and deliberated. He knew that only Walter's father had the answer to his question.

~~~

The following morning, Elliott was up early and walking down the street towards the pharmacy. The rather feeble door bell jangled to announce his presence and, once he was inside, Mr Stanford appeared from the small dispensing area and peered over his glasses, which were all but ready to fall off the end of his nose.

'Ah, Mr Elliott!'

'Morning, Mr Stanford.'

'I'll be with you in two minutes,' said Mr Stanford, precariously pouring some tincture into a small funnel over a bottle.

Elliott waited patiently and looked at the products on the counter. 'Pond's Vanishing Cream! Huh, what will they think of next?' he said, dipping his finger into the sample jar and smelling it.

'The latest fad from America, Mr Elliott. All the rage with the ladies.'

'Is it indeed?' came the sceptical response. 'I assume to rub on their husbands.'

Mr Stanford gave only a minimal titter in recognition of Elliott's joke.

'Right, I've done. So, what can I do for you? More bad news of Walter I take it?'

'No, no, not at all. I was merely hoping I might have a chat with you about something that's been bothering me,' replied Elliott.

'Is it of a private nature?'

'Pardon!' said an embarrassed Elliott and instinctively looked around the shop, hoping there were no customers, which was strange, as the shop was no more than ten foot square, and it was plain only the two of them were there. 'No, you misunderstand. It's not a medical matter, merely private.'

'Oh, I see. Well, let me drop the latch and we can talk in the back.'

'I'm not disturbing your trade?'

'It's no bother, go on through,' he said and pointed to a door leading through to the house.

Elliott waited inside the familiar parlour for his host, and once again he studied the picture frames on the mantelpiece.

'Please take a seat, Mr Elliott. Would you like some tea?'

'No, thank you. I won't keep you long.'

'Very well. So, how can I help with whatever is bothering you?'

'When we met last, Mr Stanford, we talked about Lucinda Trevill's locket, which you gave to Walter and his twin sister.'

'Yes, I remember the conversation.'

What had played on Elliott's mind since seeing Mary's locket the previous evening was its clasp. It was on the other side to the half he'd held in safekeeping for Walter.

'Well, I'm sorry if this sounds intrusive but, when Victoria died, was her half of the locket buried with her?'

Mr Stanford gave him a very puzzled look, although not one that suggested he was offended in any way. 'I think there's been a bit of confusion, Mr Elliott. You see, Victoria wasn't Walter's twin; no, she was adopted by us a little time after the twins.'

'So, who is Walter's twin?' asked Elliott, but he knew the answer before it came.

'She was called Hannah Mary. An adorable little thing but so weak and ill when we took the pair in. I could see that she needed specialist care beyond just medicines that I could give her. Good fresh air is what her little lungs cried out for, not breathing in foundry sulphur day in and day out. I learned of a doctor in Ireland who specialised in children's chest conditions, so we arranged for her to go to him and his wife. They fell for the lovely mite straight away and I knew it wouldn't be long before they would want to adopt her. I'm very sorry, Mr Elliott, I should have made that clear when we spoke previously.'

Elliott wasn't at all worried, only pleased to have finally got to the bottom of the mystery, and he hoped his next question would prove his instinct about Mary's parentage beyond all doubt.

'Would you happen to remember the doctor's name, Mr Stanford?

'Yes, of course! It was Henry O'Driscoll.'

A very happy Elliott gave a broad smile before beginning to tell him all about Mary.

Walking home, his dilemma was now only whether he should mention anything to Mary. 'Would it only raise questions that nobody would benefit from?' he asked himself. Mary was now in a new life with Tom and, therefore, what right did he have to blunder in to upset things with his news?

~~~

Tom woke with a pounding headache. He looked at the time on the small alarm clock, which confirmed he'd had no more than a couple of hours' sleep. His mind, once more, had run riot and refused to switch off. The only thing that helped him was whisky and he'd sat in the armchair, swigging away at the large hip flask that invariably accompanied him nowadays. He had then slumped back into bed and, when the alcohol had worked through, had fallen fast asleep again. When he next awoke, it was 10.15, and although he would have given anything to fall back to sleep for just a few minutes more, he knew the splitting pain in his head wouldn't let him. He fumbled to find his trousers and eventually dragged himself out of bed. There was no Mary: she had long since been woken up by his loud snoring and made her way downstairs. He staggered down the corridor to the bathroom, where a sink full of ice-cold water was his saviour. How he relished the feeling of numbness as his head submerged beneath the surface.

Back in the bedroom, eventually shaved and properly clothed, Tom felt a bit more organized, although from the smell wafting up from the kitchen, he wondered whether he would be able to manage the cooked mackerel that was on offer. He made his way downstairs to the dining room.

'Ah, good morning, Tom,' said a bright and upbeat Robert Elliott, who'd been up since well before six. He folded up his newspaper in anticipation of a chat, but immediately saw from Tom's bleary eyes that he was either not a morning person or hadn't had a good night's rest. Having heard their raised voices from downstairs the previous evening and now smelling the aroma of whisky, he opted for the latter and realised all was not well with Tom and Mary.

'Oh! Morning, Tom,' declared Ann, as she entered the room with a pot of tea. 'You've surfaced then.'

'Sorry. Had we arranged something?'

'No, I'm teasing! It's just we're early birds. Tea?'

'You don't have coffee?' he asked hopefully.

'Of course. I'll get Lily to put some on. Can you manage a cooked breakfast?' Ann enquired, but saw Tom was less than enthusiastic. 'The room and bed were comfortable? It's just…,' she continued, fearing there had been something wrong.

'Oh absolutely, Ann. Do forgive me but I don't sleep too well in a strange bed and pay the price the morning after.'

She suddenly also got a whiff of whisky and looked over to her husband in surprise. Like him, she sensed all was not well.

'Where's Mary?' Tom asked.

'Oh, she's just gone for a walk with Cecil and the dog. It won't be too long now before they're back, I'm sure.'

Tom looked worried and desperately hoped that what he'd said to Mary about an accident with Cecil wasn't a

281

premonition.

Ann wasn't one to pry but had to ask, 'Tom, is everything all right with you and Mary?'

'Yes, we're fine.'

She wasn't convinced but gave him a pleasant smile. 'Good, I'm pleased,' and walked off towards the kitchen.

With his wife gone, Elliott wasted no time in giving his opinion and, with his usual tact, took a sledgehammer to the nut.

'I hope you don't mind my saying, Tom, but when a man comes down to breakfast smelling of whisky, I would say there's something troubling him.'

Tom looked up. 'That bad?'

'Facts are stubborn things, lad.'

'And I thought only consultants were forthright.'

'A habit which is second nature, I'm afraid!'

Ann returned, as Tom put his hands over his face and sighed. This wasn't the weekend he'd envisaged – emotions laid out for dear friends to witness.

'Oh, I'm sorry. I'll leave you to…' She sensed she'd arrived in the middle of something fraught.

'No, please, Ann, sit down. I owe it to you both to let you know,' said Tom and, again, pushed his face deep into his hands. This time his fingers opened wide, revealing his anguish.

Ann sat down cautiously. 'Whatever is it, Tom?'

'The fact is I have been drinking for some time, more than I care to admit and certainly more than Mary appreciates.' He paused, wondering how best to say it. 'You see things between Mary and me…well, let's just say they've been tense for some time.'

'But that's understandable, Tom. I mean, after all you've been through.' Ann gave her opinion in a sympathetic tone and touched his hand.

'It's not just the loss of the baby, Ann. No, it's more than that.'

'Oh! I see.'

'Mary has been having strange dreams and vivid visions for, well, quite some time.'

'About what? Is it serious?'

Ann wanted to ask even more, but Elliott intervened. 'Let Tom explain, dear.'

'Do you remember Walter Stanford, Robert, the badly injured man Mary brought into hospital that night?' Tom asked Elliott.

Elliott sighed inwardly. If only Tom knew what he knew about Walter. Nevertheless, he nodded and innocently replied, 'Yes, of course, I remember.'

'Well, you see…'

Tom began to explain everything from the very start. For ten minutes, he described things, event by event, including every intimate detail of Mary's dreams, despite

Ann raising an eyebrow at some of these. He poured out his whole heart, feelings and frustrations until, finally, he confessed that Mary was suffering a form of psychosis. 'Mary is ill, I'm afraid!'

'Oh no, dear Lord!' sighed Ann. She certainly hadn't been expecting that.

Elliott sat rather expressionlessly, his chin resting on his clasped hands. It was if he was still assimilating things and trying to work them out. He wasn't. Instead, he was working out how best to tell Tom what he knew.

'There's good reason, Tom, for all this with Mary and Walter.'

'And what is that, Robert?' came Mary's voice, taking them all by surprise. She had been standing behind the door for the last five minutes, listening to her husband laying bare all their troubles. None of them had heard her return through the front door.

'Seeing as you now know all my problems, you might as well give your theory. Everyone else has!' she said.

There was a long painful silence, with nobody really sure what to say next, least of all Tom, who couldn't bring himself to look at his wife.

'I would like to know, Robert!' Mary snapped, and so curtly it made Robert give her a glare that Ann had not witnessed in her husband for a long time.

'I'll go and see what's happened to that coffee,' Ann said

gently, seeking an opportunity to leave the room. Never had she seen Mary so distressed; but then never had she imagined her problems were so deep. Equally, she knew her husband did not suffer curtness lightly and she had no desire to see them lock horns.

'No, Ann,' Elliott declared. 'Please sit down. What I have to say you need to hear.' His insistence took her by surprise, and somehow she sensed that what he was about to say she wasn't going to like. Gingerly, she sat down again.

'Close the door, please, Mary,' he asked.

She did so, then calmly held onto the back of a chair to listen.

'Mary…I once knew your mother.'

Mary thought for a moment before, finally, pushing her eyebrows together and leaning her head to one side in confusion.

'I didn't know you'd visited Ireland.'

'No, I haven't.'

'Then, sorry, Robert but I don't quite follow.'

Elliott raised his hand to his mouth and squeezed his lips together. He looked her straight in the eyes, took a breath and sighed down his nostrils.

'You're frightening me, Robert!' Mary exclaimed.

'I'm talking about your real mother. I once knew your real mother.'

His words didn't quite register, and she again pulled her eyebrows together. 'I'm sorry!' she retorted, wondering if she'd heard him correctly.

'Your real mother was called Lucinda. You are adopted, Mary.'

'No,' she laughed nervously. 'No, I think you must be mistaken because I…I'm…,' she stuttered.

'There's no mistake, Mary.'

Mary slumped onto the chair in bewilderment and grabbed at Ann. With wide, tear-filled eyes, she begged Ann to confirm it wasn't true. 'Please, Ann, tell me this isn't right.'

Ann was as shocked as Mary was at her husband's revelation and could only shrug her shoulders, tears streaming down her face. Mary looked over to Elliott, his expression unrelenting.

'I'm sorry,' he spoke softly.

Mary flopped into Ann's arms, burying her head. 'No, Ann, noooo!' she cried.

Ann cradled and rocked her back and forth, as if nursing a baby. She glared at her spouse with incredulity. 'You'd better explain yourself,' she said.

Elliott did explain, but never was there a man more adept at prolonging a story without getting to the point. So much so that the local Sunday School had long since begun politely declining his annual offer to recite the story of Moses to the children. Still, Mary's story would be told his way and off he set, occasionally stopping to assess if he'd missed any detail. As soon as the locket was mentioned, Mary felt around her neck.

As he explained about Lucinda being pregnant, Mary wailed and begged, 'Please, Robert, no. Don't dare tell me you are my father!'

'No! Why ever should you think that?' Elliott replied, taken aback.

A relieved Ann looked at him and shook her head in exasperation at his story telling. 'Why ever indeed,' she muttered.

Tom, although eager to hear everything, couldn't help but wish the coffee would arrive to make the ordeal a little easier to endure.

Finally, Elliott came to the other bombshell but, in truth, they had all but worked it out. Mary pulled herself up from Ann's comforting embrace and sniffled, 'My twin is Walter!'

'Yes, Mary…yes he is,' said Elliott and watched her lay her head back on Ann to sob.

It was a heart-wrenching scene to see, as Ann kissed her head and once more rocked her like a baby.

Tom found it hard to bear, watching his wife clinging tightly to Ann for comfort. How he wished he were the one she was seeking reassurance from. Elliott also choked back his own tears in the ensuing silence, knowing he couldn't do anything other than give Tom a sympathetic smile. Eventually, Mary raised her head to ask, 'Where is

Walter now, Robert?'

'I honestly don't know, my dear. The last news I had was from Captain Smith, who took Walter on as a deck hand. By all accounts he jumped ship in Aden some time ago.'

Mary didn't give a response. She was simply numb.

Of course, there was still the story of Newsome Street to tell her and, unusually for Elliott, he gave only an abridged version of the place's horrors and actually got to his point quite quickly. Mary simply clutched at her locket as she listened. Finally, she gently took it from her neck and handed it to him.

'Then you'd better take a look behind the velvet, Robert,' she said, not really sure what anything meant anymore.

Elliott gently teased back the velvet lining and, just as he thought, there it was: a little scrap of paper lying neatly folded underneath. With care, he opened it and flattened it out on the table. Unfortunately, just as on Walter's note, the writing was badly faded and affected by foxing. Only the odd word was legible, but there were not enough to give any clue as to what Lucinda's was trying to say.

Mary suddenly released herself from Ann. 'Please excuse me,' she simply said and ran to the door.

As his wife fled upstairs, Tom, visibly moved by the whole affair, stood up to say, 'I'd better go to her.'

'No, Tom. Leave her be for a while,' Ann suggested. 'Trust me,' and she touched his arm, 'I'll go and check on her in a while.'

Tom heeded her advice and sat back down. Mary's explanation the night before kept running through his mind. Could it possibly be that she wasn't ill and actually did somehow connect with the spirit world, he wondered. Her visions, in a paranormal sense, were something that he couldn't easily accept and, until now, had dismissed as pure fiction. However, events had now brought him to the point where he would at least consider a more psychic theory.

When Ann did check on Mary, she found her sitting on the end of the bed staring into space, a woman lost in thought. Ann sat beside her and held her hand tightly. No words were needed, no more tears shed. They just sat holding hands for a while. In the end it was Mary who broke the silence.

'Ann, can I ask you to do me a favour?' she asked.

'Of course.'

'Will you telephone for a taxi cab? But please don't say anything to Tom.'

'Oh, Mary, whatever for?'

'Will you do it, Ann?'

'Well, yes but…there's no need, you can stay here as long as you like, you know that.'

Mary turned to look at her. 'And I do appreciate that, truly. But it's better if I return home. I want to be alone for a while.'

'But what about Tom?'

'Tom's a good man, Ann. I don't want to burden him with my thoughts right now.'

'I'm sure he doesn't think…,' Ann started to reply but was cut short.

'Please Ann.'

'Very well. If that's what you really want.'

'Thank you…yes, it is.'

Ann stood up and walked towards the door, then stopped and looked over to the suitcases on top of the wardrobes. 'What about your luggage?'

'Tom will bring it home. I'll just take my attaché case,' Mary responded, quite matter of factly, as if she'd already thought it all through methodically.

As the telephone was in the hallway, Ann kept her voice as low as possible, so as not to raise any suspicion. After much repetition, she finally made the man in the taxi company understand she wasn't suffering from a terrible sore throat and ordered the cab to wait at the end of the avenue. She was sure her husband and Tom would be furious with her, but she'd deal with that later.

The two women gave each other one last hug at the back door.

'You're absolutely sure?' Ann asked.

Mary nodded. 'I'll call you.'

'You must. Let me know you've got back safely.'

With that, Mary walked with determination to the back gate, all the while tears rolling down her face. Before going through, she stopped and gave her dear friend one last wave and mimed, 'I love you.'

Ann bit her lip and sensed it would be a good while before she'd see Mary again.

CHAPTER 21

FAMILIAR SURROUNDINGS

'Would you please turn left here?' Mary asked the cab driver, who duly obliged. 'Then right at the end, and up the hill. Here! Please stop here.'

The taxi pulled up outside the Dog and Partridge Tavern. She didn't know why she'd asked him to stop here, instead of at the railway station: it was a spur of the moment decision. Perhaps, with all that had happened, she just needed to be in old familiar surroundings.

'If you don't mind, I'll get out here. How much am I in your debt?' Mary enquired.

'Oh, call it two bob, luv,' the driver declared and got out to open the door for her.

She stood on the pavement and looked over to the house, her eyes scanning upwards towards the little window of the room she'd once rented. With her attaché case in her hand, she wandered across the road and stopped outside the door she knew so well. As she peered up the street, she remembered the many times she'd run down it, either late for work or, in winter, desperate to get back to her room. She turned around to view the tavern, which held less-treasured memories. Two drunks swaggered out of the door and she could see nothing had changed.

'Does it interest you then, luv?' said a voice that took her by surprise.

'I'm sorry,' she replied.

'The flat, does it interest you?' said a man, tapping at a sign on the window stating 'Room for Rent'.

'Oh, I see.'

'Number 8, it's the top one,' said the man, opening the front door.

'Do you currently stay there?' Mary asked, more out of politeness than anything.

'No, I own the building.'

'Oh, where's Mrs Walsh gone?'

'Know her, do yer?'

Mary smiled. 'Yes…well kind of.'

'She sold up last year and, well, I bought the place. So can I tempt you to take a look?'

The man was nothing if not an enthusiastic salesman. Mary looked far too respectable to be on the lookout for this type of lodging, but he reckoned nothing ventured, nothing gained.

'Number 8 you say?' Mary asked, the number being the

same one she'd previously rented. 'Do you know what, I will take a look if you don't mind,' she said, though quite why she didn't really know.

Stepping inside, the memories came flooding back.

'Mr Entwhistle,' the man introduced himself and held out his hand.

'Oh yes, Nurse O'…I'm sorry, Mary Sharpe,' she replied and shook his hand.

'It's a bit of a hike, I'm afraid,' said the landlord.

Mary laughed to herself, remembering the time she'd helped the injured Walter stagger up the stairs. As they passed Mrs Walsh's old room, she closed her eyes and just for a moment could hear her voice, 'You'll not be having any company up there, will you now, Mary?'

At the top, Mr Entwhistle turned the key and swung the door open. Except for a few things belonging to the current occupier, everything was just how it had been before she'd left: the sofa, the table, the bookcase – even the old screen divider she'd detested remained.

'Five shillings a week,' stated Entwhistle, as she continued to look around.

Peering through into the bedroom, she saw the old Georgian wardrobe she adored and wished she could have taken it with her.

'Five shillings a week, that's quite reasonable. Does the heating work?' Mary asked cheekily.

'Well, it's a bit temperamental but I'm looking at fixing that,' he replied.

Mary had to smile, for how many times had she heard that line during her stay. Just then, a young nurse dressed in her uniform, came through the door.

'Aah, Miss Davies. I hope you don't mind but I was just showing this lady around the flat,' said Mr Entwhistle.

'I do hope I'm not intruding, Miss Davies,' remarked a slightly embarrassed Mary.

'Not at all, ma'am,' replied the young woman. Mary was taken aback. Did she really look so stuffy as to be referred to as ma'am?

'Listen, if Miss Davies doesn't mind, I'll leave her to show you the rest of the flat. I'm in Number 2 if it's of further interest. Five shillings a week remember,' said Mr Entwhistle and left, closing the door behind him.

'The robbing devil, it's gone up a shilling!' cried the nurse.

Both of them burst out laughing. Mary suddenly realised she was laughing and it felt good; despite everything she had been through that day, she was still able to laugh. She introduced herself. 'I'm Mary Sharpe.'

'Ruth Davies,' responded the young woman.

'Well, as you can see, it's not very big. But let me show you around, Mary.'

'I'm afraid I've not been entirely honest with Mr Entwhistle, Ruth.'

'Oh!'

'No. I am not really interested in renting the flat. It's just when he offered for me to take a look, curiosity got the better of me. You see, a few years ago I used to rent these rooms.'

'Really!' said Ruth, seemingly not at all bothered at Mary's admission. 'Well, has it changed?'

'No!' Mary laughed. 'Not one bit.'

Mary watched as, just as she once had, Ruth pulled the grips from her cap and threw it on the sofa. The pins holding it together popped out and the cap sprang open.

'Damn! It takes me ages to work out how it fixes back together properly,' declared Ruth.

'Don't worry I used to be exactly the same.'

'You're a nurse?' Ruth asked in excitement.

For the next half an hour, the pair sat chatting about the City Hospital, nursing, the flat, Sheffield in general, in fact anything and everything and Mary loved every minute. Finally, she looked at her watch.

'Will you look at the time. I really ought to get going or I'll be missing my train back to London,' Mary stated and stood up. 'Thank you for your time, Ruth. I really have enjoyed our chat. You will find some excuse for Mr Entwhistle, won't you,' she finished, with a guilty smirk and part frown.

Ruth laughed and promised, 'I will... Sorry, Mary, but you did say train to London?'

'Yes, I live there now.'

'You are aware the last train leaves at three o'clock on Sundays?'

'Three o'clock!' Mary shrieked in disbelief.

'Yes. It's since the war started, everything finishes at three so they can transport all the steel.'

'Oh dear! Well, I guess I'd better find a hotel for the night.'

Ruth pointed over her shoulder to the Dog and Partridge and declared, 'There is the pub across the road.'

Mary opened her eyes wide and gave a jovial look of disgust. Ruth acknowledged this and grimaced back. 'Yes, I don't blame you! Listen, Mary, I've been asked to cover tonight, so I'm back on duty soon. Why don't you stay here?'

'That's very sweet of you, my dear, but I couldn't possibly... Besides, you're very trusting of someone you've only just met.'

'Oh, I think you're trustworthy enough. And look around you, apart from my books and a few personal bits and bobs, nothing in here is mine, so you're welcome to steal what you like,' Ruth summarised flippantly.

'But it would mean staying in your bed. I couldn't...'

'It's not my bed, Mary,' Ruth reminded her with a laugh. 'Look, there are clean sheets in the cupboard and, if it really bothers you, sleep on the sofa. It's up to you.'

Mary thought about it for a while as Ruth went down to the bathroom. Never could she have believed this was how her day would end.

The offer was most generous and genuine, not to mention convenient, and if she did stay in a hotel, would it be any more comfortable? 'Oh, I don't know…I don't know anything anymore,' she said and felt anxiety coming over her until, finally, she forced herself to make a decision. 'Mary Sharpe, you will be strong and you will stay here tonight, so just get on with it!'

'Ruth, I will take you up on your kind offer – I will stay here the night,' Mary said, firmly in control of herself, when Ruth returned to the room.

'Excellent. Five shillings a week, mind.'

They again burst into laughter.

Alone that night, Mary stoked the fire and put a little more coal on, just as she'd done hundreds of times before. It seemed so strange to be back in the rooms, yet so reassuring. All she wanted at this moment was to be alone, to make sense of this morning, her life, Tom. Oh dear God, everything, she thought.

She decided she would sleep on the sofa after all. Although Ruth didn't mind her bed being used, to Mary a bed, whether owned or not, was somehow most private. She did, however, need to go into the bedroom to get a sheet and blanket but got no further than the tallboy chest of drawers, when she burst into tears. Seeing Ruth's possessions on top of it brought back the memory of the casket containing her parent's letters. Perhaps, this wasn't such a good idea after all, she thought.

Finally, curled up tight in front of a roaring fire, she began to write. She wrote three letters: one to thank Ruth for her hospitality, the second to Robert and Ann apologising for her strange behaviour and, lastly, a letter to Tom, which read:

Darling Tom,

By the time you read this letter, I know you will be sick with worry and, for that alone, I am deeply sorry. I wanted to telephone to let you know I was safe but knew hearing your voice would break my heart and I can't take any more heartache, Tom.

What Robert revealed today has struck at the very core of me and I pray you'll understand my decision. To find out I'm adopted is in itself such a blow; but to also discover Walter is my twin brother is almost too much to bear. And, Tom, how can I burden you any longer with him? I so worry that my early dreams of him were anything but dreams. And you know what that means: that I have accidentally… Sorry, but I can't even bring myself to write the words. I know you'll say we'll bounce back, dear, but honestly how could we? It is my desire to be a true wife and all that means. How can we lie together and it not rip at your heart, knowing what may have happened. I would rather die than see you troubled with such thoughts.

Believe me, there is nothing more I want right now than for you to cradle me and take my pain away – just to lie in your arms, defenceless like a child, for you to keep me warm and close. No woman could fail to feel the love and understanding you so openly give. But I have to fight my demons, and it is too much to ask of you to make that journey with me.

My thoughts and visions of Walter have robbed us of so much, my love. Visions that caused my stupidity the day of the accident and meant I killed the baby you longed for. Yet, still, I have a yearning to find him, to stand and hold my brother and, one day, I will, or I shall die trying. I know you'll have a rational theory because, bless you, you always do, so I won't expect you to accept it. I refuse to burden you any more with all my frailty and belief in the spirit world. Perhaps, as you told Robert and Ann, I am simply ill.

I beg you to forgive and, now, forget me. Don't wait for me, Tom. Remember me but please live your life without me, as I will now live without you.

I love and adore you, Tom Sharpe, and kiss you one last time, with all my heart,

Mary

Mary had no real idea how she was to start her search for Walter. All she knew for a fact was that he'd gone to sea and eventually jumped ship, according to Elliott, in Aden. Other than that, everything was a visual representation of a place she imagined him to be – just ships, desert and a plantation, all of which could simply be no more than a romantic fantasy land in her mind.

The idea for where to start came when, after writing her letters, she took out an atlas from the bookcase and, in curiosity, thumbed through to find the Middle East. Whilst she had heard of the place, Aden, she wasn't sure exactly where it was. After studying the atlas, she began to browse through the other books, deciding what to read, knowing she wouldn't sleep easily and needing to keep her mind occupied. Opening up one book, a folded-up leaflet acting as a bookmark fell out. When she studied it, she found it to be a small recruiting pamphlet about enlisting with the Voluntary Aid Despatch. The campaign urgently sought nurses for duty, and what caught her eye were the locations, in particular, Mesopotamia.

Three days later, Mary, in a highly emotional state, had purchased some clothes and a suitcase with the little money she held in a savings account, and was sailing to a war zone in a far distant land, where conditions were to be as desperate as she could imagine.

That same day, Mary's letter arrived for Tom. After he sat and read it, he simply tossed it to one side and poured himself a large whisky, then another and another. The man was destroyed: his wife, his one true love, all he cared for, had broken his heart.

CHAPTER 22

A Mute Restored

Whether it was God's will to spare him, or simply that the cat had nine lives, Walter did survive the attack on the harbour at Fao. After being tossed into the sea, dazed and battered, he clung onto a strip of wooden debris and drifted for twelve hours. Only then would the sea give him up and wash him ashore into marshland, some twenty or so miles south of Basra. It was by sheer chance he was discovered by a travelling Bedouin tribe, who had stopped to gather reeds. For days, he was nursed by the women until, finally, he was able to crawl and nothing more.

As for his father-in-law, Macca, he too would live to tell his tale. Luckily, the dhow had floated out to sea and was eventually boarded by sailors of the British Fleet. Ironically, it was the dhow's cargo, once the cause of ill-fortune, which now came to his rescue, as the naval officers, not wishing it to fall into enemy hands, decided to tow the dhow back to Muscat. Macca, suffering a shattered collarbone and a broken leg, would experience firsthand the care of his son-in-law's 'noble race'.

For two months, Walter travelled with the caravan as they made their way through the desert, and slowly he became strong enough to walk again unaided. With three broken ribs and swollen vertebrae, he wasn't as fortunate as Macca in receiving the best medical attention available. Still, he was nothing if not positive and tried his best to assist his Bedouin benefactors. Feeling sufficiently fit, he decided he would leave them when they got as near as possible to Basra and then, somehow, he'd try to get aboard a vessel bound for Aden. In dreams, he walked there with his beloved Iza and their children.

As the sun rose over the dunes, the silhouette of what appeared to be spikes appeared in the distance. The Sheikh pulled up his hand and the camels slowly came to a halt. Intrigued, he dispatched a tribesman to investigate. Minutes later, he was signalling it was clear to proceed. The caravan once more trudged through the sand, as the baking sun lifted into the sky and its intense light illuminated the desert. At last, they reached the spikes. But they weren't just spikes: they were something much worse, something that caused the tribesmen to herd the women together where they could not see.

Walter dropped from his camel, his eyes ablaze with rage, for what lay in front of him was the crew of the dhow, attached to the wooden points. Some had literally been skewered. After initially being detained in a camp, one day they had been rounded up and force-marched through the desert. Here they met their fate, and for what? Merely to show passing Arab tribesmen the outcome that awaited any man choosing to side with the enemy. As he looked around the pitiful scene, he witnessed the most horrendous sights of what must have been tortuous deaths. Tears rolled down his cheeks as he saw how his innocent friends had been butchered. The crescent moon carved into a man's chest served only to raise Walter's blood, once again, to boiling point. Now he had to seek revenge; and revenge he would have, in the most subtle yet effective way.

The tribe prayed to Allah and then the dead were mercifully taken from the spikes and buried in shallow graves. As the caravan prepared to move on, Walter realised the time had come for him to say farewell. That afternoon, after a hearty feast, the Sheikh gave him an embrace of friendship and placed two sling bags made from camel skin, around his neck: one contained water, the other food, enough to last no more than three days.

Now alone, Walter wandered through the desert towards what he thought was Basra. But, in fact, he was soon drifting further west and straight towards the front line of the conflict. Day and night he trudged on until, finally, he realised he was utterly lost. On the third day, he ate his last scrap of food and picked himself up for another day at the mercy of the sun and the barren landscape. He knew this day could be his last in his blessed land.

However, this cat had yet more lives to come and, as he stared through the haze, he caught sight of small buildings way, way ahead. He could only pray he wasn't seeing a mirage. If he was, then he was in trouble: to survive further in the open desert required skills he certainly hadn't attained.

By nightfall, he had reached a position where he could see the odd twinkle of light and calculated he was no more than a few miles away, so decided to press on. At last, he came within a few hundred yards of what was a Turkish military stronghold. He could hear the talking and muted laughter, as he looked towards the trenches being dug. Thoroughly exhausted, he decided he would rest here until daybreak; but no sooner had he laid down his head, than a rifle dug into his temple. He heard the awful sound of the gun being cocked and slowly opened his eyes to see two soldiers standing over him. The rifle moved to one side and gestured wildly up and down, indicating for him to get to his feet.

'Get up! Get up! Put your hands above your head,' shouted the soldier and forced Walter's hands up with the point of his rifle. 'What are you doing here? Speak!'

Walter then felt the thud of a rifle butt on the side of his face and fell to the ground. Once more, the two soldiers towered over him, holding a bayonet perilously close to his stomach.

They shouted repeatedly, 'Why are you here? Speak! Speak!' He understood all right and knew he had to do something – and something very inventive – or the bayonet would be pressed into him. All he could think of in that split moment was to somehow fool them. He had a flashback to when he was in the prison cell in England, and how effective his mute trick had been with the police.

'Speak! Or I will kill you,' the soldier shouted again.

Walter waved his hand to his ears and gestured he was deaf, then to his mouth, indicating he could not speak. It seemed to work, as one of the soldiers lowered his rifle point and asked his colleague, 'What is he saying?'

The once more mute Walter acted like he had never done before; and, after three days in the desert, covered in sun blisters, and with torn, dirty clothing, he looked very much the afflicted beggar.

'He's just a deaf and dumb beggar. Shall I kill him?' said one of the soldiers.

'Nah, leave the pathetic creature,' said the other, who, luckily for Walter, had an ounce more humanity.

However, as the soldiers turned to walk away, Walter wasn't done. He played the role to perfection: begging for food and water, then remonstrating more and more as they shunned him. Only at the point where he was sure he would be run through with a bayonet did he fall away and drift towards the Turkish camp. He was surprised how easily he could wander through the troops. Finally, he was thrown some scraps of bread, which he ate like a man possessed. If ever Walter had sought a career on the stage, with a performance as good as this, he certainly would have achieved rave reviews.

For two weeks, Walter passed himself off as the mute beggar and, by now, he had added the extra quirk of being mentally disturbed, all of which enabled him to secure enough food to survive. But survival was all it was: he was on the brink of starvation. It was only when supplies were replenished, some six weeks later, that he started to scrounge enough food to nourish his emaciated body back to a standard that gave him hope of being able to move on. As he further improved, it became common to see Walter wandering about, begging in the role of the deranged idiot. Such was the amusement he brought to the troops that he was hardly paid any attention when he made his way through the labyrinth of trenches out towards the big guns that were being brought in. There, he surveyed the gleaming steel machines of destruction, all the while noting their locations and shell capacity.

Another three weeks on and the British offensive to

take the Turkish stronghold began in earnest. Some four hundred yards or so in front of the Turkish lines, the British dug in and soon the daily exchange of artillery fire whistled back and forth. However, to the surprise of the British Generals, the Turks seemed well-equipped and disciplined. Before long, they had the upper hand in shellfire, causing considerable loss of life in the British trenches and substantial destruction of British artillery. In contrast, the Turkish lines and weapons appeared relatively unscathed.

One thing Walter couldn't work out was a curious structure about one hundred yards to the left of the camp. From a distance, it appeared to be a super gun, with its barrel set at $45°$ degrees. He had been stopped from going there three times during the shelling and became ever more intrigued as to what it was. However, some of the troops were becoming wary of him. So in order not to raise suspicion, he decided to lie low for a while.

Food again became scarce but Walter had a plan for that! Having been in the Turkish camp now for going on three months, he was a familiar sight and caused less and less interest. Many was the time he just wandered into the desert for hours on end, and then back into the camp, without arousing so much as the blink of an eye. One quiet evening he hatched his plan and slid away towards the British lines. How strange it was to hear his mother tongue again after all this time.

'Where the bloody hell have you come from?' shouted a startled soldier, suddenly seeing the beggar. 'Go on, piss off!'

So charming a welcome, and from a fellow countryman at that, thought Walter. Within minutes, he was pushing his fingers into his mouth, begging for food once more, and so the whole charade began again.

'Give him some of your snap, George,' called the private, biting into a chunk of bread.

'No – give him some of yours!' came the reply.

The private finally threw down a piece of bread, which Walter scampered after and ate like a rabid dog.

'Bloody hell, easy old son,' chirped the soldier.

A further few chunks of bread saw Walter ravenously gnawing away like a squirrel. Then he did a strange thing and spat out the bread, in front of the two men, as if shunning the infidel.

'You ungrateful bastard!' cried the soldier.

Of course, it was just one more instance of Walter playing his character for his own amusement. Within an hour of wandering into the British lines, Walter had had his fill of nourishment, including chocolate, which could only have dreamed about weeks earlier. Over the next few days, he pottered from camp to camp, unchallenged, and made himself such a familiar sight that he could get within speaking distance of the British General's command tents.

It was during a heavy shelling session that Walter got to understand the significance of the funny structure away from the Turkish lines. It was a simple yet ingenious contraption and one that used cunning to great effect. In the mayhem of activity, he found he had easy access to the big gun, as it was known. Before it was fired, he watched as the gunner pulled furiously at some string. Then, he observed how the responding British shells landed all around the structure. He scurried over to take a closer look.

What he found was a large steamer funnel jutting out of various bits of solid timber and positioned just below a large sand dune. Beside the funnel was a soldier eagerly watching for movement of a tin can, which was filled with pebbles and attached to a length of string. On hearing the can rattle, he would open a panel and release plumes of dense smoke up the funnel. The British officers, viewing the battle scene through binoculars, would see smoke rising here every time the proper gun fired. Obviously, it was here the British believed the main shelling was coming from, and hence the area their guns were trained.

The following day, Walter was again in the British lines and near the General's tent. As usual, it was blisteringly hot and a trio of officers sat on folding chairs eating rations. Walter glared at them, like a wolf, with every bite they took.

'Do we have to have that barbarian here?' asked the General.

'Sorry, sir, I'll move him on,' dutifully replied a Lieutenant.

Walter suddenly spoke. 'A bit of chocolate for my secrets, sir.'

The officers looked at him agog.

'What did he just say? Bring him here,' exclaimed the General.

Walter was paraded in front of the General, who took his drill stick and moved his chin from side to side, studying every inch of his face. 'Who are you?' he asked with curiosity.

'Well, I'm not the Duke of Devonshire, sir, that's for sure.'

'My God! You're English,' pronounced the flummoxed General.

With that, Walter was bundled into the tent and, for fifteen minutes, gave an abridged version of who he was and how he came to be there and, more importantly, how he could help 'Dear old King George.' He sat for a further half an hour drawing maps of the Turkish trenches and explaining the gun trick; and then he disappeared, a mute once more.

Walter had become an unofficial spy and the next day's shelling saw his work reap revenge on the Turks, the revenge he'd so long desired. It wasn't long before the Turkish stronghold was on the brink of defeat and it was only the fact that the British needed to wait for more ammunition supplies that saved the enemy in the coming days.

Meanwhile, Major Koln, a German officer, was drafted in from Baghdad to spearhead a new Turkish strategy. As usual, Walter was wandering the trenches and playing the fool around the Turkish officers' lair when he heard the familiar Germanic tongue. He crept nearer to listen.

'Three! Three!' hollered Koln at the officers. He took off his gloves and threw them in disgust onto a table, then beat down his cane onto a map. 'Three artillery placements totally obliterated in as many days. How can that be, Lieutenant?'

The officers hung their heads in embarrassment and shame, until one, finally, had the nerve to say, 'I think it is just fortuitous shelling on their part, sir. I'm sure they don't yet realise the trick, sir.'

'And am I to write that in my report to Field Marshall Von Der Goltz, Lieutenant?' the German spat out angrily.

'No, perhaps not, Major.'

'No. Not unless I want to be paraded as a failed fool on the Russian front!'

Trying to get a little nearer, Walter lost his footing and came crashing down onto a pile of rifles, stacked upright.

'What the...?' cried the Major.

Walter was dragged up and paraded in front of him.

'And who...or what, is this?' the Major asked, looking

over Walter with as much disgust and contempt as it was possible to give.

'Oh, it's just the beggar, sir. By the hand of Allah, he cannot hear or speak. He wanders oblivious, looking for scraps – totally harmless,' confirmed the Lieutenant.

'Is he indeed?'

Koln circled around Walter, looking him up and down with suspicion. 'Deaf and mute, you say! Very interesting.' Then from behind, he tried to make him jump with a sudden loud clap of his hands. Walter didn't flinch a muscle.

'And how long has our Bedouin beggar friend been wandering, oblivious, as you put it?'

'A couple of months, I guess. He comes and goes.'

'Comes and goes, hey,' Koln remarked with some sarcasm. 'I wonder from where and where to? Perhaps we should examine your Allah's affliction on him a little further. Tie him and take him to the gun.'

It was at nightfall that Walter would discover his fate. He was taken and placed next to the big gun, untied, and positioned in such a way as to feel the full force of the air concussion in his ears.

'Forgive me, Major, but what is this to prove?' enquired the Lieutenant.

'Well, let's see shall we? If he can hear, he'll try to protect his ears.'

'Fire!' shouted the Major.

The gunner tugged on the string, waited for the plume of smoke from the decoy and then fired the gun. Walter's head took the full force of the air discharge and noise, his keffiyeh flying off to one side. To the Major's surprise, the beggar hadn't raised his hands.

'Again,' bellowed the Major and, once more, Walter was placed by the gun.

'Fire!'

Walter rocked as soot splattered on his face but still he didn't protect his ears. Twice more he suffered the torture until, finally, he slumped to his knees but without appearing startled at the noise. Blood began to trickle from his ears and nostrils.

Koln looked on frustrated. 'Leave him in the pit; we'll pursue this tomorrow,' he said scornfully.

The pit was a ten-foot deep dug-out in the sand, near to the decoy structure and used to dispose of the trenches' effluent. Walter was thrown into it and left there, shivering. Throughout the night, shells sporadically rained down all around him. He prayed for one to be a direct hit and relieve his pain, but he wasn't that fortunate and the following day had to endure worse torture.

In the scorching heat he was taken, still shaking and bemused, stripped naked and his hands tied to wooden planks trussed into a crucifix. His eyes opened wide with fear as Koln arrived. It wasn't fear of the man himself, more of what he was about to do. He didn't have long to wait and find out, as Koln walked over to a fire and raked a branding iron through the white-hot coals.

'So we have a deaf beggar it appears. But can he speak after all?' said Koln callously, as he took out the burning hot iron from the fire and proceeded over to his victim. Walter closed his eyes and waited. The horrible smell of his own burning flesh went up his nostrils as the iron branded his chest. He writhed in agony but remained silent.

'A brave mute indeed,' observed the evil Koln and branded him again. 'Where do you wander to? The British lines?'

He continued branding him all over his body, including his genitals.

'Are you a spy?' he kept asking.

Walter, although in excruciating pain, didn't utter a word or moan. Koln walked over to a table and picked up a pair of industrial pliers and a bottle of ammonia. Slowly, he walked back to Walter and held them in front of his face.

'I ask you again, are you spying for the British? Do you give them the location of our guns?'

Walter gave him no response.

'Very well,' said Koln, quite calmly, 'untie a hand.'

With soldiers holding Walter tightly, Koln callously tore out a fingernail from Walter's finger. His pupils rolled up as his head reeled around. Still he never spoke a word. On the verge of passing out, Koln brought him round with a whiff of ammonia.

'You see it's quite simple,' explained Koln and showed Walter his bloodied fingernail. 'You speak and I stop, remain silent and…well, then I continue!'

There was no speaking, not even a guttural moan and, consequently, three more fingernails were torn out but, for Walter, there wasn't any more pain. He had collapsed into unconsciousness that even ammonia couldn't bring him round from.

As Koln walked away, Walter was untied and left in a heap to perish.

When he came to, some two hours later, he found himself lying alone in a small room, no more than four yards square. There was a tiny shaft of light coming from a horizontal slit high on the wall. He looked down to see his clothes piled on top of him. What Walter didn't realise yet was that, once again, he was in a prison – or at least a building used by the Turks to house any prisoners. Mostly they were their own men, captured after desertion, and waiting to be ushered before a firing squad. However, there were also a few prisoners of war, who had been spared and would be used for propaganda purposes. This was what Koln intended for Walter: to keep him alive and parade him for all the locals to see, so they would understand the tyranny of their superbosses.

Three days he spent in that hell, so hot it was nothing short of an oven, until suddenly the door burst open and in walked a British army private wielding his rifle. The Turkish stronghold had finally been overpowered and all the troops had fled northwards.

'Jesus Christ!' said the private, smelling the air. He looked down at the pathetic body of Walter, all but dead. The overriding smell was that of gangrene!

'Here, Arthur, give me a hand to get this poor sod out,' was all Walter would remember hearing, until he awoke in a field hospital outpost, thirty miles away.

CHAPTER 23

You've Made Your Bed, So Lie In It!

Unfortunately, Mary didn't share Walter's view of his blessed land. Her heart sank as she disembarked from the ship and climbed onto a rickety old truck that proceeded to the hospital. The winding streets, full of shouting and noise, starkly showed her the poverty, squalor and sheer desperation of the town. First impressions were certainly not good, and she quickly decided she hated the place. In those early days, she thought she had made such a terrible mistake, and it took several weeks before she could appreciate anything positive about Aden. It was certainly a case of 'she'd made her bed, so now she must lie in it'.

She missed everything about England, especially Tom. Her heart ached as she thought about what she'd done and how she'd treated him. Every night she would cry herself to sleep, desperately wishing she could turn back the clock and once again lie safe in his arms. She would most likely have taken the next ship back home if it had not been for her absolute belief that Walter was in Aden and, hence, her dogged determination to find him.

'If he's here, I'll find him,' she kept saying to herself.

But how naive she was. It was like looking for a needle in a haystack. She had no contacts, nobody to guide her, and even if she did, what would she say? 'Well, he's English, my age, looks similar to me. I think he may have a wife and children. No, sir, I'm not certain he lives in Aden, it may be somewhere else!'

In truth, Walter could have been in Outer Mongolia – she just didn't know. It was all so preposterous as to be laughable. Yet there was something in her face that could convince you she was destined to find her brother.

Because of her past experience, Mary had been recruited as a sister with the VAD, and because of her desire for a posting in Mesopotamia, where getting volunteers of any sort was always a challenge, she had quickly been snapped up by Matron Clements. Luckily for Mary, Joyce Clements was a great matron, and between them they were soon running a very efficient hospital that treated the war-wounded before their return home.

As with any war hospital, there were many pitiful sights and no shortage of heart-wrenching outcomes for the volunteer nurses. Mary took the raw, inexperienced ones under her wing and was always there to help them cope, even on the days when she herself was struggling with her own troubles.

In terms of making any progress tracing Walter, Mary found she had precious little time. However, when she did get an afternoon off, she would go down to the port and make enquires with any English sailors she could find. Not that she got very far: she spent most of her time fending off advances from high-spirited seamen. In a bar, on one such visit to town, she did come tantalisingly close to learning something. It was just a throwaway comment, which she didn't pick up on and, in fairness, didn't hear properly, because of a parakeet that was constantly squawking.

'I was wondering if you gentlemen could help. Have you ever heard of a young Englishman who jumped ship here a year or so ago? Walter Stanford was his name.' Mary asked her usual question and waited for the equally usual humorous answers to come back.

With the jokes out of the way, most sailors would try to help and rack their brains as to who it could be. The trouble was that most of the merchant ships that had travelled to the Middle East back then were now engaged in European activities. A young man, however, suddenly chirped up, 'Didn't old Sheikh Ibraham have some English crew, Reggie?'

'No! You're thinking about that swarthy guy who always gave us a brilliant impersonation of a fine English gent,' Reggie replied.

'Ah yes,' recalled the young man.

Had Mary heard properly and enquired about the Sheikh, she would have certainly been told where to find the popular trader and all would have been revealed. But she hadn't.

As always, she gave a pleasant smile to hide her disappointment and made the lonely journey back to the hospital. However, her fortune was about to change when one day she was asked to visit Matron in her room.

'Yes, Matron, you wanted to see me.'

'Oh yes, Mary, do come in…and please, when we're not in earshot, call me Joyce.'

How different things were from her days back at 'The City' in Sheffield.

'We've been asked to provide a detachment to a field unit. I'd like you to lead the nursing staff, Mary,' explained Matron.

'Oh! Right, well, I'm flattered…but aren't I more use to you here?' Mary enquired.

'You are and, as soon as the new recruits arrive, trust me I'll be pulling you back.'

'Well, yes, all right, if it helps.'

'Thank you, my dear. Oh! There is just one drawback. Major Forbes is going as surgeon!'

Both women gave a grimace at each other and began to laugh.

During Mary's time in this strange land, her visions and lucid dreams of Walter had ceased. Now the truth about Walter and her was known, she clearly understood any feelings and yearnings she'd had merely represented an unbreakable bond between twin brother and sister. However, she was still tortured by the thought of what might have happened between them back in Sheffield. Her heart sank remembering the event; but she had learnt to rationalise it, and now longed to see Walter again simply to talk to him and embrace him as a brother. Only then could she finally rest.

As for Tom, her thoughts of him continued to bring her great sadness. Only now did she realise that he was the lover she was truly destined to find.

~~~

It came as no real surprise to Tom when he got the phone call from Dr Jefferies, the Chair of the Hospital Board of Governors, requesting a meeting in his office. 'Just a quick informal chat, you understand,' he'd said; but Tom wasn't naive enough to believe that for one moment. He knew it was about his drink problem, and that it was justified, because this was something that could have serious implications for him, his patients and the hospital.

Since Mary had left, his drink problem had in actual

fact increased to become a bottle of whisky a day. It was killing him, but he didn't seem to care. When something or someone breaks your heart, all common sense and medical knowledge can go out of the window, and from Tom's window, it was a long drop.

'You must realise, Tom, that the Board…and I have concerns, though this is not without due appreciation of your…well, personal circumstances,' stated Dr Jefferies, in his usual ingratiating, shallow way, as he strutted around the large austere office.

Tom sat in the high backed leather chair, playing the attentive schoolboy awaiting his reprimand and wishing the so-called 'learned' Jefferies would get to the point. For the last five minutes he'd played the game, but his body language now suggested he wouldn't suffer much more pussy-footing around.

'You see, when one has a crisis in a relationship, such as you do…,' continued Jefferies.

It was the final straw! Tom certainly had no intention of being preached to about the ebbs and flows of a relationship.

'When exactly do you intend to come to the point, Mr Jefferies?' interrupted Tom, in an abrupt, condescending tone.

He'd learnt by observing Robert Elliott that, in order to bring matters to a quick conclusion, a spade should be called a spade. Jefferies was shocked by Tom's forthright manner, which clearly ruffled his plumage.

'Very well, Tom. It's about your problem with drink,' he said.

'My only problem with drink, Mr Jefferies, is that I'm consuming too much of it – a bottle a day to be precise. I'm bordering on being an alcoholic and, if I carry on, I should say I have six months, perhaps a year.'

Jefferies' eyes opened wide, as if Martians had just landed. 'Yes, quite,' he finally declared in astonishment.

'If I can be so bold, I'll make the conversation a little easier for you,' said Tom, pragmatically. 'As I see it, there are currently two options: I resign or you dismiss me.'

'Well, I wouldn't have been quite as blunt, but seeing as you have…'

'Facts are stubborn things,' Tom replied. Elliott would have been proud of him.

'There may be a third option,' said Jefferies.

'Carry on.'

'It is only a suggestion, you understand.'

This suggestion, however, was more for Jefferies's benefit, because he knew that if St. Thomas's were seen to be releasing surgeons to operate on soldiers in the field, then his credibility with the Board, and therefore his future career prospects, would be so much the better.

'The Board has been asked if they could second surgeons

to the cause in the field…in a purely civilian capacity, of course,' explained Jefferies.

'For how long?'

'Probably six months. It would give you time to sort out your troubles,' Jefferies said, as if the war would become his magic wand, '…and I'm sure they would accept one's slight fall from grace!'

Tom lifted his eyes up to meet Jefferies's. 'Of that, one has no doubt,' he retorted with derision.

As they parted, Tom was given a card with the telephone number of a Captain Stewart, lead surgeon in the Fifteenth Hampshires.

'Your choice…but don't leave it too long to decide, there's a good chap,' Jefferies concluded and gave Tom a gentle and belittling pat on the shoulder.

Tom spent that afternoon propping up the bar in the Dickens public house. The afternoon led into the evening, and by 10 o'clock he was slumped in a corner seat, incoherent and not a good proposition for the landlord's guests arriving from the theatre.

'Come on then, Tom, let's be having you on your way,' the landlord called and helped a thoroughly drunk Tom to the door. 'Goodnight, fella.'

Tom stumbled out of the door and bounced against the tiled wall of the little entrance lobby. He tried to say goodnight, but his tongue struggled to get round the word and he sounded like a gurgling baby. Aiming himself down the street, he eventually staggered off, only to stop at a lamppost to which he made a proposal of marriage! The once fine figure of a man now looked exactly like the caricature of a drunken, drooling fool on the advertising hording ahead of him. It was only a matter of time before he met trouble.

'Got a match, 'ave yer, Guv?' said the voice.

Tom stood and fumbled in every pocket before, suddenly, being pushed forward and dragged into a side alley. He didn't really feel the pain of the punches, just a stinging sensation. Within two minutes, he had been beaten and robbed. Rather than try to get up, he decided it was easier to just roll over and close his eyes.

The following morning he awoke to the noise coming from the bustling street and it dawned on him what must have happened. He looked at his wrist for the time but, of course, the watch was gone. It was the thing he treasured most dearly and was a wedding gift from Mary. At the street he looked at his reflection in a shop window and realised he had hit rock bottom.

When he was finally safe back in his house, he took the card off the table and picked up the phone. He looked down at a photo of Mary and himself. It looked so wrong now she wasn't here any more.

'Is that Captain Stewart? Yes, hello, my name is Tom Sharpe...'

CHAPTER 24

FIELD DUTIES

The thing Mary would always remember of the desert, for all of her days, was not the trauma and horrific injuries: she'd seen all that before. It wasn't even the horrendous conditions they had to work in. It was the stifling Arabian heat that never seemed to relent until nightfall when, conversely, the cold was almost as unbearable.

It was nearly two months since she had arrived at the hospital transfer unit, which had been set up in a little village on the road to Baghdad. Here, the wounded from the battle fields could be operated on before the arduous journey back to Aden and then, if they were lucky, home to England. Mary was relieved when the new sister and her volunteer nurses had arrived, for once she got them fully conversant with the unit, she hoped to return to Aden, where at least there were fans! She didn't envy the new girls, but they seemed to have quite a bullish attitude, and they soon adapted.

The one exception was a young girl, Emma Tully, who had volunteered at just eighteen, and was like a rabbit caught in headlights. Mary made Emma stick to her like glue, until she could finally manage a day without shaking and could dress a wound without vomiting. It could have been a long haul, but the girl tried hard and learned quite quickly.

'This is where we'll be tonight, Miss Tully,' Mary said.

It was the receiving area for admissions and was full of bodies lying on stretchers, most of them badly injured and near death. The scorching heat only added to their misery. Miss Tully's face went white as she looked around. A comforting arm from Mary made her slightly more relaxed.

'I'm sorry, my dear, but there is no easy way to prepare you. We just have to deal with it,' Mary had to say.

'It's just…well, all these poor men with such appalling injuries…I've never seen such horrors before,' the worried Miss Tully replied.

Mary took hold of her hand and squeezed it tightly, 'I know. Just keep telling yourself you're making a difference, and you will.'

Miss Tully took a look at a soldier, lying on a stretcher, badly wounded. 'Doesn't he need surgery?' she asked in innocence.

'Sadly, most of them do, my dear. The trick is telling who needs to be dealt with first, to sort out the nearly dying from the dying.'

Miss Tully looked so afraid, as Mary walked her on to a corner unoccupied by bodies.

'Don't worry, I'll be with you. It's our job to send them through in order of urgency.'

'But how will I know?'

'Instinct and experience, dear. You get to know how they feel to your hand.'

'Feel to my hand?' replied the confused trainee.

'That's right. You see most of the fighting is done at night and, as you know, the nights here are so dreadfully cold.'

'I am sorry, Sister, but I don't really follow!'

'You will, you will. It's all about telling one kind of cold from another – to know the difference between what is just bitter cold and what is the coldness of death.'

Miss Tully's face took on a forlorn look; but three days later she was organising the men unaided, and with ruthless efficiency.

Mary was attending the receiving area one morning, thankful there weren't any casualties yet, when two soldiers brought in a body on a stretcher.

'One 'ere for you, luv… Where do you want 'im?' said the stretcher bearer, as if handling a sack of potatoes. To him, transporting the sick was just a job that someone had to do.

Just then, Major Forbes appeared, up to his armpits in blood and, on seeing the new patient, vented his frustration. 'Oh! Bloody hell, not another! I thought it was too good to be true!' Walking across to have a quick look, he saw the unconscious man was dressed in a kaftan and assumed he was an Arab. 'Who the hell is this?'

'Dunno, sir. Lieutenant Heaton just said to bring 'im in,' commented the bearer.

'Did he indeed,' said Forbes. 'Well, Lieutenant Heaton should know better. We are full to breaking with our own. We can't take in Arab wounded as well.'

'Shall we just dump 'im, then, sir?' the bearer asked, quite seriously.

Mary was appalled by his callousness. 'No, you won't just dump him, soldier. We may be at breaking point but in God's name we are still human.'

Forbes let out a sigh. 'Sister's right, take him through,' and he grimaced at the smell as the patient was stretchered past him to the operating-room and laid on a table. The patient waiting for attention was, of course, Walter, whom Lieutenant Heaton had recognised as the beggar spy when they overran the camp. Mercifully, he had given orders that Walter should be treated.

'Good God, what a mess!' proclaimed Forbes as he took a closer look at the beleaguered body. 'Aah, well, scissors then please, Sister,' he announced.

Mary brought across a tray of instruments and watched as the Major cut through the blood and pus-stained kaftan. Finally, Walter's torso was exposed.

'Jesus Christ!' Forbes uttered, seeing all the burns. He lifted up Walter's hand and looked at the torn-out fingernails. 'The poor man's been tortured. Right, iodine please.'

There wasn't a response from Mary.

'Can I have some iodine please, Sister!' Forbes insisted with increased volume. As there was still no answer from Mary, he turned around to look at her.

Mary was staring intently at Walter: not at his burns, but at the chain and locket around his neck. She went to lift it up and started hysterically screaming at him, 'Where did you get this locket? Tell me! Tell me!' She began to weep. 'Did you take it from an Englishman?' Again, she started to scream, 'Do you understand English? Tell me, do you hear, where did you get it?'

Forbes was astonished and started to pull her away, 'Sister Sharpe, what in heaven's name do you think you're doing?'

Through all the blood and burns Mary suddenly recognised Walter's scar from his operation in Sheffield years earlier. She finally realised that the man in front of her was actually Walter. The man she had come half way around the world to find was suddenly lying before her, at death's door. Her stomach churned with a horrible sensation: this was not how she'd painted the picture of their next meeting; that was supposed to be somewhere lovely and bright, in springtime, with him giving her that mischievous smile. Her colourful painting suddenly turned to black and white.

She promptly fainted and fell into the arms of Forbes. With her dead weight, it took him all his strength to drag her to a chair. As she slumped, he called out 'Nurse! Nurse!' until finally Miss Tully arrived.

'What is it, Major Forbes?' she panted and looked over to see Sister on the chair. 'Oh dear! Is everything alright, sir?'

'She just passed out, that's all. Hold her steady,' he instructed and went to get some smelling salts. 'Here, keep wafting them under her nose while I deal with this.'

After a final look at Walter, Forbes concluded nothing more could be done without operating and he called the bearers to take him out into the receiving area. Forbes was washing his arms in the sink when, eventually, Mary started to stir and opened her eyes. It took a moment to recall where she was. Miss Tully fanned cooler air into her face.

'Are you alright, Sister?' asked Forbes.

'Where is he?' Mary enquired in alarm, looking over to the operating table.

'There isn't a deal I can do. He has a severe infection and advanced gangrene in his arm. At the very least he would need amputation,' explained Forbes.

'Then you must operate!'

'Sister, we have barely enough anaesthetic to last the week. Besides he most likely wouldn't survive the operation anyhow.'

'No, sir, you don't understand. You must operate.'

Forbes gave her a look of indifference. He cared little for what she thought and proceeded towards the door.

'No, no, Major,' she said, blocking the door. 'You really don't understand.'

'Sister, get out of my way!' he snorted with some authority.

Mary grabbed a scalpel from a tray and held it firmly to her wrist, her eyes wide open in anticipation of what she was prepared to do. Miss Tully's jaw dropped in sheer amazement. She couldn't believe she was looking at the same person who, only ten minutes earlier, had been a model of calmness and gentility. Forbes was equally shocked but managed to maintain the look of a man in control.

'Please, Sister Sharpe, put down the knife,' he said and moved forward a pace, fully expecting she would immediately drop it, like some obedient dog.

'As God is my witness, I will do it, Major. If you refuse to operate, I will do it.'

He took a pace back, realising she was deadly serious.

'You know the rules, Sister…we can't…'

'Will you operate?' she interrupted with a shout, bracing the scalpel ever harder to her wrist.

'Whatever is it about the man? What is he to you? And why on earth are you so desperate to save him?'

Mary stood with tears in her eyes, her face full of distress. With a sigh of hopelessness, she cried, 'Because he's my brother!'

Forbes was expecting any answer but that and could only repeat her words in utter amazement. 'Your brother?'

'Yes, my brother, Major Forbes, and I beg of you to try and save him…please!'

He let out an almighty sigh, thought for a second, and then shrugged his shoulders. 'Very well,' he finally declared, '…but please, first the scalpel,' and held out his palm. She gently took it away from her wrist and handed it over.

'Nurse, go and get the bearers to bring him back in,' he said to Miss Tully, who was still transfixed, never before having been in a situation of such tense drama.

'Thank you, sir,' Mary wept.

With Walter anaesthetised, Forbes was less than optimistic for his patient. 'I have to warn you the chances of him surviving an amputation are almost nil.'

Mary simply said with a smile, 'Oh! He'll survive, sir. He always does.'

With that, the Major cut through the flesh to expose the bone and carefully positioned the saw.

~~~

With the trauma of his injuries, and after the major surgery of an amputation, Walter's body all but shut down and he began to develop a high fever. It was days before he finally stopped drifting into unconsciousness.

All the while Mary nursed and cared for him in any spare moment she had, cradling him late into the night as he thrashed about in delirium. At long last, though, he did pull through and one morning he heard voices, loud then soft. He recognised the Irish lilt, now firmly etched into his subconscious, the one that reassured him everything was going to be all right. His eyes opened but the room was blurred and it took him all his effort to watch a silhouette as it moved by. He slurred some words until, in the end, he could shout, 'Mary!'

But he had only imagined it to be her, as a young nurse came over to him. 'Hello, sir,' she said.

His eyes slowly came back into focus. 'I'm sorry, I thought you were…,' Walter muttered and looked around the room. 'Where am I?'

She wiped his brow. 'Don't worry, you're safe in a field hospital. Just rest. I'll get you some water.'

Walter's head, the only part of him that didn't feel battered, bruised or numb, fell back onto the pillow. He then remembered his torture and lifted his right hand to look at his fingers, now heavily dressed. With his left hand, he went to touch them, but only a bandaged stump moved to meet it. In horror, his eyes opened wide.

'My arm! Where the hell? Who gave permission to cut off my ruddy arm?' he demanded to know.

'I did,' came the answer, in a soft Irish tone. With a

broad smile across her face, she greeted him: 'Hello, Walter Stanford!'

He took a moment to take it all in, then gave her a big grin. 'Well, I'll be. Mary! It is you?'

'Yes, it's me, Walter. It's me,' she replied and moved gently to kiss him on his cheek. Tears of joy rolled down her face as two years' worth of emotion poured through her body and she held him as tight as she dared, with all his injuries.

'Oh! Walter…you've no idea how much…,' she spoke softly but never finished, as the lump again entered her throat.

Walter was slightly overawed by everything and did not quite understand the intense out-pouring of elation from Mary. He remained dazed and wondered whether all this was happening or if it was just a cruel trick of his mind. Looking at her elated face, as she cried and laughed in equal measure, he felt humbled by her joy but couldn't even offer a hand in appreciation. Instead, all he had was that smile of his, so charming and magnetic, that made her reach out to stroke his face.

'I can't honestly believe this! How are you, Mary?'

'I'm fine…just fine,' she beamed back.

Walter looked down at his stump and his bandaged body and said, 'I wish I could say the same.'

'You're alive and that's all that matters,' she replied, cradling his face with her palm once more.

'Yes, I suppose there is that!' he agreed, and leant into her hand to laugh. 'Mary O'Driscoll...my angel nurse. Who'd ever have thought it?' Finally, he laid his head back down.

'Well, not exactly Mary O'Driscoll any more...but that story can wait. Right now you need to rest,' she said, then straightened his sheets and gave him another kiss on the cheek. 'It's so good to see you again, Walter,' she continued, staring into his dark eyes.

'You will tell me, before you take any more limbs off, Mary,' he joked as she began to walk away.

The next fortnight, as Walter recovered, was sheer delight for Mary and just like old times back in Sheffield. At any opportunity, she would check on him and, when off duty, would quietly sit and listen as he described his beloved Iza, his children and the plantation. She was amazed at just how accurate all her visions and dreams had been. All she'd visualised was eerily real; but now the significance of it all was at last understood. She felt the love in Walter's voice for his family and the heartache it brought him to have been parted from them for what had now been over six months.

'I do so love Iza, Mary, but she doesn't mince her words. I dare say I'll get an ear bashing for losing this,' he said, lifting his stump.

'I'm sure not,' she replied, imagining how wonderful it would be for him to hold and cherish his wife again. How she longed for the same with Tom, but alas, that was not going to be. She thought of him and wondered how he was doing.

In truth, Tom was doing just fine and, like her, was sometimes working around the clock, saving and mending the many courageous men who needed his skills. In the three months he'd been in France, he had all but conquered the demon drink, and was slowly accepting his life without Mary. He loved to do what he did best – be a surgeon, without the politics and the rigidity of process of a hospital board. Here, he was free to take chances to save a life and wondered whether he should enlist for regular service.

All the time that Mary sat with Walter, she wanted to tell him, to break the news of them being brother and sister, but she forced herself to hold back until she felt he was strong enough. Besides which, she wanted to be somewhere tranquil, like the walled garden at the back of the hospital. Here, she imagined they could gently stroll and sit under the palm tree to chat openly.

She had played the scene over and over in her head but, somehow, nothing quite sounded right and she worried just how Walter would react. In her moments of reflection in her room, she took hold of her locket and twisted it round endlessly, in nervousness. Eventually, she decided that the time was right and that, on her next afternoon off, she would walk him through the garden and break her news. However, as always in their lives, fate was to show its hand and affect the outcome.

That morning had been tremendously busy and the hospital had taken in over twenty badly wounded soldiers from the battle zone. As usual, Mary was in the thick of things, trying to keep order in the utter chaos of the receiving room. Miss Tully was doing a stalwart job but struggled as the bodies just kept coming in.

'Over there, please, soldiers,' Mary said to the stretcher bearers bringing in a poor young fusilier, his leg blown clean off in a shell attack. He screamed and cried so much in pain.

'Nurse…fetch me some morphine, please,' she called out and bent down to try to reassure the petrified boy, who was no more than eighteen, but had the face of a thirteen-year-old. 'I'm getting you something for the pain, as quickly as I can,' she said.

'Oh! Dear God, help me, help me!' was all he could shout out until, finally, the needle arrived with the nurse.

'I need you to sit up slightly if you can. Nurse, help me please.'

Both women put his arms around their shoulders and lifted him. Finally, Mary was able to sink the needle into what was left of his leg and push hard on the plunger. As the drug took effect, he rolled his eyes and slumped, dragging his arm around Mary's neck. She didn't notice her chain snap and her locket drop to the ground. In all the subsequent shuffling, it was knocked to the side of the boy, now docile under the effect of morphine.

'Sister Sharpe,' called out Major Forbes from the operating room. 'Can I borrow you for a moment?'

On her return, she saw the nurse holding the limp body and realised the poor lad had not made it. She felt his pulse to confirm this.

'I know it's hard but at least he had a hand to hold before he passed over. Well done, Nurse,' Mary said, to comfort the distressed girl.

'What do I do with his belongings, Sister?'

'Miss Tully will give you an envelope and show you, dear.'

By afternoon things had calmed down enough for Mary to take a few moments for herself in the sink room. She was splashing her face with water when Walter appeared and took her totally by surprise.

'This heat, does it ever relent?' she cursed to herself.

'This is nothing,' said his voice.

She spun around to see him standing there and clasped at her racing heart. 'Dear Lord! Walter, it's you,' she panted in shock. 'Is it your aim in life to always surprise me?' she jested.

He gave her his usual smile of innocence. 'A few months more, then it gets hot!'

'No, please don't tell me that,' she said, drying her face.

'A busy morning, by all accounts,' he observed.

'Yes, that's one way to describe it,' and she put her arm through his. 'Come, let's walk a while and talk.'

Off they strolled through the little garden, lovingly tended by the staff to give the recuperating soldiers a sense of home. Mary stopped along the pathway to take in the array of colourful plants, all giving off a gorgeous smell.

'Well, I have to say you look much, much better. Another week or so and you'll be good as new. Then we can get you back to Aden. You will let me visit you on this plantation of yours. I do so want to see it.'

'Of course. You can be Auntie Mary,' he suggested in jest.

She smiled at the irony of his comment and thought how she could lead into breaking her news. But she needn't have worried, for Walter would do it for her.

'Mary, I do appreciate all you've done…not just here but also in the past.'

'I only did what I would for any man.'

'Not a brother then?'

His words stunned her and her face showed it.

'Mary, I may have only one arm, a body riddled with burns and heavens knows what, but I can assure you there is nothing wrong with my hearing.' Although there certainly should have been, with all he'd had to endure at the hands of Major Koln.

She looked at him with confusion.

'It's common talk. I'm not meant to hear it but I do. "That's Sister Mary's brother," they say. A master stroke, but one you needn't have ventured to invent just to get me treatment.'

'Walter, let's sit under the palm. I have things I have to tell you.'

In the shade, she sat and tried to explain.

'The nurses…they were…well they, the nurses that is…,' she babbled until Walter interrupted.

'Mary, you're not making a deal of sense.'

'The nurses, Walter, they aren't wrong. What you hear is right.' She took a deep breath, 'You are my brother! We are brother and sister.'

Walter let out the heartiest laugh. 'I beg your pardon,' he gasped with incredulity.

'It is true!' she implored.

'What do you mean, "It is true!" Don't be ridiculous, how can it be? I think this heat has affected you, Mary.'

She steeled herself as he got up.

'What do you know about your mother, Walter?'

He turned to her, puzzled. 'I don't know what game this is, but I'm finding it quite disturbing.'

'Tell me,' she insisted.

'I haven't seen or contacted my mother since leaving England. I don't even know if she's still alive; a fact no son should be proud of, least of all me. There, are you happy now?' he hissed.

Mary braced herself for the reaction to what she would say next. 'I mean your real mother, Walter.'

'This is ludicrous! I can't believe we're talking like this,' he said and began to walk off.

But Mary was fired up to breaking point. She would have her say, make him realise she was telling the truth. She wasn't going to be rebuffed as a stupid woman, and she stood in his path.

'Your real mother. You never knew her, did you?'

'Oh please, Mary,' he snorted.

'…because just like me, you were adopted; only I was sent to Ireland and you stayed in Sheffield.'

Walter finally stood still and volleyed back his response. 'All right! So we were both adopted. That hardly makes us brother and sister.'

Mary started to explain Elliott's discovery until Walter stopped her, 'No, Mary, I refuse to listen to any more of this nonsense. I know my real sister died as a baby.'

'That's what you were told by Canon Brockwell. But it was all lies to disguise the truth of our past. Oh, Walter, look at us. Why can't we tear ourselves apart? Because we have a deep yearning to be part of each other's lives – like twins. We have to be together, Walter, as brother and sister. We're soul mates.'

'Are you mad? If, and only if, I was your brother, have you forgotten what happened that night in your rooms?'

Mary bowed her head. Finally, her torture was over. She had confirmation that it did actually happen. 'So, we did make love?'

'Yes, Mary, we did make love. I'm sorry it was so memorable,' he snarled. 'I won't accept your findings, Mary. Incest is for the sick of mind, and whatever vices God has given me, incest is not one of them.'

She grabbed hold of his arm and pleaded, 'No Walter. Listen! As vulgar as it is, can't you see that it was just confusion in our feelings, just like all the years I've dreamt so vividly of you. It's all been mistaken feelings. That night, we unearthed emotions we mistook for physical need! Yes, it was wrong, of course it was wrong, and something we will always regret. But we simply didn't understand because we didn't know of our past. God will forgive us, Walter.'

'You're right, Mary. It is vulgar. The whole sordid notion is very vulgar! What is it you're after? Am I now to learn that not only am I your brother, but also the father of a child born of that night?'

She looked at him with deep hurt. 'You beast! You horrible beast! How dare you think of me that way!'

'I don't know what to think anymore,' Walter simply replied.

'Perhaps this will convince you…,' she said and felt for her chain and locket. Instead, all she could feel was her crucifix. 'Oh no! My locket, it's gone.'

Walter watched her fumble around her neck in a blind panic. 'This locket… It wouldn't be the other half of mine, by chance?' he said, with so much sarcasm it should have burnt his mouth.

'Walter, you have to believe me! Every word I've said is the truth,' she pleaded, watching him walk away. 'No, please, Walter, don't leave.'

'Mary, I am truly flattered by your infatuation, but to fabricate such a story is hardly endearing.'

Tears rolled down her face as she realised, without the locket, her agony would now only continue.

That night she tried to retrace her every move that day, thinking where she had last had it. She remembered having it after washing in the morning, and the only place she had been since, apart from the sink room, was the receiving area and operating theatre. There was nothing to be found near the sink, so she followed her footsteps back into the hospital, looking at every bit of an object with fervour. In the receiving room, she got on her hands and knees and scoured every inch of the place. After two hours of searching in vain, she finally dropped against the wall and sobbed her heart out in despair.

'Whatever is the matter, Sister? called the young nurse who had helped her earlier in the day.

'Oh, ignore me, I'm just a silly woman looking for something.'

'I could help you look, if you'd like?'

'Bless you, dear, but I've searched everywhere.'

'Well, as my mother always says, "two pairs of eyes are better than one", the nurse replied optimistically, and she got down on her hands and knees. 'What exactly are we looking for, Sister?'

Mary had to smile at her helpful endeavours. 'It's my chain and locket… Well, half a locket actually.'

'Oh!' replied the nurse with hesitation. 'I'm afraid I might be at fault then, Sister. I'm so sorry but, you see when I saw it, I thought it must have belonged to that boy that died, so I put it in the envelope, just like Miss Tully instructed me.'

Mary felt all the tension suddenly lift off her shoulders and her heart skipped a beat. She sighed with relief. 'My dear girl, please don't apologise – if only you knew!'

It was with trepidation she went to the ward, her locket clasped firmly in her hand, to see Walter. However, when she arrived, she found he wasn't in his bed.

'Nurse, where is Mr Stanford?' she enquired.

'I don't know, Sister, I haven't seen him since this morning.'

Her heart sank once more, as she looked to the floor to see his spare set of sandals were gone.

CHAPTER 25

A STRANGE PARCEL

Lily, the maid, brought in the rather battered paper parcel and announced, 'A parcel for you, Mr Elliott.'

'Oh thank you, Lily. Leave it on the table please.'

'Another parcel, dear?' quizzed Ann. 'I dare say we'll soon have enough to start our own little sorting office!'

What Ann referred to were the many letters and packages her husband received from the grateful men he'd helped who were now serving overseas in the forces. It seemed strange to her that, when faced with life away from home, these men had an urge to send him all manner of things in which he was not the least bit interested. Still, she knew he was grateful to be remembered.

'I do hope it's not anything like those dreadful beetles or worse, spiders! Where do they get the notion you know about such things?' Ann remarked, interrupting the reading of her book.

Elliott couldn't help but agree and went to investigate

the postman's latest offering. Neither the writing on the label nor the postmark revealed much, the latter being heavily smudged. Opening it up, he found a collection of coarse grasses surrounding a single stalk of a dried orchid. It was most strange and could hardly be described as an attractive flower arrangement.

'Shall I fetch a vase, Mrs Elliott?' Lily enquired.

'I fear not,' Ann replied, peering over her glasses at the assortment of grasses now spilt over the table. 'What on earth is it, Robert?'

'I'm not altogether sure,' commented Elliott, while taking a closer look at the leaf, which, instead of holding a flower, contained dozens of fragments of paper rolled into pellets. He took some of them out and began smoothing them flat. 'It appears to be writings, a letter of sorts!'

Ann took a quick look and, unimpressed, went back to reading her book. 'I'm sure it will keep you amused for a while,' she said and, looking across to Lily, gave her a wink.

And keep him amused it did. After half an hour, he was totally engrossed trying to put the little pieces into some sort of order. Finally, he rolled out another yellowish pellet and stood in amazement as he read what was the start of the letter. He recognised the poetic style in an instant.

'*Mr Elliott,*

'*Somewhere in blessed Mesopotamia, a poor deaf mute has wandered and experienced so much that it enables him to send his writings in a puzzle. He is a slender, swarthy and agile Bedouin about my age and so like me that, but for the clothing, I could own him as my brother.*

'*I have often wished to write to you, sir, just to let you know I am doing my bit for Britain, under this scorching sun...*'

'Well, I'll be! If it's not from Walter,' Elliott shouted out, making Ann nearly jump out of her skin. He should have known from the very start that only Walter, with all his eccentricity, would go to the trouble to send a note in such a way. The fact that the lad had still got his sense of humour, as strange as that sometimes was, made him smile. He could easily imagine Walter tearing up each little piece and laughing in mischievousness, wondering if his joke would be understood.

It would take the rest of the evening and into the early hours before he finally had all the pieces in the right place, so that he could make out Walter's letter in its entirety. But Ann wasn't there to see his triumph; she'd long since left her husband to his jigsaw of torn bits of paper.

'Please make sure it all gets cleaned away, dear,' she'd said, more in hope than in certainty.

Elliott sat back. At last, he could read through Walter's writings in a logical manner. It was an account of his time spent since jumping ship, and written at various stages during his journey home from the field hospital, a journey that proved most gruelling and took him four weeks to achieve. Finally, he had made it to the River Tigris and, ultimately, found passage back to Basra and then onward to Aden, though, to add to his bodily misery, he was now stricken with dysentery. Perhaps his own words best describe his homecoming:

'July 20

'There I stand and look up to my little place, glistening in the morning sun. It has been a long, long time. I fall to my knees, the emotion so great to see my bairns running around screaming at each other. Suddenly, they stop. Who is this strange, one-armed man, tearfully watching them? They run inside to fetch their mother, who begrudgingly comes out to see what all the fuss is about.

'How sweet the sight: my splendid Arab wife, as lovely a face as I ever looked upon, her astonished look to find her love is still alive and then the wondrous smile of joy as I walk to greet her, the man she thought had been sacrificed to this vengeful business of war, a war she wishes not to comprehend. It is me, my love, the father taken from his bairns at such a tender age that they now don't

know who he is. We don't speak, only let our lips gently press together. I close my eyes. Finally, I am home!'

'August 5

'This cursed dysentery has redoubled in its severity. At times, I'm as weak as a kitten. But for the attention of my beloved Iza and the bairns, I surely would not see many more days. If only you could see my family, Mr Elliott. No man, for certain, could be luckier to be blessed with wife and mother full of goodness and of such kind heart. And how fortunate is this fellow to hear the music of his children's voices once more. Nestling darling heads with sweetest lips breathing into one's ears the magic word "Father".

'There is also another from my circle I have to contact. Another, I fear, I have treated very ill, and who must now surely only consider me with bitter disappointment. How utterly stupid of me to immediately discount her findings, thinking them only lies and wickedness! You remember Nurse Mary, sir? That Irish gem who saved my life in that prison cell and, again, in that brawl. Well, by chance we met again a few months ago. An angel nurse once more tending my wounds, as I lay clutching onto life in an army hospital. She did all she could to steer me to recovery – like a mother to her child or sister to a brother. Then, how incredible her notion – she my sister, we to be *from the same flesh and blood! But of course, you know that only too well, Mr Elliott.*

'Oh, how I fought her notion! But illness makes a man see that denial is not a virtue, only an excuse for his flaws. Now I see that all she told me adds up so perfectly. If only I had known the tale before venturing to this promised land.

'I have much more to inform you of, sir but, alas, paper is short so I will write again when father-in-law returns with supplies.'

'August 9.
'Utterly prostrate. I write lying on the ground. Wife and father-in-law plead with me to seek medical help at an army hospital in Aden. But it's easily thirty miles, and I fear God will not spare me such a journey. However, I have no more strength to argue and no desire to see my wife and bairns in distress, so will be docile.

'Thank you for many a kindness, Mr Elliott. Good-bye. Father-in-law may get what I have written through, somehow'.

Elliott, for the first time since the loss of his daughter, felt a tear slowly trickle down his cheek and all for a man in whose company he'd not spent more than a few days in total.

~~~

After her three months in the field, Mary returned to the hospital in Aden in sombre mood. Her hurt over Walter had turned to anger, then to tears, and, finally, to an increasingly desperate feeling that they would probably never meet again. She didn't even know if he was alive. In her final analysis, she had to be content with the thought that, if he were dead, then at least he had died having been told the truth about them and somewhere deep down having accepted it.

All she did know for certain was that she couldn't return to England without attempting to find him or gain news of his situation. Now, at least, she had some detailed information about his home village of Zinjibar, some miles east of Aden. Hopefully, this would make the task a little easier; and fate found her a friend willing to help in the form of the new Hospital Chaplain. With some knowledge of the area, he had agreed to make enquiries with his contacts and soon brought her news that Walter's plantation was indeed just north of the village and he and his family were well known there. More important was the fact that Walter had been seen in the village very recently. It was the best news Mary could have hoped for, and she positively overflowed with excitement at the prospect of seeing him once more. The following Sunday it was arranged that the Chaplain would drive her to Walter's plantation. However, their journey was to prove unnecessary.

Nurses often assisted in the collection of supplies from the docks and it was usual for the truck to be besieged at the gates by dozens of native Arabs: a pitiful sight to see, as the men, women and children begged for medical attention, and one that the nurses had to become hardened to. Driving through the gates, one needed nerves of steel and particularly today, when the truck had decided to give up the ghost short of the gates, so they had to walk through the crowds.

'No, we don't have enough medicine,' cried a nurse, as a baby was thrust in her arms.

'I'm sorry I can't help!' shouted another. 'No, please don't touch me!'

'English,' exclaimed a little Arab woman to a nurse.

'What?' replied the harassed nurse.

'English?'

'Of course I'm English.'

'Please, to man of English,' begged the woman and pointed to Walter.

'No, we can't. And it's Englishman, not man of English!' rebuked the nurse with condescension.

The woman grabbed hold of the nurse's arm.

'Take your filthy hands off me! I've told you we can't help. Do you hear, we can't help!' the nurse screamed hysterically.

'Whatever is the matter?' asked Mary, trying to calm her down.

'This…this woman wants help for that man. I've told her no, but she won't listen.'

'Please to English – man?' pleaded the woman, this time to Mary.

The woman pointed to a man hanging over a horse; beside him, an elderly man held two bemused young children by the hand.

'We can't help, I'm so sorry,' said Mary and turned away.

'Please to Walter!'

That final word caused her to stop in her tracks. She turned around to look again at the man lying over the horse. It dawned on her who it must be and she raced over. She picked up Walter's head and cried out, 'Mercy God, nooooo!'

The other nurses were stunned as she called out, 'Quickly, help me! We have to get him inside.'

'Sister, what are you doing? You know we can't help them,' a nurse shouted and watched in amazement as Mary helped Macca to lift Walter from the horse.

'Sister, no! Please stop.'

'Just do as I say and damned well help me,' snarled Mary, with every ounce of assertiveness she could muster.

Finally, Walter was carried through the gates and onwards to a small annexe room where he was laid out on the floor. His family were beckoned in. Iza stood traumatised, as Mary shouted at her, 'Why didn't you bring him in earlier? You should have brought him in earlier.'

Of course, Iza didn't understand a word and just stared at her. Mary felt so guilty and went over. 'I'm sorry, I didn't mean to…,' she said and held out her hand but Iza pulled away.

'You must be Iza? Please, don't think me unkind. We will do all we can. Do you understand me?'

It was only when her father, Macca, spoke and interpreted Mary's question that Iza gave her a faint yet trusting smile and offered her hand. Mary took hold of it.

'You understand English?' she asked Macca.

'A little.'

She looked over to Walter. 'What happened to him?'

'Much worse in dysentery,' he answered in pigeon English.

Mary bent down, 'Oh dear God, Walter, I cannot bear this.'

'He live?' said Macca.

She stared at her brother, now only a shadow of his former self, and pushed back his hair, then looked up to give Macca a sweet smile. He knew the answer.

Mary gestured to the children to come over to her but they wouldn't move and held steadfastly onto their mother.

'Will they help me?' she looked at Macca and asked.

As Macca spoke to them, they shook their little heads and clung more tightly to their mother. No amount of encouragement from Mary would get them to come close to her, that is until she started to mop their father's brow, when a tiny hand was suddenly placed over hers and began to help her gently wipe his forehead. She pulled away and let the boy continue alone. Walter stirred, knowing his son was close to him. Before long, the little daughter was dragging her mother towards him. Iza knelt down, wrung out a cloth in a bowl and gave it to her little girl so she could join her brother soothing their father's discomfort.

Walter tugged at his wife's arm and beckoned her close to his lips.

'Beloved, my lord awaits me now... One day we shall whisper together again,' he struggled to say in her ear.

With every bit of strength he had left, he then beckoned Mary to his side. She gazed into his dark eyes, which even near death could still tell a story of mischief.

'My sweet sister,' he managed to say and struggled to lift up his locket from around his neck. Mary guided his hand and then took off her locket and pressed it together with his.

'Forgive me!' he muttered.

A tear from her cheek fell onto his lips. She touched it and wept, as Walter slowly closed his eyes for the final time.

'Dream of me always, my dear brother, in that place far away from here,' she murmured.

CHAPTER 26

Remembered With Affection

Water lapped gently at the ship's side as it pulled away from its mooring and, to the sound of the horn, came loud cheering and shouts of farewell from the dockside. Mary turned away from the rail and sought a quiet corner of the deck. She stood and watched as the sun broke over the bow, bathing her in a warm glow. The breeze caught her face and, closing her eyes, she leant her head back. It was final closure to a chapter of her life she would truly never forget. There wasn't much Mary would miss about this land; but as she opened her eyes again, she couldn't help but marvel at the glorious red sun hovering just above the horizon. A shaft of intense light cut a perfect line across the sea to the shoreline, where the dark buildings would soon burst into life and bask in the brightness.

'Soon be home now, miss,' said a passing soldier.

'Indeed,' smiled Mary, not really sure where home was to be. Should she settle again in London? Or maybe move somewhere different? Perhaps even go back to Ireland, for after all she had no ties to speak of. In the end, it was Ann Elliott's letter, received just before she left, that convinced her to spend a little time with her and Robert back in Sheffield, at least until she had found her feet once more.

Mary had written as often as she could to the Elliotts during her stay in Aden, always apologising for her uncharacteristic behaviour months earlier and describing all of the adventures she had encountered. Of course, there was still the news to break of Walter's death, which she knew Robert would take with heavy heart. As she wasn't aware of Walter's letters to him, she wouldn't know that Elliott was expecting the worst.

It was Ann's idea to surprise Mary at Southampton and give her a precious hug as she disembarked from the ship. Apart from love, there can be no better feeling than true friendship, and how lovely for that friend to travel over two hundred miles to greet her. Mary fanned her hands in front of her face with sheer joy and emotion, trying to catch her breath, when Ann suddenly appeared in front of her and said, 'Do you need a taxi, miss?'

On the long train journey back north, Mary described Walter's final hour to Elliott, who showed his sympathy with a gentle embrace and spent the rest of the trip looking out of the window, silent and deep in reflection.

Finally, at the end of a very long day, Mary stood at that little gate again and, looking across the garden towards the house, knew she had made the right decision.

Inside, young Cecil wasted no time in bouncing down the stairs and hugging her to death.

'Ooooooo!' cried Mary and spun him around in her arms before giving him a big kiss. 'Hello, my little scallywag.'

'You look brown!' he commented.

'Do I? Well that's because I've been somewhere very hot.'

'I know…Mesopo…something'

'Meso-pot-amia,' she laughed, helping him to pronounce it.

'Just remember what I said, young man!' said Ann, and gave her son the look that all parents have in their repertoire of warnings. But, of course, to a nine-year-old boy, a glare would not stop his curiosity.

'Why isn't Tom coming? Mother said I wasn't to mention it but I want to know!'

'Well, because Tom…'

'Cecil! What did I just say?' Ann interrupted. 'It's like talking to a brick wall.'

'It's all right, Ann…he's only being inquisitive.'

'Yes, quite!' said Ann, again with a look to Cecil to signify this wasn't the end of the matter.

'It's a fair question and one that deserves an answer,' stated Mary, and she reached out to hold the small hand.

'Tom isn't here…well, because he's busy.'

'Are you not friends anymore, and that's why you went to that place?'

Ann closed her eyes in desperation.

'No! It's just we don't see as much of each other as we used to,' Mary explained, trying to be as tactful as she could.

'But isn't that strange when you're married?'

'Right, I think that's quite enough questions!' Ann cut across her son, wanting to spare Mary any more awkwardness. 'Cecil, go and let the dog into the garden. And don't let him wee on my plants, please!'

'I'm sorry, Mary,' Ann declared, after he'd made his exit. 'I should have known better than to ask him to keep hush.'

'I'm sure he would have asked anyway,' Mary replied and smiled.

'Have you had any contact with Tom?'

'No,' replied Mary and then asked, 'Have you?'

'We had a letter about a month ago saying he was well and helping the medical corps in France,' Ann remarked. 'Oh! Mary, why don't you make contact?' she continued with hope.

'No, Ann. What I did to Tom was hurtful and selfish of me. I chose my path in finding Walter and forced Tom to bear the brunt of that.'

'But Walter was the brother you never knew. Tom

would have supported you in trying to find him!'

'I had to do it my way, Ann. I wasn't going to burden Tom with my demons any longer.'

'Do you still love him?'

'Of course,' she sighed anxiously. 'I never stopped loving him.'

Ann took hold of Mary's hand, 'Then find a way to tell him… Perhaps I could help…'

'No! Please! I want Tom to be happy. I've made my bed… And, furthermore, I won't burden you and Robert for long either.'

'You listen to me, Mary Sharpe! This house is your home for as long as you need it. Promise me you will never feel you are a burden to us. Promise!'

Mary smiled in appreciation and said, 'I promise.'

Within a couple of weeks Mary was rested and adjusted to normality, or as much normality as the war would allow. She turned her attention to her long neglected trust fund and discussed the problem with Robert who, after an evening of pacing the carpet, came up with a plan – one that revolved round George Mills and his father's commercial house. In his opinion, who would be more pleased than George Mills to learn of Walter's escapades; and even more pleased to assist Mary, once he learned that she and Walter were siblings?

Whilst the meeting with Mills started in sombre mood,

dealing with the news of Walter's death, they were soon remembering him with affection.

'I'm thinking we should replace that empty plaque space of his in the hall of your old school, Mr Mills; if, of course, you hold any sway there,' suggested Elliott, massaging Mills' importance as influencer extraordinaire.

'I should certainly give it a go,' replied Mills, taking the bait.

It was a good hour before they even got around to discussing Mary's trust fund problem. However, Mills declared he was indeed very happy to help Mary in any way he could. Elliott was convinced there was no better man to assist, as his father's company was not without power in the legal and commercial sector.

On a bright sunny autumn day, the scene was set at Rugby School. A polite young student saw Mills, Mary and the Elliotts to their seats on the stage of the great hall. Elliott was armed with the plaque and his speech; for the headmaster had kindly suggested he should say a few words in honour of their redeemed former boy. A throng of boys waited patiently for this special assembly and, as the headmaster strode across the stage and towards the lectern, all fell silent.

'Mr Elliott,' he simply said and gestured for him to take the stand.

Ann was mortified when her husband brought out

from his jacket pocket what must have been at least twenty sheets of foolscap writing.

'Lord have mercy on their poor ears,' she muttered to Mary, who struggled to keep a straight face.

Elliott cleared his throat, plumped out his chest and began in earnest. 'Of all the multitude of men named in my registers, none has been more loveable and done more nobly than Walter Stanford...'

He was up and running and soon delivering his lines as if playing King Lear. 'Men like him, who once occupied your seats in this hallowed establishment, know very well what to look for in a protagonist...'

Ann could only close her eyes in embarrassment.

Finally, after twenty minutes, the headmaster felt it his duty to spare his students, with their glazed expressions, further suffering of what was no longer the story of an old boy but now more a full-blown lecture on the good of probation for the fallen man.

'I don't wish to sound ungrateful, Mr Elliott, but I'm wondering if an end is imminent,' whispered the headmaster politely into Elliott's ear.

'Of course,' responded Elliott, not the least bit perturbed, and he skipped some pages to move to his last sheet. 'My registers cannot be amended. Here, Walter remains a criminal; but a high place is now finally given him on these walls.'

As the relieved clapping died away, a small plaque was revealed, and he read out the inscription:

Walter Stanford
Old boy of this school 1903-1905.
Beloved Deaf Mute, Enigma, Bedouin Brother,
Spy And Above All – Hero

CHAPTER 27

SINISTER MOTIVES

The folders in front of Elliott were old cases, outside of his normal court circuit, which he had been asked to study, then provide a report on, detailing where the use of probation would have produced a better outcome than that of prison. It was an appealing prospect to him, albeit one that he knew would eat up much of his spare time. However, a promise was a promise, and he sat down to begin the task.

As he flicked through the paperwork, he found the usual situation: a of lack of guidance and help at the very beginning of trouble; and, most often, a lack of tolerance by Victorian fathers. Elliott sighed. As always, the approach taken had simply been to use a stick to beat the problem. He skimmed through the folders, looking for one that held most scope for his report, and finally chose quite a bulky one containing the police and court records of Bessie Palmer. The file was littered with trivial charges and statements, and detailed a woman who had been in and out of custody, the workhouse and prostitution since an early age. He sat back and thumbed through the first few pages and picked up his pen to make notes: mother died; father a drunk; endless cautions for petty theft. It was an all too familiar story.

His eyes were then drawn to a police statement taken in Sheffield, at the very same station in which he now visited offenders, and the one where he first encountered Walter. He began to read on and was surprised to see the charge of 'accessory to child murder.' Continuing, he then hit the words '24 Newsome Street' and drew up his head in shock as he read the awful truth of the place. Leaning back in his chair, he let out a huge sigh and immediately went over in his mind the visit he had made to Mr Stanford, remembering the conversation about where Walter and his sister had been taken from. It dawned on him that he was reading the account of the night the house was raided.

Bessie Palmer was arrested there on suspicion of aiding and abetting Ellie Hart in the illegal activity of baby farming, and the lengthy statement went on to give an account of her association with Hart. Then Elliott came to the bombshell – her accusation against the Reverend Charles Brockwell for his use of prostitutes and, more seriously, his involvement with Mrs Hart. He was utterly stunned as he read on, and could not believe his friend was implicated in such activity. Thoughts of Alice Harper's comments and loathing of the man came back to him. Also, there was the renting of 24 Newsome Street. Did Brockwell cunningly steer him and Mary away from the place? And Mary's unease whenever she met Brockwell. Finally, he remembered the piece of paper in Walter's half of the locket, which mentioned Hart. Could it be that the piece of paper was actually referring to Mrs Hart?

Elliott's mind went into overdrive about his friend, and his instinct troubled him. He simply had to investigate further to reveal the truth and, as he turned the last page of the statement, he knew exactly where to start. He looked down to the name of the police officer who had taken the statement – Constable Drake.

Fortunately, Sergeant Drake, as he now was, had a memory like an elephant, and when Elliott met him he found that Drake could remember the incident in startling detail, hardly needing to read his statement to remind himself of the facts.

'Aye, I remember it very well, just as it's written.'

'Nothing you'd add, with the passage of time?'

'Nay, I was as thorough then as I am today, Mr Elliott,' replied the proud sergeant.

'Of that I've no doubt,' commented Elliott, whilst taking the statement back and sliding it into the folder. 'It implicates Canon Brockwell, Sergeant. Did you investigate that?'

Drake huffed.

'From that I assume you didn't take the allegations seriously.'

'Prostitutes will say anything if it means they get off. You know that.'

Elliott pulled out the statement again and studied it before giving his observation: 'I would say Bessie Palmer wasn't exactly trying to get off, Sergeant. More giving facts about who else was involved.'

'Smearing the name of a good man, and someone of the church at that, merely in an attempt to divert attention away from her own sins.'

'Perhaps…but what if the Canon wasn't innocent?'

Sergeant Drake looked up with incredulity. 'Mr Elliott! Are you seriously suggesting there was any truth in her story?'

'Just because he is a man of the cloth doesn't mean he's beyond reproach,' Elliott replied and turned his head to one side, playing devil's advocate.

'Canon Brockwell is a most wholesome man, who visited those girls purely in an attempt to bring them back to the path of rightful thinking, just as he still does today.'

'I'm sorry?' said Elliott in alarm.

'I said, Canon…'

'No, the last part,' Elliott interrupted.

'Just as he still does today,' Drake confirmed. 'He'll often visit them in the cells and have a chat.'

'Does he now!'

'Yes, sir, he does and I've no reason to suspect him of anything other than Christian reasons,' said Drake, with authority and an expression that let Elliott know he didn't care for his inference of wrongdoing.

'And would the girls always be amenable after these visits – no bawling or shouting as is usual?'

'Well, yes.'

'And am I right in thinking that most prostitutes are addicted to laudanum, Sergeant Drake?' Elliott concluded. He didn't need a reply, for he knew the answer.

~~~

Mary stood peering into what was now a hardware shop window and tried to imagine how it would have looked as a pharmacy. She allowed herself to drift into thinking how different things might have been, had she not been ill as a baby, and had the Stanfords been able to adopt her. She pictured herself growing up with Walter and imagined just how much fun they could have had – he the adventurous rogue, always up to his tricks; she the steadying and influencing sister. Then she thought, perhaps they might just have been two bickering siblings always at odds with each other. Eventually, she realised her picture of them could be anything she chose it to be and smiled, deciding that each day she'd make their past different; but always it would be colourful and have at its centre a smiling, trouble-free Walter.

She turned and made her way across the street and headed towards the church. There was one thing she wanted to do: to pay her respects to Walter's adopted parents and lay the small bunch of flowers she clutched in her hand, on their grave. It would be a gesture from Walter.

Eventually she found the modest headstone, quite near the church entrance, and gently laid the flowers down. Closing her eyes, she offered a small prayer and held onto the locket round her neck. The silence was broken by a familiar voice. 'Mary O'Driscoll, isn't it?' It was Canon Brockwell. Mary spun around. Immediately the feeling of unease came over her.

He caught sight of her locket and his thoughts flashed back to the lying-in house. The memories for him were still so strong; his vision, one of her mother lying naked whilst he played his game of twisting the locket chain. Even with all the years that had passed his perversions had not dulled, nor his desire for a young woman. He gave his usual sickly smile and said, 'I was so sorry to hear of your brother's parting.'

Mary looked at him with surprise.

'Mr Elliott told me all about your discovery and subsequent journey.'

'Did he indeed!' she replied, not exactly pleased that details of her personal life had been discussed openly with the Canon.

'The truth is though, Mary, I did already know as much.'

Even more surprised, Mary could only answer, 'I see.'

'Yes, as I once remember telling you, I knew Walter very well, as indeed I did your mother, Lucinda.'

Normally Mary would have had no inclination to continue their conversation. But, if the Canon had information about her brother and estranged mother, then she was compelled to listen further.

'Please, come into the church,' he said, offering a guiding hand, 'I have some papers which I know you'll find most interesting. I'd be happy for you to have them.'

Although nervous of the man, Mary had to concede she was perhaps over reacting, to what, after all, was most likely a genuine offer to give her information about her past. She accepted his invitation and turned towards the church. Brockwell watched as she walked ahead, his heart beginning to pump a little faster, his sick mind now only thinking how wonderful he would soon feel.

~~~

Elliott returned home from his visit to Sergeant Drake quite angry, his mind busy working out just how he should confront his old friend, Charles Brockwell, with his findings. He was quietly pondering at his desk when Ann interrupted, bringing him a cup of tea. She sensed he had had a fraught day.

'Here, a cup of tea.'

Elliott didn't immediately respond, his thoughts far away. Eventually, he smiled, 'Yes, sorry. Thank you, dear.'

'Is everything all right, Robert? You look awfully troubled.'

Elliott didn't want to tell his wife about his findings just yet, not until he had gone over things thoroughly again. Besides, the children were downstairs. 'Yes, I'm fine. I've just had a bit of disturbing news, that's all,' he said and gestured towards the boys within earshot. 'I'll tell you later.' Then, changing the subject swiftly, he asked, 'No Mary?'

'No, she wanted to go and see Walter's parents' old shop and said she might also stop at the church and pay her respects at their grave. I must say, though, I was expecting her back well before now.'

Elliott's look turned to one of concern. He went into the hallway and picked up the telephone.

'…All right, Elizabeth. Thank you anyway,' he said to Mrs Brockwell, who'd confirmed that her husband was still over in the church somewhere, despite being told dinner would be ready for 5 o'clock.

An increasingly flustered Elliott then called the local butcher, Harry Fletcher.

Alarmed at her husband's sudden uncharacteristic panic, Ann shouted, 'Robert, whatever is it?'

'It's Mary, I think she may be in trouble… Oh, yes, hello Harry, it's Robert Elliott. I was wondering if I could ask you a great favour…for you to run me somewhere in your van?'

~~~

Brockwell slowly closed the door to the vestry and invited Mary to go through a little further, into the small annexe room. Once inside, he began play acting. 'Right, where did I put them?' he said and started to pick at the registers on a shelf. 'You see, when you were both adopted, I was asked to witness things and I have the original letters from your parents in Ireland, requesting your adoption be considered.' He gave a smile, '…Somewhere here. I just need to remember exactly which register.' He kept up the pretence. 'Please take a seat.'

Mary began to feel a little less uneasy and accepted the Canon's offer to sit down. Finally, he placed a big book on the table in front of her. 'There you go.'

He left Mary to open it, whilst he moved to the various vestments hung on the wall. He picked up two stoles adorning the cassocks and slowly walked towards the door.

Mary was consumed with eagerness for what she was about to read and didn't hear the key quietly turn in the lock.

'Where exactly am I supposed to be looking, Canon?'

Brockwell stood behind her in readiness, the stole now twisted tightly at each end and wrapped round his wrists.

~~~

Travelling in Harry Fletcher's van was nothing if not an experience for Elliott. He had at least expected a seat but instead was greeted with an upturned crate, which he sincerely hoped would hold his weight. He had his doubts. Eventually, within a mile of the church, Elliott managed to get in time with the rhythm of the crate bumping up and down. But all the same, he wondered how many splinters he would need to remove from his rump that evening. The van suddenly gave a loud bang and the rumbling of the wheel signalled a burst tyre.

'I'm really sorry, Mr Elliott,' proclaimed Harry, getting out and kicking the tyre. 'You see, I don't carry a spare!'

Oh no, isn't that just great! thought Elliott but didn't say so, as he was grateful for Harry's help in getting this far. 'Listen, I'll carry on walking and, when I get into the village, I'll have a word at the garage and send you some help.'

With that, he bid Harry farewell and began to walk the final mile to the church. His numb buttocks at long last returned to normal. As he walked, he had an all consuming sense that Mary was in great danger, and he started to quicken his pace.

~~~

The longer of the two stoles flicked over Mary's head, pinning her arms to her body. She instinctively screamed, until a hand came over her mouth to silence her. She struggled as best she could but the stole pulled ever tighter into her, restricting her movement. The hand moved away but, before she could scream again, an apple was forced into her mouth and then the smaller stole was tied around her head to keep it in place. Brockwell moved around to the front of her and Mary sensed what was going to happen next. He tied each of her ankles to the chair legs with embroidered tie-backs, rendering her totally unable to move. Her eyes opened wide with horror as Brockwell leered at her, just as he'd done at her mother, many years ago. He pulled the hip flask from under his cassock and started to unscrew the top.

Slowly he began to trickle the laudanum and spirit mixture into the small gap in her mouth, talking to her as he did so. 'You see, God has given you beauty, just like your mother. But I'm afraid the dear Lord didn't give me the strength to resist such temptation.'

The last drops of drink drained into her throat and she felt a weird sensation coming over her. Still able to grasp reality, she hoped that whatever was about to happen to her, would be over quickly. Then the laudanum began to take effect and she drifted into a hallucination. Brockwell watched her head slump and then he untied the scarf from her mouth and released the apple. She was now his to do whatever he wished with. He tore at her blouse and pulled it down over her shoulders. There, lying still around her neck, was the locket. He gently ran it through his fingers in anticipation.

Just as Brockwell was about to remove his cassock, there came a loud knock on the outer vestry door.

By great good fortune, Elliott had heard the Number 16 bus bound for Ecclesfield approaching behind him and had flagged it down. Had it not been for the bus, he would still have been a quarter of a mile away from the church at this point. The overriding feeling of something being wrong was fierce within him, in a way he had never felt it before. He hammered ever harder on the door.

Brockwell clenched his fists in exasperation, but knew he couldn't ignore the knocks, which were becoming louder and louder. His sordid fantasy would have to wait. He checked Mary was fully unconscious and then exited into the main vestry, locking the door behind him. The knocks were now quite frantic. Eventually, he turned the key and opened the door to a distraught Elliott.

'Robert!' Brockwell exclaimed.

'Where is she?' Elliott shouted and barged into the room.

'Robert, please calm down. Whatever is the matter?'

'Where is she, Charles?' Elliott repeated with determination.

'Where is who?'

'Mary Sharpe. She's here at the church.'

'Aah, now I see. I'm afraid she left me about an hour ago, Robert. Come sit down for a minute, please.'

Elliott began to realise his behaviour was a little aggressive and his assumption of Brockwell's doing anything wrong to Mary perhaps unfounded. However, with what he'd discovered about his friend, he couldn't hide his unease, and his body language said as much.

'Whatever is wrong, Robert?'

'There are a few things I'd like to discuss with you,' replied Elliott, with a less than friendly inflection in his voice.

'Listen. I've just got some bits to finish off here. Why don't you go across to the house and we can talk over a spot of dinner,' said Brockwell, hoping he could persuade his friend away, so that he could fulfil his evil intentions.

'Perhaps, but I would rather talk first. As it's quiet.'

'Sounds rather desperate. I hope it isn't anything too serious.' commented Brockwell.

Elliott drew in a deep breath in preparation for what he had to say. Even with all his suspicions, he had known Brockwell as a friend for the last twenty years, so this was not going to be easy. Although Elliott's trademark was always to speak as he found, on this occasion he chose to skirt around Brockwell and tease out his reactions.

'Walter Stanford, Charles. You never mentioned that he was adopted when we spoke of him.'

'Well, I never thought it relevant,' Brockwell batted straight back.

'Just like it wasn't relevant to tell me that Mary O'Driscoll was his twin sister?'

Brockwell looked very guilty, but gave an honest response, 'All right, I did know of her, Robert. I should have told you. But I would never have found out who she was, if she hadn't looked the image of her father. Many times I encountered him over the years and I couldn't forget that face. Thank the Lord the girl only inherited his looks and nothing else!'

'So, you knew Mary was adopted in Ireland?'

'Yes, by a Dr O'Driscoll.'

'So that's why you asked her all those questions at the flower festival – to tease out her name.'

Brockwell had no defence and simply confirmed, 'Yes.'

'And what of the mother, Charles? What do you know of Walter and Mary's mother?'

'Well, only that the poor mite had the unfortunate pleasure of meeting their father and found herself pregnant by him. Should I know more?'

Elliott took out a sheet of folded paper from his pocket. On it he'd written the words discovered on the little note behind the velvet lining of Walter's locket.

'What do you make of this?' he said, and handed the paper over.

Brockwell studied it but eventually frowned and shrugged his shoulders. 'Well, they're just words, Robert. Am I supposed to make something of them?'

'They're words taken from a little note found in a locket Walter's mother gave him.'

'I see. Well, is it some sort of message?' Brockwell asked, acting as if he had no knowledge whatsoever of the locket.

Elliott began to play him further. 'I would say so. I was thinking "Hart" was perhaps a misspelling of "Heart".'

'Yes, that's good, Robert. I'm sure you're right,' commented Brockwell.

'There again, it could be something quite different. "Hart" could be referring to a Mrs Hart. And "seek" might go on to say "justice". Perhaps it's all a clue to Walter and Mary's past,' Elliott said and walked behind Brockwell's back. 'It appears they had a tough start in life.'

'Yes, terrible, terrible affair,' Brockwell agreed, now realising Elliott knew something.

'But happen they were the lucky ones that survived that place. You know where I'm talking about, Charles, don't you? The house at 24 Newsome Street.'

Brockwell wasn't facing Elliott when asked the question, so he was able to hide the anxiety that appeared on his face.

'And perhaps this was the reason you steered me away from trying to rent it, Charles? So I wouldn't unearth the truth of the place.'

Eventually Brockwell had to turn around and respond. 'No, as I said at the time, I was in negotiations to rent the house.'

Elliott raised his eyebrows and frowned. 'Aah, yes, of course, the diocese was going to use it for hardship cases. Strange then that it's lain empty all this time! And stranger still that it is you who is actually renting it and not the diocese!'

There was a brief silence. Brockwell needed time to think of a plausible reason but struggled. What he ultimately came up with, he knew his friend would immediately reject, but he had to say something.

'Very well, Robert. I admit I was hiding the truth. You see, I've been rather selfish and wanted to rent the property ready for when I retire.'

'Hardly, Charles. Not with your association with the place,' Elliott said, rejecting the explanation with ease, just as Brockwell had suspected he would.

'I see you've been doing your homework,' Brockwell replied and went to sit by a table. He sat tapping his fingers together nervously. 'So you know of the allegations against me?'

Elliott walked over to the table, spread his broad hands out and calmly said, 'Yes, I'm afraid I do, Charles.'

Brockwell looked hard into his friend's eyes, which were unforgiving and held his firmly, never blinking to break the intensity. He made a last attempt at bravado, but deep down he knew the time had finally arrived for the truth to come out. 'All right, so I was there during that time. But only to help those girls to a better life.'

'By giving up their children to a baby farmer?'

'I swear I didn't know what she was up to!'

'Don't insult my intelligence, Charles. You knew exactly what you were subjecting those babies to. The question is, why did you do it?'

'I've told you. Giving over their child was the only chance the mothers had for a better life.'

'No, no, Charles. That's too convenient. My belief is that you were getting something in return.'

'Don't be ridiculous!'

'Tell me, as well, why should you choose to go thirty miles out of your parish to help young girls at a lying-in house? Does that responsibility not fall on the local clergyman, or, more appropriately, a nurse?'

'Well, because…,' Brockwell started to bluster.

Elliott was happy to finish for him, 'Because you knew what came after those girls gave birth, didn't you? A life of drugs and prostitution, and you saw this as your opportunity.'

'No!'

Elliott banged his fist down hard onto the table, making Brockwell jump. 'Don't lie to me! You couldn't resist the temptation any more than a dog can resist chasing a cat.'

'All right!' Brockwell snapped. 'All right, so I tasted the sin of their flesh on occasion. They wanted it as much as I did.'

Elliott pulled himself up slowly and declared in disgust, 'No Canon. They had to do it, because they didn't have the choice, unlike you.' He began to pace around the vestry, partly in frustration but mostly in anger. Brockwell, for his part, simply sat in silence with his head bowed in shame.

'You knew Walter and Mary's mother, Lucinda, from there, didn't you?' Elliott asked, with a tone so cold. Brockwell simply didn't answer. Instead, he chose to keep his head bowed, not wanting to make any more eye contact with his inquisitor.

'Damn you! Answer me!' shouted Elliott and banged the table once more.

'Yes,' sneered Brockwell, 'Yes, I knew her. Yet another one that succumbed to opening her legs to the charms of gypsy travellers.'

Elliott began to turn red with rage. Brockwell realised there must have been some affinity between the pair and seized the moment to paint a lurid vision for him to contemplate. 'Yes, Robert, I knew Lucinda very well,' he said, with spite and, finally, stood up tall in defiance. 'And she tasted and did it sweeter than most!'

Elliott lunged and took hold of the Canon by his throat, pinning him to the wall. 'As God is my witness, I will see you hang for your crimes,' he snarled. For the first time in his life he felt pure hatred. However, as much as he was affronted by what he'd heard, he knew he must calm down. Having to listen to lewd details was all too common in his line of work, and experience told him that only by being composed could he bring this horrible abuser to the courts. He slowly let go of Brockwell and turned away.

'I think you're forgetting that we have stalemate, Robert – simply your word against mine!' said the Canon, brazen to the last. 'Who is there to testify against me?'

'I believe your old housemaid might have a few things to say in court,' Elliott replied, with disdain.

Brockwell let out a laugh. 'Well, if they bring her back from beyond the grave, then yes, I'm sure she would!

Such a tragic accident, bless her.' He could see Elliott looked rather baffled and continued with sarcasm, 'Oh! Did you not hear, Robert? Alice Harper was run over and killed last year.'

Elliott could only assume the contemptible man he had once called a friend had had some sort of involvement in the event.

Brockwell was revelling in the fact that there appeared to be no one else who could be called on as a witness to his sinister past and scoffed, 'Oh, but I'm forgetting those words on the note in that locket, Robert. Yes, they will surely incriminate me.'

Despite wanting to punch the man, Elliott held his control and with steely resolve said, 'That locket is just the start but, regardless, my report to the court will be most thorough, Charles, you can be assured of that.' He moved in uncomfortably close to the Canon's face and very calmly vowed, 'I will dig and dig, then dig some more, until I find the evidence. For the sake of all those women who had to suffer your obscenity, and for those poor dear babies, I will see you swing from a rope, if it's the last thing I ever do.'

Brockwell knew Elliott only too well and had no doubt the man would pursue him relentlessly. The dread that his one-time friend would unearth the whole truth was all too real.

Suddenly, there was an audible moan from the annexe to the vestry. Elliott's expression hardened. How could he have been so stupid as not to check. 'She's in there, isn't she?' he shouted and ran towards the door.

The Canon saw his opportunity and made a dash to the other door. Elliott turned and flung himself at Brockwell to stop him getting out. Once more he held the man by his throat. 'You sick creature,' he spat. 'The key! Where is the key?'

Mary gave another moan from beyond the door. 'The key, damn you! or I swear I'll run your head against the door to break it down.'

'All right! All right! I'll get it,' responded Brockwell pathetically.

Elliott released his grip and allowed Brockwell to go over to the bureau. Opening the drop-down lid he fumbled with some papers in a corner. Buried underneath was a Webley revolver, which he picked up. Releasing the safety catch, he stood facing a stunned Elliott.

'Don't look so worried, Robert,' he calmly announced, 'I'm told the pain is only momentary.' Slowly he pulled back the hammer. Without any warning, he then turned the pistol on himself and held the barrel against his temple. 'You see, the Lord giveth and the Lord taketh… but I'm afraid I will choose the way he taketh me.' With that, the trigger clicked and Elliott watched in horror as Brockwell wobbled and a fountain of blood spurted out from the bullet exit wound. Brockwell's large frame slumped over to one side and then fell to the ground, like a slaughtered animal.

CHAPTER 28

Closure

Mills had kept his word and had made very good progress in dealing with Mary's trust fund, ultimately securing a settlement with the administrators that she was happy to proceed with. All that was now needed was a trip to the administrators' offices in London to sign the documents and have them legally witnessed. It seemed such a waste of a full day for what was literally five minutes of formality; but it was yet another piece of closure in her life, and one that meant she could rest, knowing she had some financial security for the future.

As she returned to St Pancras Station to catch her train home, she found it absolutely jammed with soldiers returning north and had to push and jostle to get anywhere near the train. 'Excuse me... Excuse me, sir! Thank you... Excuse me!' she continually repeated, until she came to a clearing on the platform. Looking down, the reason was clear: badly wounded soldiers lay on stretchers waiting to be taken into the carriages. She stopped and waited as boarding began. As one patient without legs was carried past her, he accidently dropped his cigarette, which she promptly picked up and gave back to the grateful man.

'Much obliged, miss,' he said, then suddenly shouted out to beyond her, 'Goodbye then, Dr Sharpe, and thank you for everything.'

Mary froze as a familiar voice replied, 'Yes, you take care now, soldier…do you hear!'

Their eyes met and it was hard to tell who was more shocked. She suddenly felt that familiar churning sensation hit her stomach and her heart began pounding like a set of pistons. Tom was similarly affected and his legs began to tremble.

'Mary!' he was at last able to say.

'Hello, Tom,' she muttered breathlessly.

She moved to one side to allow the boarding to continue. Tom walked over and they stood facing each other, their eyes locked. To them, it seemed they had been gazing at each other for an eternity but, in fact, it was literally seconds.

'Well, what a surprise!' said Tom, pushing his hair back as he always did when anxious. 'How are you?' he asked. It was all he could think of to say.

Mary's heart was still beating as hard as she'd ever experienced in her life. 'I'm fine, thank you for asking…and you?'

'Yes…good, well as good as…'

She held her hand to her face and cut across him. 'Oh! Tom, I'm so sorry but I can't…,' and she turned to run away.

He ran after her and grabbed her by the arm, 'Mary, please!'

'I don't know what to say to you,' she wept.

'You're shaking,' he said and put his palm around her cheek.

'No, please Tom, don't do this…because…' She closed her eyes and allowed her face to feel the warmth of his touch. 'Because I'm liable to fall into your arms and I can't do…'

Suddenly, his lips made contact with hers and she felt herself delicately opening her mouth and then pressing hard.

As the guard's whistle blew, he held her face and kissed her forehead as she sobbed uncontrollably. Then wiping away her tears, he said, 'I won't let you leave, Mary. Do you hear? I won't let you leave…ever again.'

She looked into his eyes, saying, 'Then you ought to see a doctor, Tom Sharpe,' and buried herself in his embrace, as the train chugged forwards without her.

~~~

Sergeant Drake was hardly known for having much sympathy with prostitutes but, when the truth about Canon Brockwell came out, he couldn't help but feel some guilt, knowing that he had been fooled into making many of the women available to feed the Canon's perversion. There was one woman in particular who had been in and out of custody so many times over the years she might as well have had her own cell. He reflected on the day when she had finally passed away in the station a few years earlier. With just a cloth over her face, the ragged old woman had been carried away.

'Come on then, let's get the paperwork done,' Drake had said callously, and thumbed down his sheet to the section "Personal belongings". 'Huh! This should be good. Right, go get her bag, lad.'

The constable returned with a filthy, threadbare carpetbag and hesitated.

'Well, go on, open it up and tell me what's inside,' barked the impatient Drake.

'Do I have to, Sarge?' grimaced the lad.

'Get on with it.'

He placed his hand into the bag with some trepidation and pulled out a dirty shawl, which obviously hadn't been washed in years. Underneath this there wasn't much else except a pair of fingerless gloves and a charming little pebble – hand-painted as a ladybird and wrapped

394

in a grubby lace doyley. Finally, he pulled out a piece of folded paper.

'What's that?' asked Drake and prompted the constable to open it out.

'It's a drawing of some sort, Sarge,' he proclaimed.

It was in fact a child's sketch of a tinker's caravan in a woodland clearing, with a toll bridge in the background. Outside the caravan sat a man sharpening a knife on a grinding wheel, whilst a young girl laid out her lace goods. At the bottom it read:

'*Me and Daddy – Lucinda Trevill, aged 13 years.*'

~~~

The new vicar of Ecclesfield, Brockwell's replacement, was proving to be most popular in the village and was never happier than when asked to perform a christening service, particularly one where God's gift of childbirth had been so long in coming. For Tom and Mary, this day was a very special one and they stood, proud parents, holding their newborn daughter.

Mary's face was radiant. She was healthy, beautiful and, above all, happy again. It was so very far away from her troubles over the last few years. She had been on an incredible journey of self-discovery, one that she could only have dreamed of.

There was, however, just one more thing she would experience before her closure was complete.

As they waited for the Vicar, Tom gave her a loving smile. She responded by leaning her head against his shoulder. It was a moment of sheer content and she closed her eyes. On opening them, she naturally expected to be looking at her husband with longing; but he wasn't there, next to her; instead, he was standing some distance away, on the other side of the font. She looked so confused, as she observed herself next to him and the rest of the congregation. From behind her, a woman's voice suddenly spoke to her.

'You look so gorgeous, my dear.'

Mary turned around and gasped, staring at Lucinda, her mother, but, of course, she didn't know that. All she saw was a ragged, wrinkled old woman, although she did recognise her as the woman she'd met in the police station cell years earlier.

'I do remember you,' Mary said and began to study Lucinda's withered face with curiosity.

'You do, Mary. This is what I became, I'm afraid. You have to see what effect he had on me. Why justice had to be done. But I want you to remember me so differently.'

The woman's face suddenly began to get younger, slowly becoming more and more attractive, until, finally, she stood in front of Mary as a young woman, in a time before the ravages of drugs and prostitution had befallen her. She looked so lovely and untainted, just as she was when Elliott started to court her.

Mary held her hand over her mouth in shock, seeing the young woman who had mysteriously appeared in her previous visions. Eventually, she asked, 'Who are you?'

'I'm Lucinda, your mother!' replied the woman, holding out her hand. With apprehension, Mary took it. Their dreamy eyes locked. It was such a bizarre situation – a daughter to be looking and talking to her own mother, but her mother at an age almost ten years her junior.

'I have so wondered about you over all these years, Mary. My little girl, who I couldn't hold and cherish, couldn't watch grow into the fine woman you've become.'

Mary didn't answer. Instead, she felt a tremendous urge to embrace her. Tears trickled down her face and she held her mother so tight, feeling every bit of raw emotion tingle through her body. The sound of the Vicar's voice welcoming the congregation finally broke them apart.

Standing watching herself from afar, brimming with delight at the start of the service, she asked, 'Am I dead? Are we watching past events?'

'No, Mary! You're still very much alive.'

'So it's a vision?'

'Not exactly.'

'Then I don't understand. How can I be physically here, yet also over there?

'You aren't physically here, Mary. It's just your spirit that is here, but in a form you can understand,' explained Lucinda, holding her daughter's hand again. 'You see in death, we are all able to seek closure before we move on. And my closure is…' She paused, looking so sad and forlorn. Eventually, with a tremble in her voice, she managed to finish her sentence, 'Well, mine is simply to hold you and Walter one more time, and ask for your forgiveness.'

Mary felt her mother's distress and remorse eat into her. Hugging her close, she became lost in a sensation that she had truly never experienced before.

'There is nothing to forgive,' Mary said tearfully.

Lucinda pulled back slowly and smiled. 'I really did love you both. If only I could turn the clock back.'

'But you can't, Mother. Things are what they are,' said the very familiar and philosophical voice of Walter, who suddenly appeared from nowhere and stood smiling in his usual mischievous way. 'Hello sweet sister!'

Mary pulled her hand to her mouth in shock yet again, then slowly started to laugh with absolute delight and ran to hug him. 'Walter!' she cried. 'Oh, dear Lord.'

Lucinda smiled with joy and watched her children squeeze each other. She looked across to the congregation and saw Elliott. Through her thoughts, she reversed his age until, like her, he appeared as an eighteen year old. 'Oh! Robert, you were such a fine and handsome young man,' she said wistfully. 'If only I hadn't been such a stupid, flirty butterfly, then perhaps, things might have been so different.'

As Mary cupped Walter's face, his body began to fade.

'It's time now, Walter,' called out his mother.

'No, please,' shouted Mary in desperation.

'Our world has rules I'm afraid, Mary. Once closure is done we have to move on.'

'But...' answered Mary, looking so worried.

The images of Lucinda and Walter faded more and more.

'Don't fret, Mary. Where we go, there is only happiness,' said Lucinda, now almost translucent. She held out her hand to Walter, 'Both of us will always be there to watch over you. I do so love you, my dear child.'

Then they were gone. Mary closed her eyes and sobbed.

When she did open them again she was back in the real world and watching Tom hand over their daughter to the Vicar to be baptised. He held their treasure, a girl with a thick head of gorgeous dark hair and deep brown eyes. Dabbing the baby's head with holy water the Vicar announced, 'I name thee Charlotte Dorothy...'

Mary suddenly interrupted, 'Stop!' and turned to Tom, 'Darling, would you mind awfully if we just call her Lucinda?'

Tom gave his wife a playful look of exasperation, his expression reminding her of the hours they'd spent going over different names; but then he gave her a loving smile and a nod of agreement. What did he really care? To him, their daughter would always be called precious anyway.

In the congregation were proud and tearful godparents, Robert and Ann Elliott. Robert smiled with so much admiration at Mary and gently squeezed the little baby bootie always in his pocket. Although he would never forget the loss of his own daughter, Amy, he knew he had the best possible replacement in Mary.

'I name thee Lucinda Sharpe,' said the vicar finally, and with some relief.

Mary felt a rush of air pass by her side, followed by the feeling of a hand, gently brushing against hers. She closed her eyes and gave a soft sigh. At the church door was Walter, beaming a smile. Beside him, a very beautiful and contented Lucinda.

When she opened her eyes again, she wanted so much to believe her spirit really had joined that of her mother and Walter, for those brief moments in time, but she couldn't help thinking that perhaps she had just wished for it all to happen.

One thing is certain: the mind is a most fascinating and wondrous thing.

~~~

CHARACTERS
BEHIND THE STORY

The plot in my novel and the central characters of Mary, Tom and Brockwell are wholly fictional. However, Walter and Elliott are loosely based on real people and their relationship, as depicted in the writings of Robert Holmes. In describing some events in my story, I have, in part, included quotes, text and extracts of letters from Holmes's work and wish to credit him as the originator.

Robert Holmes was Sheffield's first probation officer and wrote about Walter Greenway in his book, 'Walter Greenway – Spy and Hero.' Here, he recounts his time spent as a police court missionary and the actual encounter with Walter, whom he gives a false name to conceal his true identity.

Walter was indeed a most intriguing man and his experiences in Mesopotamia included many acts of heroism. He was never recognised for his unofficial spy work during the First World War, but the commemorative inscription I give him in my novel: *A Beloved Deaf Mute, Enigma, Bedouin Brother, Spy And Above All – Hero*, seems most worthy.

Follow Elliott's further Police Court experiences in the sequel to 'Entanglement of Fate'.

Coming soon…

'REVENGE'

To follow progress and get sneak previews please visit: www.chrisbrookes.info

Lightning Source UK Ltd.
Milton Keynes UK
UKOW02f2255131116
287528UK00002B/3/P

9 781910 667231